THIRST OF THE VAMPIRE

Emily was halfway back when she heard something behind her, a kind of shuffling. She didn't bother to turn, but she did stop.

She waited a moment, listening. She heard another shuffle, like a thousand hungry insects moving along the floor toward a pile of spilled garbage.

"Food! Need food!"

Emily's eyes bulged and her skin erupted in gooseflesh. She wheeled around, and her breath caught in her throat.

Martin, grinning, his fangs the size of walrus teeth, his eyes feverishly intent, stood only a few feet away. He reached out to her and Emily screamed.

"Food! Need food!" Martin said.

Her legs were almost useless, but she did manage to fall onto her rearend and crabwalk slowly up the aisle, Martin moving ever so close, arms outstretched, fangs glistening, hungry for a proper meal . . .

IMMORTAL

Jason Nickles

Zebra Books
Kensington Publishing Corp.

Prologue

The White House
In The Cabinet Room
5:43 A.M.

Avery Krist shoved a cassette into a VCR to the president's right and turned off the lights.

A woman's fully clothed body lay on a table in a light blue, sterile-looking room, about twenty feet from the camera. No special precautions had been taken because the virus could be passed only through close physical contact, or so the scientists had concluded.

The camera moved closer and the attorney general, Robert Martinez, said, "As you can see, the body is that of a young female. Her name is Christine Fuller, and she turned twenty-three a couple of days ago."

Keith Pohlan, the chief-of-staff, looked puzzled. "What do you mean, turned twenty-three? She's dead, isn't she?" he asked.

"Sorry, Keith, we can't confirm that."

"Jesus," Keith murmured.

The camera panned the body slowly, starting with her feet. Christine had on a pair of black pumps; the heel of one had broken off. Her black stockings and pleated tan skirt were both shredded. She had on a black silk blouse, unbuttoned, and a black bra. A string of pearls hung around her frail neck. From a distance, she looked almost normal, but when the camera stopped at her head, everyone gasped. They knew what the virus could do, but until now, no one here had seen any real proof. The right side of her skull looked like she'd run into a telephone pole, her features shoved toward the other side of her face like something in a funhouse mirror. Her vibrant blue eyes were open wide, and her lower lip looked about three times its normal size.

A disembodied hand reached in and placed the woman's driver's license next to her head. In the picture, Christine Fuller looked as normal as anyone in the room.

"Striking," the vice-president mumbled.

The camera moved back, and a few seconds later, the screen went black.

"Thanks, Avery," the president said, with a wave of his hand.

Avery turned on the lights and took the tape out of the machine.

"Bob?" the president said to the surgeon general, who cleared his throat.

"What you've seen," he said, "is the first real proof that these, well, these *beings* actually do exist. They've been seen before now, but this unfortunate young woman is our first . . . for lack of a better term, our first prisoner of war. The body itself is as hard as stone, as I'm sure you've heard. Needles are useless; we haven't been able to extract body fluids from any cavity. We can't rule out the possibility that she's still alive, in a state of suspended animation, somehow, although she hasn't got a pulse and she's not breathing.

"The problem is this: people are leaving New York City by the thousands. As near as we can tell, the virus hasn't spread beyond the city's borders, not yet—"

"Which is why," the president interrupted, "I'm ordering a quarantine. Once it's in effect, we'll begin the second phase of the operation, military action. We've got to find these people and deal with them. I know all the arguments about human rights, believe me, that's all I think about. There's no other way, though. Hundreds, maybe thousands, of lives have been lost already. We have to act. I just pray, ladies and gentlemen, that it's not too late."

In the minds of almost everyone present, the image of

what lay on that table lingered, but beside it, in a truly mind-numbing before-and-after, lay the driver's license photo and how normal-looking Christine Fuller had once been.

One

Six Months Earlier

A thin-faced man with a flurry of open sores on his face tapped on the right side window of the Lincoln Continental and looked inside. He couldn't see anything with the windows blacked out, but the smell of cold cash was as strong here as anywhere.

Stuck in traffic—what else was new?—Dr. Emily Kane felt a moment of compassion. She reached into her purse, took out a five, then rolled down the window and handed it to the panhandler.

The man nodded and tipped his baseball cap. "God bless you," he said. He glanced toward the driver, then trundled off.

"You think that's wise?" the driver asked.

Emily didn't like the question. She liked the tone of it even less. "No," she said evenly. "But you'll protect me from big, bad panhandlers, won't you, Larry?"

Emily's father, David Kane, the self-appointed president and founder of what he called the Anglo-American Arts Foundation, an archaeological association engaged in the study of artifacts found in England and the United States, rented space in the Empire State Building. The rent was astronomical, but he could afford it. His grandfather, a railroad tycoon, had left a large fortune.

Larry pulled the car into David Kane's private parking space, cut the engine, got out, and opened Emily's door. A few minutes later, Emily stepped off the elevator and onto the seventy-fifth floor, walked to a door directly across from the elevator, and went inside. Her father's private secretary, a large and unusually homely woman, greeted her with a tight little smile. "He's in back," she said.

Emily couldn't help it; every time she saw this woman she thought about her long-dead Aunt Victoria looming vulture-like over the lunch table, her fingers laced together in front of her. "Eat it all up, Emily, every drop! Millions of Chinese would call that simple meal food for a whole week."

Still, Nancy Richmond, she knew, was as devoted to Emily's dad as any dog to its master, and it was very comforting to have someone watching him who thought duty was a religion.

"How's he doing today?" Emily asked.

"I'd say he's in fairly good spirits."

Her father's leukemia, diagnosed two years earlier, had been in remission for the last half year. "Borrowed time" was a phrase Emily knew well.

"I'll tell him you're here, Doctor," Nancy continued, disappearing beyond a frosted glass door that read ARTIFACTS HOLDING AREA.

While she waited, Emily picked up a big, glossy book with a picture of the Pyramids on the front and started thumbing through it. Archaeology had been her father's profession and obsession before his illness. Her brother, Hal, had taken up where her father'd left off. Now he was in Massachusetts on a very hush-hush dig.

Five minutes later, Emily put the book down and let out an exasperated sigh. She hated being announced like the Avon lady. Fathers and daughters weren't supposed to operate like that. But Nancy usually got her way, and if she wanted to announce someone, she would.

Her father joined her then, greeting her with a toothy grin.

"So what's up, Doc?" he said, as they hugged.

Holding him tight, Emily thought he felt thinner this week. He looked thinner every week, though; give him a month and he'll disappear, she thought. Worry, she knew, could be a real taskmaster. She pushed him to arm's length.

"How you feelin', Dad?"

Nancy sat down behind her desk, a book open in front of her.

"Absolutely incredible," he said convincingly.

"And you look just as incredible," Emily lied. "Death warmed over" was another phrase she kept close by. There was a lot of excess baggage beneath those gray eyes; his skin had yellowed. She'd stay on her knees a little longer tonight. The length of her prayers always correlated with how her dad had looked that day.

His grin broadened—probably, she thought, because he knew she was worried. "I'm beating this thing, Emily," he whispered. "Six months now, six goddamn months! God, I feel good! Now, what can I get you to drink?"

"Just juice, Dad."

"Emily, it's dark out. Time to let your hair down a little. Hell, life's too damn short for *just juice*."

"I've got some paperwork to do. You wouldn't want me to misfile, would you? What if, I don't know, what if I gave Mr. Piggly-Wiggly's neurosis to Mrs. Cock Robin? I'd probably get sued, that's what, then I'd be out on the street selling T-shirts to pay off the debt."

"Well, hell, Emily, that's what I've always said about neuroses and delusions and all that—they probably all have the same common denominator. Who cares if you misfile? Nancy, would you get my daughter a whiskey sour?"

Nancy got up and left the room.

"Dad, I wish you hadn't done that."

"C'mon back, Emily. You look like someone who wants to get away."

Emily followed her father to one of two private rooms, outfitted with all the comforts of home, primarily because for David, this was home. There weren't any private residences in the Empire State Building, but David had a sleep sofa for when he worked late. Emily sat on the sofabed while her father sat down beside her in a wing chair placed in front of a huge cherrywood pedestal desk. By then, Nancy had a whiskey sour for her and an old-fashioned for David. Emily nodded a thank-you, then took a sip just to please him; he hated to drink alone.

"Pretty good, huh? Nancy makes a mean whiskey sour."

"No, Dad, it's awful." She smiled.

David took a long gulp and said, "Look, Emily, you doing anything important tomorrow?"

"Dad, tomorrow's a workday."

He touched her hand. "Can you get away?"

"Why?"

"I'm going out to your brother's dig and I want you to go with me."

"Out to Hal's . . . why would you do that?"

"Just to get away, that's all. And I haven't seen Hal for, God, at least six months. How about it?"

She looked into his pleading gray eyes, as persuasive as anything he could say. He wanted to see Hal, but it seemed that he wanted *her* to see Hal even more. She flipped through her mental Rolodex. She had Mrs. Murphy and her dead Pekinese. Tough stuff. Mrs. Murphy could put the grieving process on hold for a while, though. Mr. Lofton would show around one; his problems were a little more real, but nothing they couldn't put off. Tomorrow was actually a pretty slow day.

She smiled at him. "Okay, Dad, I'll probably regret this, but okay. We taking your plane?"

"Sure. We'll fly into Boston and rent a car. The dig's about thirty miles to the north. How's eight sound?"

"Yeah, that's okay. I'll just leave a message for my secretary."

"Then it's settled."

Emily looked closely at her father. Funny, how he got his way all the time. As spoiled as any button-nosed ten-year-old.

"You up to a video?" he asked.

"A video? What did you have in mind, Dad?" *Anything but Casablanca* . . .

"*Casablanca.*"

"What, you haven't got the whole script memorized yet?"

Emily called her ex-boyfriend before the movie started. He'd wanted to get together that evening, although she didn't have a clue as to why. Their relationship had ended about a month earlier; their careers got in the way. "I told you that'd happen," her father said. "You can't juggle careers and a relationship, too. Something's got to give." Trouble was, Ray and she were about as resilient as granite, and with their careers taking off—Ray was a writer breaking into the big-time—neither one had time to work on a relationship.

Ray had drifted onto the scene almost as soon as her name had hit the *Yellow Pages.* He'd seen her at Manhattan General a year and a half earlier, while he was there playing Santa. He hadn't hesitated. He hiked up his fake belly, tugged his beard down, and said, "I think we should take you on a tour of the hospital, Dr. Kane."

She bit. "Now, why would you do that, Santa?"

"Why, to heal the sick, of course. One look at you and I know I feel real good!"

As lines go, she'd thought, *that wasn't bad.* And when she saw it was paired with a man who, although not drop-dead gorgeous, smiled much more often than he frowned and also liked cats, she let the relationship continue.

"You're going home tonight, aren't you?" Ray had asked when he'd called earlier that afternoon.

"That depends."

"On what?"

"What you want to talk about."

"What about your cats?"

Emily's four cats, Alpha, Beta, Delta, and Gamma, had all been spared a quick death at the local pound.

"Ray, I'm tired. The cats can take care of themselves. That's what they do best. Now, if what you have to say is that important—"

"Okay, here it is. I have to know, Emily. Was there another guy? Is that why you broke up with me?"

She couldn't believe it. They'd hashed out their split like two sane, rational adults. He knew what had happened as much as she did. Wasn't it just like a man to get weird over something like that? Hell, he'd been her first lover and her last. Not that she hadn't been approached. She had everything a man could want in a woman; she was tall and blond, with a figure a gunny sack couldn't hide, and gray eyes, like her dad's, only sultry. Until Ray, though, she hadn't had time for men.

"Ray, there wasn't another man and there still isn't. We covered that ground—remember?"

"Okay, if that won't get us together, maybe this will. I've got a thirty-eight pointed at my temple and if you don't come home, I'll pull the trigger."

Emily didn't miss a beat. "You did make sure it was loaded, didn't you?" As soon as she said that, she wished she could take it back. There was a reason he wanted to see her. Maybe he'd received bad news about his latest book, or maybe the writing wasn't going well. Whatever it was, he didn't want to be alone tonight.

"Thanks for reminding me, Emily," Ray said. "We potential suicides can get pretty fur-brained." He made a clicking sound. "There, it's loaded. Satisfied?"

"Okay, Ray, okay. Just make sure I don't walk in on a corpse. See you later."

"That's pretty nebulous. *Later,* I mean."

"When I get there, then, how's that?"

"Much more to the point. As I always tell my students—make your point and get the hell out of there."

"Which is exactly what I'm doing now, Ray."

That sentence had ended their conversation about three hours earlier. Ray and Emily were in her living room now, on the Upper West Side, an apartment building that overlooked Central Park and the Planetarium, a place she visited about twice a month. She loved the laser light shows.

They were seated next to each other on a cream-colored leather sofa, the area lit by a gas fireplace, turned down to romance level quite by accident.

"So you're going to see Hal tomorrow, huh? How's he doing?" Ray asked.

Emily took a sip of wine. "Fine, I guess. I talked with him on the phone about a month ago. He was in England then, researching Stonehenge. You know, overkill."

"Yeah, that place has been researched to death. He specializes in weaponry, doesn't he?"

"Yeah. Hal loves anything that was used to kill at one time or another. He's got more useless pieces of weaponry than Uncle Sam."

"Well, everyone needs a hobby."

Emily looked at Ray more closely than she had for quite a while, and for whatever reason—the lateness of the hour, the smell of his Aramis cologne—she laid friendship aside and allowed lust to intervene. Casual sex went against everything she believed in, but she had a lot of catching up to do. Sex had been a cruise with all the trimmings while she was going to school—not that she hadn't had the urge. She'd just ignored that urge, concentrating instead on her studies. One consolation, of course, was that women in their thirties were at their sexual peak.

She moved closer, shuffling along at a turtle's pace and smiling like the Mona Lisa, the leather crackling like burning paper. But as she moved within range of a kiss, Ray smiled and said, "I really don't think we should, Emily," which caught her completely by surprise. Rare was the time any man refused an impromptu roll in the sack. Could she have possibly misjudged him?

She moved back to where she'd been before the hornies had hit and picked up her wineglass. "Kudos," she said, saluting him. "My respect instead of my body. I *am* impressed."

Alpha and Gamma joined them on the sofa then, Alpha curling onto Emily's lap, Gamma onto Ray's. They talked into the wee hours, the cats coming and going with feline impetuosity, and Emily discovered that Ray, in fact, missed their friendship. He had loved the sex, but sex, he said, was sex—and friendship, at least for him, was much more satisfying.

"I thought you'd be, I don't know, I thought you might be insulted if I told you I only wanted to be friends."

She thought about that and discovered that she *did* feel a little insulted. Hadn't she been a good enough lover? Didn't his knees turn to jelly every time he saw her?

"You *are* insulted," Ray said, when she didn't respond right away.

Emily grinned. "A little. Yeah, a little. I'll get over it, though, and you know what? The more I think about it, the more I understand it. Wait a second."

She got up and went into the kitchen, returning about a minute later with a corkscrew, a bottle of the good stuff, and two fresh glasses.

"Here, you do the honors," she said, handing him the bottle and the corkscrew.

"What are we toasting?" he asked.

"Friendship. Just friendship."

Ray pulled the cork out with a jaunty pop. "To friendship, then," he said, filling their glasses.

Two

They arrived at Logan around ten the next morning, later than David had hoped, because Emily'd overslept.

After they rented a Buick LeSabre they drove northwest, following the Mystic River along Route 3 to the town of Winchester, a few miles from the Middlesex Falls Reservation. They stopped at a gas station and called Hal for directions. Hal had a cell phone in his 1978 Volkswagen bus, his home while he was on a dig. Like Emily, Hal had decided to go it alone, without the benefit of the family's enormous wealth. The dig was at a place called Horn Pond, on a farm owned by a retired couple. A very early text indicated there had been a skirmish in that area during the Revolutionary War, an area littered with marshes and peat bogs.

"Where are you, Dad?" Hal asked. He wiped the sweat off his forehead with the back of his hand.

"Winchester, son."

"Okay, listen, you get onto Thistle Down Road, it's a dirt road. Take it about five miles till you get to a covered bridge. Once you get across the bridge, go right. Horn Pond and the Lerner Farm are another three miles. You'll see my microbus."

"Oh, the camper. Okay, see you soon."

Emily and David soon arrived at the site. Hal's camper was parked off the road, on the crest of an incline, the open canopy protecting a card table, four folding chairs, and a guitar leaning against the camper. Horn Pond hugged the road for about a half mile, then took a lazy right for another half mile.

Emily parked the climate-controlled Buick behind the camper and got out. "Like a furnace," she mumbled.

"Without the fan," David added.

They saw Hal at the bottom of the incline, supervising a honeycomb of dig sites: twelve in all, each one manned, everyone going about his business with exacting prudence. A path had been beaten through the waist-high weeds during the week-long dig, and Hal was reasonably proud of what they'd uncovered. Compared to, say, the opening of King Tut's tomb, Hal's dig wasn't much. He hadn't hoped for much, though, maybe a few buttons and plates—a musket, if they got real lucky. The text indicated that the area around the lake, near a stand of woods and down an incline, had been the site of a skirmish costing ten British and twelve American lives, small enough to miss mention in any history book. Hal's friends, to a man as hopeful as he, either stayed in Winchester or in the camper, where three could sleep as comfortably as they would in any Red Roof Inn. Everyone involved with the dig was an old college friend and no one worried about money; they were doing what they wanted to do, living their own personal American dream.

Hal waved. "Dad, Sis, c'mon down," he yelled.

No one looked up, intent as they were on their work. David and Emily moved carefully down the abrupt incline and there were hugs and kisses all around. Hal even gave David a kiss on the cheek, affection David welcomed any time.

David looked at his son. Hal's electric-blue eyes were as frantic as ever. His Georgetown T-shirt bore layers of dirt and sweat and a few recent ketchup stains.

He needs a bath, too, Emily thought. She didn't care, though, she hadn't seen Hal for months; if he smelled a little like an archaeologist, that was okay with her.

"So, Hal, did you find anything yet?" she asked.

Hal shrugged. "A few things. Some eating utensils, down by that stand of trees. It's pretty swampy back there. Gary—he's over there. Say hi, Gary."

A tall man with a shock of unruly blond hair waved and smiled, then went back to work.

"Gary looked around, you know, with a pole. Couldn't find anything, though. Janet and Lowell are back there now. Look, come on up to the bus and I'll get us some lemonade. It's really fierce out today, isn't it? I apologize for the way I look, not to mention the way I probably smell."

"Apologies aren't necessary, but I think I'll take you up on that drink," David said. "And what about dinner this evening? They got any good restaurants in Winchester?"

"I doubt it. There's one on the other side of Horn Pond, though—we can eat there. We've all been eating out of cans, mostly, although we did have a cookout the other night. Usually we're all too tired to mess around with cooking."

"Well, maybe we can have a cookout tonight—unless you'd rather eat out."

"You know, I've gotten a little tired of canned beans. A sit-down dinner sounds great."

They saw a woman on the path. She waved to Hal. "We got something, Hal," she yelled. "I don't know what, but it's big and it's solid."

"Wait here," he said. He met her halfway, talked with her a moment, then waved to David and Emily to join him.

"I can't promise you anything," he said, "but do you want to have a look?"

"Sure," Emily said.

They followed him around the side of the woods to a large, marshy area where they saw a man pushing a long pole through thick mud.

"Over here, Hal," he said excitedly. "It's pretty big, seven by three, maybe. I poked around underneath it a little and got it to move, but I haven't got a clue about how we're going to get it out of there."

"It's probably being sucked down by the mud," Hal said.

Hal took the pole. "Are you sure it's not a rock?"

"No, it's too symmetrical, you know? A couple feet thick, too."

Hal poked around while everyone watched. "It's in maybe three and a half feet," he said. He tested the ground behind him with his pole, walked on it. "Seems solid enough. Maybe we can get the Jeep down here. Janet, get Ed, will you?"

She ran back up the incline and reappeared a few minutes later, Ed in the lead.

"What do you think?" Hal asked. "Can you get your Jeep down here?"

Ed tested the ground. "I don't see a problem." He went off toward the Jeep.

"Gotta be careful," Hal said. "Maybe we can slide a few ropes underneath it and make a kind of cradle."

"That's gonna be real tricky," Janet said. "This is really squishy stuff."

He thought about that, weighed his options. "Go on up to the bus and get me some rope, Janet."

Ed and Janet got back about the same time. Meanwhile, Hal dropped onto his stomach and stuck his arm into the goo. He ran his hand over the object. "Christ, it's like trying to get through Jell-O," he said. Everyone watched hopefully. "Wood, I think it's wood!" he said finally. He lifted his arm out and shook it off. "Could be a case of muskets. Jesus, someone might have actually hidden a case of muskets down there."

His guess got everyone excited. A case of muskets—the grand prize, he thought. Lady luck had stepped right up and kissed them squarely on the mouth.

Janet handed him the rope. "It's gonna be tough," he said. "Wish me luck." After fumbling around for a couple of minutes, Hal got to his feet and shook his head. "I sure don't want to, but it looks like I'm gonna have to go in there." He looked around. "Anyone want to volunteer?"

No takers.

"Thought so."

"Tie a rope around your belly," Janet suggested.

"You sure about this?" David asked.

"No," Hal said with a smile. He tested his knot, then picked up the other rope. "I need a bath anyway, though. Ed, Lowell, lower me in, will you?"

They did as he'd asked, and after Hal was in waist deep, he said, "Seems solid enough. Janet, I'm going to need another rope."

Hal waited a second, watched as Janet started back to the camper, then drew in a deep breath and disappeared. The circling mud produced a wet popping sound. A minute passed.

By now Emily's heart was pounding. "He's okay, isn't he?" she said.

Another thirty seconds passed and Emily decided it was definitely time to get worried. She caught a couple of guys looking at each other funny and took a step toward the water's edge. "Hal?" she said. She looked back. "Look, don't you think——?"

Hal resurfaced then, looking like a giant chocolate bar, his white teeth gleaming like diamonds. "Got the right side," he said triumphantly. "Get me out of here, guys."

Ed and Gary pulled him out and Hal went around to the other side. "You knotted it up, right?" Ed asked.

"Solid as I can get 'er."

"Here's another rope," Janet yelled from the hillside. "It's a little smaller, but it'll hold, I think."

He took it. "Yeah, it'll hold," he said. "One more time, guys."

They lowered him in again. Tying the rope under this side took less than a minute.

"Gettin' good at this," Hal said, after he'd resurfaced. "Get me out, fellas. Ed, tie this around the frame, make a bowline knot."

Ed tied it, then got in behind the wheel. Hal tested the rope and gave Ed a thumbs-up.

"Give it some gas, just a little," he said.

Ed, apparently lost in the excitement of the moment, goosed the accelerator, spinning the wheels. "Shit," he said. He let off the gas and tried again. The Jeep responded, only a foot or so, but it was happening.

"That's it, Ed," Hal yelled. "Slow and easy."

Steadily the object began to emerge, but Ed could feel something wasn't right. The ground was softer now, the strain on the ropes enormous. "They're gonna break," he mumbled, "I just know it."

He had a choice: back off and let the thing sink again, or get everyone together and try to pull the damn thing out. He pushed the door open and got out. "Hal, we're gonna have to pull it out," he said. "Ground's too soft and that goddamn mud . . . it's too thick!"

Hal looked at the rope. "Maybe we should just let her sink," he said. "Those ropes don't look so good. Christ, if they snapped . . ."

"They're not gonna snap," Lowell said. "C'mon, we got enough muscle here. Let's just yank that sucker outta there."

Hal looked at Lowell, then at the others. He had to make a decision and hope to God he didn't regret it later. "Okay, let's do it. Gary, Lowell, get the right side. Ed, you and I'll get the left."

So they did, two on one side, two on the other.

"God, I hope this is worth it," Ed said through clenched teeth. He couldn't get a good handhold; no one could.

"Jesus, what the hell's in there?" Hal said.

No one had an answer, of course, but a case of muskets slipped a few notches from the top of their guess list.

"C'mon, dammit!" Gary yelled. "Will you just—"

The pop they heard then, as the box finally freed itself from the sucking mud, sent a shiver of relief through everyone, but the casual roll the box did as soon as it was freed sent everyone scattering. The box managed two rolls and finally stopped in what looked like a face-up position.

A circle formed, because by now the casket shape had become obvious.

"Holy shit," Janet mumbled, as everyone converged.

"Get me a rag, someone," Hal said.

Gary took a handkerchief from his pocket.

"Bet there aren't any muskets in that thing," Hal said, as he rubbed the head of the box with the handkerchief.

Finally he looked inside. "There's something in there. Christ, you guys aren't gonna believe this. It looks like a body!"

A million questions dangled from that announcement. Whose body? Where had it come from? Why was it here, in a peat bog? How old was it?

"You sure, Hal?" Emily asked.

Before Hal could answer her question, it began to rain. Almost immediately a bolt of lightning slashed to the earth nearby, followed by a clap of thunder that rattled the ground around them. The storm, born of heat and humidity, had formed against the horizon, waiting for a strong westerly wind. Another bolt of lightning rammed into the earth, this one even closer than the last, and again the ground shook.

"Jesus," Hal yelled, "get some cover. Everyone get to cover!"

"What about that?" Ed yelled, pointing at the casket.

"Forget it, dammit, get to the cars!"

They ran as fast as their legs would carry them, the ground under their feet already squishy from rain carried by gale-force winds.

Emily held her hand over her face while she fought her way up the hill, David right behind. Within twenty feet of the camper, a bolt of lightning slammed into Horn Pond, producing a clap of thunder like a cannon going off.

Emily and David dropped to the ground. "Dad, you okay?" Emily yelled.

"I'm fine," he yelled back. "Just go!"

She saw the Jeep out of the corner of her eye, Ed behind the wheel, shifting gears, trying to dig in, his face twisted with worry. *How the hell can he see?* Emily wondered. Janet sat beside him, covering her head with her hands, her body curled into a tight ball.

The rain blasted into the earth, firing mud like shrapnel at anything in the way. The last few feet were the hardest. The road was like a sinkhole, grabbing their ankles and holding on like something alive and very hungry. But somehow, exhausted, their clothing soaked with mud, they finally made it to the cars. Some piled into the camper; everyone else got into the Buick. Prayers came readily then as everyone tried to refocus and catch their breath. David sat behind the wheel of the Buick, Emily beside him.

"It's gotta let up soon," he muttered optimistically.

"Sure hope so," she said. "If it doesn't, I don't know how much longer that thing's gonna stay put. There's a lot of water out there."

"I've never seen anything like it," the woman in the back seat said. "Where the hell'd it come from?"

"Look at that," Gary said, pointing at the camper swaying like an inverted cradle.

"Christ," Emily said, "this keeps up any longer, that camper's not gonna make it!"

And if the wind had blown just a few minutes more, the camper would probably have blown away, but the storm stopped just as quickly as it had started and the sun, peeking through small, misshapen dark clouds, was a most welcome sight. Emily got out first.

"Everyone all right?" Hal asked, as they gathered between vehicles.

"Yeah," Emily said, "a little wet, but we're okay. You lost your canopy, Hal."

It had landed in one of the water-filled dig sites.

"Yeah, my guitar, too," Hal said bleakly. "That storm just plain ambushed us."

"One good thing, though," David said, "whatever you got down there is probably spic-and-span by now."

A stand of woods blocked their view of the casket. "Let's let things dry out a little," Hal said.

Janet came out of the camper. "We've only got a couple towels, so we'll have to share." She gave one to Emily, who, after she dried herself off, gave it to her father.

Three

A half hour later the air was as warm and moist as it had been before the storm. The water in the dig sites had drained out, too.

"Well, I'm game," Hal said. "Anyone else coming?"

In minutes they were all gathered around the rain-washed casket. Hal approached it first and looked inside. "Jesus," he said, "look at this!"

The top was translucent, disclosing the contents with magnificent clarity. What lay inside stoked the fires of their collective imagination.

"What do you suppose a vampire's doing in a swamp?" Hal said.

"What is this, some kind of joke?" Lowell said.

"Yeah, real funny!" Janet said.

The "vampire" looked real enough—too real, in fact. He had on a black cape with a gaudy red lining, a black bow tie, and a starched white shirt. His shirt buttons were tiny black skulls. His dark, greasy-looking hair was slicked straight back, and there were glittering rings on each of his large-knuckled fingers.

The box was a dark wood, and when Hal touched it, he discovered that the layers of sealant had done a pretty good job of protecting it.

"What *is* it?" Janet asked.

Hal forced a smile. "Looks like a vampire to me."

"C'mon, Hal!"

"Well, it does!"

Hal didn't really know what they had; no one did. *And it certainly isn't a vampire,* Hal thought. But as they inspected the casket, they found the beginnings of an answer.

"Look here," Gary said. "Tip it a little."

Etched into the underside of the casket were the words "PROPERTY OF PETRY BROS. CARNIVALS."

"You know what this is?" Hal said. "A castoff from a sideshow."

"What the hell's it doing here?" Janet asked.

"Insurance fraud, maybe," Emily said. "Perhaps the Petry Brothers Carnivals insured this thing for a lot of money, reported it stolen—when in actuality they'd dumped it here—and then collected the money. Fraud happens all the time."

Emily glanced around. She got a few nods.

"But who owns this guy?" Hal asked. "The Lerners, us, or Petry Brothers Carnivals?"

"I think we should tell the Lerners," Janet said. "We found him on their land."

"You're right," Hal said. "What we've got to do is get this thing up the hill and into the camper. Then we can drive down to the Lerners' farm and show them what we found."

"That's all well and good," Janet said, "but how the hell do we do that?"

"Carry him. There are enough of us. We probably can't carry him straight up the hill, but the ground levels off a little ways back; we'll take that route."

"This guy's heavy," Lowell said. "There are no handholds, either."

"Oh, c'mon, you guys! Four of us can carry this thing easy enough. Ed, Gary, me, Lowell. Sis, maybe you and Dad can drive down to the Lerners' and tell them we found something. Don't tell them what, just tell them we'll be there, I don't know, within a half hour or so."

"Sure," Emily said.

It took an hour. Now all they had to do was get it inside the camper. They couldn't turn it because of the stove and refrigerator, so they let it stick out the sliding doors while Hal sat on it to keep it steady.

The Lerners were waiting on the side of the road with David and Emily. After the van stopped, Hal got out, one hand on the casket to make sure it wouldn't just drop on the ground. "We found this in the swamp," he said. "We thought you might want to have a look at it."

Mary and Homer Lerner had seen a few horror movies, but nothing could have prepared them for this. "Heavens," Mary said, "you found that thing in the swamp?"

"Buried in four feet of mud. Probably made out of wax. Just something from a sideshow, that's all. Wood seems to be in good shape, though. Thing is, we *did* find it on your land, and who knows, it just might be worth something. Give me a hand, guys."

Mary and Homer stepped closer. "Goodness gracious," Mary said, when she saw what was inside.

Homer looked at it more objectively. "Made out of wax or wood, you say?"

"Probably. Look at this," Hal said, pointing.

The Lerners bent closer.

"See there, it says, 'Property of Petry Brothers Carnivals.' "

"Well, I'll be," Homer said, and stood up. "How do you think it got into the swamp?"

"I haven't got a clue. Could be insurance fraud."

"Well, that just might be it. I've heard about that. It's greed, you know, just plain old-fashioned greed. It's supposed to be a vampire, huh?"

"Well, it's meant to represent a vampire, it's not a real—"

"I know that, son . . . I know that."

"What are you going to do with him, young man?" Mary asked.

"Do with him? Tell you the truth, I don't know. It's not archaeological, and in our verbal agreement you gave us permission to remove only those items that could be considered archaeological. Actually, it's yours if you want it."

Mary smiled. "Oh, goodness, no. What would we do with him? *Him*. Just listen to me!"

"We could make a scarecrow out of him," Homer said, laughing.

Mary waved loosely. "Probably scare the corn out of growing, Homer," she said.

Everyone laughed at that. Hal said, "Anyone got any suggestions? I mean, I don't want him. It's not even good sculpture."

Silence.

Hal shrugged. "I guess the only thing we can do is call the authorities—"

"I'll take him," David said.

"You, Dad? Why in the world would *you* want him?"

He thought about it a moment, then said, "I just do, I guess. He's captured my imagination, I don't know. Will you let me have him?"

"Are you sure?"

"Reasonably so." David turned to the Lerners. "Can you folks recommend a reliable mover?"

Homer looked at Mary, then back at David. "There's Harry Fenwick, right down the road. He does a lot of hauling. Truck's a mite old, but well kept. I'd recommend him. Reasonable, too."

"Would you mind if I used your phone?"

"Not at all. Fact is, Mary and I have been wanting to ask you folks to supper. You can even put that thing on the porch if you like. If it's made out of wax, you don't want to leave it in the sun. Say, wasn't that a humdinger of a

storm? Real humdinger. So, what do you folks say to dinner?"

That evening, while everyone gathered around a big table,
eating a chicken dinner with all the fixings, Janet said, "You
realize, we don't know for certain that it *isn't* a body."

Everyone stopped eating.

Emily agreed, "I've been thinking about it, and I say we
should open it up."

Everyone looked at her.

"I know it's probably not real," she continued, "but what
if it is? If it's human, we should probably have contacted
the authorities by now."

Mary Lerner suddenly looked pale. She dropped her fork
onto her plate. A fake vampire was one thing; a dead body
was quite another.

Hal, too, had wondered if they hadn't made a mistake by
not opening the casket right away, and as the leader of the
group, he felt a sudden strong urge to do something about
it. He pushed his chair back and got up. "Mr. Lerner," he
said, "I need a hammer and a screwdriver."

"In the drawer," Mary said.

"What are you going to do?" Homer asked.

"I'm going to make sure whatever's in that casket is only
make-believe."

Hal took out a hammer and screwdriver. "C'mon," he
said, "let's open him up and see exactly what we've got."

On the porch, Homer flipped on a light while Hal removed the tarp. He paused, looking down at the thing, felt
his eyes begin to water. Funny, how it looked more menacing. *Probably the light,* he thought. *Just the light. Shadows dancing. Night shadows.*

Hal slipped the business end of the screwdriver between
the lid and the wood near the top of the casket and drove
the point home. It made a sound like ice cracking, but sound

was all they got. The top didn't budge. He went around to the other side and tried again. Still nothing.

"Tight as a drum," he muttered under his breath.

He tried the foot, parallel to the vampire's spit-shined shoes. This time the top gave about a quarter inch and an ominous, ear-splitting screech filled the room. Encouraged, he went about his business now like a man possessed. He hurried around to the other side, rammed the screwdriver into place, and drove down onto it with the hammer. The top exploded into the air about three feet, grazing his chin and knocking him on his butt. The top slammed down cock-eyed across the casket.

Hal got to his feet. "Christ," he said, "scared the hell out of me!"

Nervous laughter made the rounds.

Hal moved closer. "Smell it?" he said softly, glancing around.

"Smell what?" Emily said.

Another sniff. "Wood."

"Wood? So what?" Lowell said.

"Don't you see?" Emily said, "If this really *was* a body, there'd be an odor. Fecal matter, decay. But the only thing we smell is wood."

"Give me a hand, Ed," Hal said.

They moved the cover to the other side of the porch. When they were done, Hal stood over the vampire, and after a few nerve-steeling moments, reached in and touched his cheek. "Hard as stone," he said, looking into the vampire's flat blue eyes. He looked around the room, then back into the casket. "One thing's for sure, he's not human. I don't know what he is, but he's not human. Thank God."

"Well, then," Homer said, "if it's not something to call the sheriff about, I say we have dessert."

After they replaced the plastic cover, and prodded by the odor of Cherries Jubilee, everyone except David went back into the kitchen.

Alone with the vampire, David stood over the casket, looking in. The light was off. Finally, he smiled and said, "You're very ugly, did you know that? And anyone as ugly as you are needs a name. Not just any name, though . . . something appropriate." He thought back to his college days and to his roommate, a man as ugly as any man he had ever seen, at least until now. "Martin," he said. "I think we'll call you Martin. How does that suit you? In honor of my old roomie."

He laughed lightly, pleased with his choice of names, then went inside and joined the others.

Alone again, Martin simply stared at the porch ceiling and listened.

Four

Martin watched while a man with a long, waxed mustache, a Red Sox baseball cap, and the stub of a cigarette dangling from his mouth straddled his casket and covered it with heavy brown paper. Effectively blind now, Martin could only listen while the man secured the paper with postage tape. "Put this sucker back in the swamp, you ask me," he heard the man say. A short time later, Martin's world turned a dry black as the man added another layer of paper. Again he heard the sound of tape being yanked out and then stuck to the sides of the casket.

"There, that oughta hold 'er," the man said.

Get it right, Martin thought.

"Okay, you got the key, right, Harry?"

Martin heard the squeak of sneakers on hardwood.

"Jesus, like to scared the crap out of me! Shouldn't sneak up like that, Mr. Kane."

"You have the key, right?"

Martin recognized the voice as that of one of the men who'd rescued him.

"Yeah, I got it. Right here in my change pocket."

"The Empire State Building, Room 750. You wrote that down, didn't you? It's the Anglo-American Arts Foundation. Write that down, too."

"Yes, sir."

Silence then, and Martin vaguely heard the sound of graphite gliding on paper.

"Good. Be careful."

"Oh, sure, always am."

"I'm taking you at your word, now. You said you'd driven through the city before. If you haven't, I want to know. There's tougher driving than in New York City, but I'll be damned if I know where."

"Like driving in a combat zone. I heard that. Well, I'm not going to tell you I been there when I haven't. All told, this'll be my fourth, no, fifth trip. Got a cousin lives there. In Queens. Been to see him three times, and one other time—"

"That's fine. As I told you, we'll be staying here for a while. That's why I gave you a key to the office."

"Bein' a Saturday, your help's at home. That's what you said, right?"

"Take the casket through the outer offices and into the artifacts holding area. You'll recognize it. And don't take the paper off."

"Don't take the paper off. Gotcha."

"And relay that to your help. You do have someone to help you, don't you? He's awfully heavy."

"Yes, sir. Got my sister's husband, Sam. He's a big man. Probably lift this thing all by himself."

Martin heard a screen door open, then slam shut. A short time later, he felt his casket being lifted, followed by the sensation of movement. *Feels like being on a boat.* "Watch that last step," he heard. "Looks kinda weak."

"Maybe we can sue," he heard another man say.

A few moments later, Martin felt the casket scrape along what he thought was a metal truck bed.

"Hope these springs make it," Harry said.

"How's he fastened? He's not gonna fall forward and break the glass, is he?"

"Nah. They got it braced around the middle and secured to the back with bolts. Top's made out of plastic, anyway."

This was the first time Martin realized how he had been put on display: trussed at the middle. It made sense. If some clumsy kid bumped into his casket, at least he wouldn't fall. He guessed the casket itself had been bolted to the floor.

A few seconds later, he heard the engine turn over.

For the next few hours or so Martin tried to sleep, but he couldn't. He was being taken someplace new, and he couldn't help wonder what that place was like. Over the years he had gone everywhere they had taken him—having no choice—and on those trips he had tried, in his special way, to talk with Bobby. He had tried to tell him that he wanted to go to New York City, that they should have a carnival there. Bobby'd heard him, he knew he had, but Bobby'd only laughed. "You can't move, Martin," he said. "You're so dead you can't even move! How does that feel, Martin?" He hadn't even tried to disguise his impatience. That's why they'd thrown him into the swamp in the first place—impatience. "You know," Bobby'd told him, the day before they'd gotten rid of him, "there was a time when I found you . . . amusing. I wish to hell I could remember when that was."

Someday, after I've finally puzzled through all this, Martin thought . . . *Someday . . .*

After a while, Martin tried to catch snatches of conversation between people in cars going the same way. He got a mixed bag: music with conversation, music only, conversation only. *Pretty boring stuff,* he thought, *boring enough to listen to what Sam and Harry are thinking.* He'd tried that before, with other people. Sometimes it worked, sometimes it didn't. He did know that thinking voices always matched speaking voices, so he at least knew whose thoughts he had tuned in to. Harry's thoughts came in fits and gasps, like a dream, first something about a kid's birthday, then darkness, then glimpses of a baby's smile, then more darkness, before he saw tiny hands clapping and a two-candle, lopsided birthday cake. *Interesting, though,*

Martin thought, *how images of violent sex overlap.* A blend of innocence and indulgence that gave him a feeling of comradeship.

Sam's thoughts came in a little better, but still not as good as he'd hoped. From Sam he got only sex; Sam and Harry and a woman named Marge all pretzeled together, the images again laced by frequent and annoying blackouts. He went back to Harry for a second and got an image of the same woman standing behind the birthday boy. *Probably the kid's mother. Sam was probably having a fantasy about the three of them getting it on. Interesting, if he wasn't para-lyzed. Always better to participate than watch.*

Participation wasn't about to happen, though, not in his condition, so eventually Martin gave up listening to Harry and Sam and went back to listening to real conversations.

Lying there in the dark, he thought about when he was a kid, a human, and when his family went on Sunday drives and how they counted cows. He smiled, or at least tried to. *Even vampires get bored on long trips,* he thought. *Are we there yet, Dad?*

"I've got a thing about tunnels," Sam said. "You sure there isn't a better way?"

They were coming into New York City, via the New Jersey Turnpike and then through the Lincoln Tunnel to West Side Drive. They'd gone miles out of their way, but Harry told Sam that driving from the top of Manhattan to the middle would be a real hassle. "There's another way, but it sure ain't better," he said, "so you're just going to have to suck it up till we get through. It won't be long then, down the West Side Drive to Thirty-fourth and then up Thirty-fourth a coupla blocks. Can't miss it, Sam, it's a real tall building and there's this big ape holding onto the side for dear life."

"Very funny."

The trip up Thirty-fourth Street took them a lot longer than they'd anticipated, but Martin knew when they got there. The air crackled with noise: horns blaring, cursing and yelling, brakes squealing, bicycle chains whirring. Cop whistles. Confusing stuff at first, but after a while, Martin figured out how to tune in to one sound and push everything else to the background.

The truck stopped and Martin heard Harry say, "Glad we're almost there," and Martin thought so, too.

A little while later the traffic noises died down and Martin heard the back doors swing open. *We're in an underground parking lot,* he thought.

"Get the back, Sam, I'll get the front," Harry said.

Sam climbed into the truck—Martin felt the bed sag a little—and lifted the foot end.

"Got it?" Harry asked.

Martin pictured Harry outside the truck, a hand on either side of the casket.

"Got her."

Careful, Martin thought.

"Heavy son of a bitch," he heard Sam say.

"Gotta go three hundred, three-fifty with the box."

"Freight elevator, right?"

"Yeah."

When they got to the elevator, Harry said, "Okay, let's stand this guy up."

Sam laughed. "Can't get over how we're callin' this thing a guy."

"Statue, then. Just do it, Sam."

"Sure. No need to get short, Harry."

Martin felt the elevator rising. A little while later he heard the elevator doors open again and then the sound of the box being dragged.

"Office number seven-fifty. Off to the right, looks like," Harry said.

They carried Martin to Room 750 and Harry took out

his notepad to make sure the name on the glass door jibed. "This is it," he said.

The door into the artifacts holding area was already open.

"Jesus, will you look at this place?" Sam said.

"Don't you steal anything, Sam! I told you about stealin' stuff from clients."

"Hell, it's all boxed up, anyway, Harry. Bet this stuff's worth a fortune! Jesus, oughta be a crime, anyone gets to have stuff like this. What kind of business you say it was?"

"Hell if I know. But I'll tell you, you so much as pocket a breath mint, I'll can your ass."

Martin was amused. The world was full of crooks.

"Yeah. Okay. We take the paper off when we get him— Jesus, there I go again. We take off the paper when we get it situated?"

"No, Mr. Kane said he'd do that. C'mon, let's get outta here."

Martin listened to them leave, to the front door being locked, and for any other sound during the next hour. He couldn't help but admit that he was excited. Harry and Sam had said something about how nice this place was, and he very much looked forward to being part of that. Sure, he'd still be on display, but these people would have the capacity to appreciate his workmanship, the lifelike quality of the wax that wasn't wax. That was something, at least.

As the second hour started, Martin heard the front door open, followed by the voices of David Kane and a woman and one of the people who had rescued him from the swamp. More excitement. Footsteps. Then he heard, "He's in here, Dad. Want me to take the paper off?"

David was in the outer office, poring over the mail. "No, I'll do it. He is out of the sunlight, isn't he? I didn't tell those guys to put him in the shade, I just thought they'd do that on their own."

"Assuming again, huh, Dad? Yeah, he's out of the sunlight."

During summer months the sun made an afternoon semi-circle across a bank of tall windows. It was almost six now, late enough. Martin was out of danger.

Looking at the paper-covered casket, Emily heard her father on the phone. She had a good idea who he'd called.

"You called Ray, didn't you?" she asked, when he came back into the room.

He put his hands in his pockets and looked up at Martin's casket, then back at her. "As a matter of fact, I did. I didn't tell you, did I? Ray's going to write my memoirs. I just thought he'd get a kick out of this. I invited him over for dinner. You know what, I think I'll wait till then to take the paper off. Kind of an unveiling. What do you think?"

"Sounds interesting. And I suppose you'll be doing the cooking?"

"You suppose correctly."

"Well, despite that, I guess I can make it."

"A vote of confidence—thanks loads, Emily."

"No problem, but first I'm gonna go home for a while. The cats haven't been fed. I'll see you tonight, okay?"

"Great. Sevenish?"

"Okay—I'll bring the wine."

He smiled at her. "Okay," he said.

After the offices were quiet again, Martin thought about some things, remembering.

In his dormant state, he wasn't as vulnerable to sunlight, he knew that well enough. He thought about something that had happened just a few days before they'd left him in the swamp, remembered it as if it had happened ten minutes ago.

With his mind's eye, he saw a boy holding a tent flap open, his mouth open wide in amazement. The sun lay low on the horizon, catching Martin on the left side of the face. For a moment then his mind screamed at the boy. "You're killing me, dammit! Close that flap. Close that flap!"

But what had happened yesterday—the overhead sun dividing him like a thousand knives—had been potentially far more dangerous. Two minutes, that's how long the boy had left the flap open, maybe a little longer. Yesterday he had spent at least half an hour staring up at that blazing sun, and although the pain had been excruciating, he had come out of it relatively unscathed. The question now was, how long could he withstand the sun's rays? But there was another question, too, a far more important one—would he ever move again, or was this the way he'd spend his last days? And nights. Just a statue with a brain and a little more tolerance for the sun. Given a choice, less tolerance and the ability to actually move would be far more preferable.

Five

Ray Timmerson had come a long way in twenty years. He'd started as a reporter for the *Albany Herald,* covering politics, after which he'd gotten a job at the *New York Times.* At the *Times* he'd written about political issues again, not as a reporter, but as a columnist. Like most reporters, though, Ray had a dream—he wanted to write the Great American Novel. In 1982 he'd left his job at the *Times* and isolated himself in the family room of his suburban Connecticut home, where he'd slaved over a sweeping epic of the American frontier called *Fathers and Sons.* His research had been perfect and his smooth style had caught the attention of every major publisher. The book was an instant hit with everyone, critics included. He followed that with three more books just as ambitious.

David and Ray had met through Emily, and David had liked him right away. Despite his success, he had a quick and sincere smile and he listened intently. He never talked about his writing, either—unless someone asked, and even then he was the soul of brevity. A male Dorothy Parker. But David hadn't invited Ray over because he was going to write his memoirs. Ray had also written two horror novels under the pen name A. K. Shriber. And although they had been written in just a few months, as a change of pace, the Timmerson wit was hard to miss. The horror novels were the reason David had invited Ray.

Ray and his date had arrived at about eight-thirty, and at first glance they'd seemed to be the proverbial odd couple. She was at least a head taller and gorgeous, while Ray's stringy brown hair was as thin as he was. He wore a white suit with bell-bottomed trousers that Travolta would have sneered at, while she wore an above-the-knee, very tight Paris original. Passion was blind tonight, though, and as they stepped off the elevator, grinning, she hurriedly worked at her hair while Ray defogged his glasses.

Ray smiled at her, then knocked on the door.

David opened it. "Ray, really glad you could make it," a long look at Ray's date, "so glad *both* of you could make it. Come on in."

Emily was in back, drinking a black Russian, wondering if Ray would bring someone. At the same time, she found out that she didn't really care whether he did or not.

The others joined her and Ray said, "Emily, David, it's a very great pleasure to introduce Kathy Winestead. Kathy's a Rockette."

Kathy smiled; she had teeth like Chiclets, clear green eyes, and a very nice figure.

"A Rockette," David said. "Well, that's just fascinating. Kathy, you know, I've always wanted to know—what's the height limit for a Rockette?"

"Five-eight to six feet. David, you're not going to ask me to do a kick, are you?"

"Yeah, I was, actually."

Kathy shrugged, hiked up her skirt, and did a classic Rockette kick with the left leg and then the right.

"My God," Emily said, impressed. "Talk about limber!"

Kathy smiled and with a wink and a touch of Emily's elbow said, "None of us has any bones, Emily. That's another requirement."

Emily laughed out loud. She was going to like this woman.

Everyone grabbed a seat then, prepared to make small

talk until dinner was ready. After a few moments, Ray got up and wandered to the door leading into the artifacts holding area.

"Drink?" David asked from the doorway into the makeshift kitchen.

Ray turned and looked at him. "So you're going to make us wait, huh, David?"

"What?"

"To see Martin."

"Oh, that. I thought we'd wait till after dinner."

"That might take another hour. Do me a favor, I mean, I've written about these things, but I've never actually seen one up close and personal—wax or otherwise. Let's do it now, what do you say?"

David had wanted to get everyone satiated, then bring on the floor show. And with a face like Martin's, appetites might disappear.

"Kathy, how about you?" he asked.

Kathy had taken a seat on the sofa beside Emily. She shrugged and chewed on her lower lip, then smiled wanly. "Oh, I know they're not real—vampires, I mean. But I've always been somewhat impressionable. Know what I mean?" She smiled again, naturally, and her apprehension appeared to dissolve. "I'm being silly. Let's have a look. He's only wax, right?"

"He's not much to look at," David said. "Harmless as a kitten, but ugly as a stump."

"Lacking the romantic mystique of the classic vampire, is he?" Ray said.

"Ray, you're the expert—you tell me. After you," David said.

Ray led the way, and within a few seconds everyone had gathered around the paper-covered casket. A bank of fluorescent lights provided a harsh wash of pale light.

"Tall, isn't he?" Ray said, and delicately touched the front of the casket.

"About six and a half feet," David said.

Despite himself—he was an intelligent twentieth-century man, after all—Ray felt uncomfortable. *Martin,* he thought, *is probably nothing more than a huge candle without the wick, but the circumstances surrounding his discovery are pretty fascinating.*

"Well, let's see him," Ray said, his hands joined in front of him, a curious blend of enchantment and studious concentration on his face.

"Drumroll, please," David said.

David picked at the tape along the sides, pulled it down, and the paper began to fall away in large sheets. Finally Martin came into view.

"My God," Ray said. He took an involuntary step back. "I've never seen anything like it."

He steeled himself against what stood before him, his imagination telling him one thing, logic another. He stepped closer and ran his hand over the plastic that covered Martin's face. "He looks sad, doesn't he?" he said.

"If I looked like that, I'd be sad, too," Kathy said.

Emily noticed it, too, a sadness that hadn't been there before. *It's just the lighting,* she decided.

"How do you think his face got so misshapen?" Ray asked.

"You got me. We did have to leave him in the sun at the swamp. That's gotta be it, because he sure didn't look like that when they pulled him out. Hideous, isn't he?"

Everyone laughed, and when they stopped, Ray stepped back. "No fangs," he said, more or less to himself.

"What?" David said.

Ray kept looking at Martin. "Teeth, David. No teeth. Vampires are supposed to have very long, very sharp fangs. Martin doesn't have any. Here they went to all that trouble and they forgot the most important feature."

"Well, no teeth that we can *see.*"

"Isn't that the point, though? No pun intended. You're

supposed to see them. I mean, you can dress him up and give him a great backdrop and bloodshot eyes, but if you forget the teeth, you've kind of missed the point."

Kathy rolled her eyes.

"You get my drift, don't you, David?"

Ray looked at David, at how his attention seemed to have been diverted; he had his nose to the air.

"Dinner," he said, almost whispering. He touched Ray's arm. "Hold that thought and excuse me."

David left then, leaving Ray and Kathy alone. Finally Kathy said, "Coming, Ray?" sounding a little anxious.

Ray looked at her. "You cold?" he asked.

"Yeah, a little. You coming or not?"

Ray smiled. "Go on. I'll be right there."

"Supper in five minutes," David yelled.

"Great, I'm starved," Kathy said. She left Ray and Martin alone. After a minute or so, Ray took out a notepad and a pen and after only a few seconds' thought, he started writing.

It is the eyes, I think, that drew me first. Eyes that are as penetrating as any mesmerist's, as intuitive as any scholar's, and as coldly blue as an Arctic dawn. The forehead is broad and deformed, appearing very much like a rotting melon, and the nose, bent and hooked, with nostrils flared, fairly dominates the face. The skin is the color of March slush, and the lower lip is jutting and huge, spilling over a remarkably weak chin that almost disappears into the creature's neck. The ears are a boxer's, and veins crisscross the hairless skull like lines on a road map.

His breath is the wind blowing over a desecrated grave, lifting the odor of the dead to the noses of the innocent, who lie unknowing in their warm beds.

His arms are grotesquely long, dangling his blunt and thick hands to his knees, and the nails of his fingers have been chewed to the quick; but hopefully not by Martin, for he is a wax concoction, a being of the mind and not the womb. A creature sent to us by another's imagination and given life by our own.

But although he is a creature of wax, of the mind, if the devil were a man, I suspect his name would be Martin and that his legions would be many.

Ray reread his description, then tore the pages out of the notepad, crumpled them up, and threw them into a wastebasket near the door. Shaking his head and smiling at himself, he joined the others.

About the same time, Martin, who had read Ray's thoughts, started to get a little frantic, wondering if he really did look like that.

Six

At about two in the morning, Martin listened as David pulled up a wingbacked chair and sat down in front of him. Martin couldn't see David, but he could hear him. *What the hell are you doing?* Martin wondered. A reasonable question, he thought, considering the lateness of the hour.

Martin tried to read David's thoughts, but all he got were jumbled phrases and an occasional name: Emily, Ray, Martin. Martin frowned—he never had liked one-sided conversations.

Finally David said, "You were a hit, Martin, you know that?" A pause. Then, "But God, you sure are ugly, and you're getting uglier by the day."

Ugly, Martin thought evenly, having come to grips with Ray's description. Ugly was okay, but ugly was such a strong word. Different would be good, or at least, better than ugly. Or maybe unusual. Or unique, especially for his kind. There were probably a few mortals as ugly as he was, but no vampires.

"Okay," David said, interrupting Martin's train of thought. "Maybe ugly is a little . . . harsh. Unusual might be better. Highly unusual. Even for a vampire."

Martin realized then that he and David were actually communicating, that David had broken into his thoughts, or maybe vice versa. While David prattled on about Martin's nonexistent teeth, wondering what had happened to them,

Martin drew a mental picture of David moving his casket to a window, someplace where he could see something other than crates. He even had sweat breaking out on David's brow in his vision. But David, it appeared, hadn't heard or seen. He kept talking and talking, so eventually Martin gave up, allowing his mental painting to simply pop into nonexistence.

"You know, I wish you were real, Martin," David said. "I'd have quite a conversation piece then. The only nonlethal vampire in existence."

A pause, and Martin suspected that David was frowning.

"You're not real, though," David continued. "You're just a hunk of wax, the world's largest candle. If I had any sense at all I'd put a wick in you, stick you next to a window and watch you melt."

Martin saw through that remark—the homicidal nature of it—and wondered if maybe, just maybe, he hadn't gotten through, after all. When David got up, he was sure he hadn't.

"Goodnight, Martin," he said tiredly. "We'll have to chat like this more often, only next time, don't let me do all the talking."

Very funny, Martin thought.

Martin saw David smile and watched as he turned and walked slowly away, listening while David went into the bathroom and brushed his teeth.

While David was in there, Martin caught snippets of thought, again a wild mix. He did think about him again before he finally crawled into bed. He thought about the woman, Emily, too, those thoughts rimmed by a strong feeling of comfort and love. But when David thought about him, Martin got only ambivalence and even frustration. *Strange,* Martin thought, *that having him here should actually be frustrating.*

After David went to sleep, Martin discovered that if he tried hard enough, he could tap into his dreams. He saw a

boy in a field and a large man and a kite, and then he saw
what he thought were a hospital and lot of people in white.
The images were muddled and frazzled, though, so he finally tuned out and thought about New York. This huge and
captivating place where so much happened, where so many
people laughed and cried and died for so many different
reasons . . . he was thinking about Radio City Music Hall
and the Rockettes when he heard David stir and then get
up. He focused on the door, one of the few things he could
see, and within a minute or so the door opened and David
stumbled, half asleep, into the room.

"I'll bet you're bored silly," he said.

Martin didn't answer, afraid to.

"Give the neighbors a scare, they see you," David said
matter-of-factly. "Ah, but what the hell, I never did like the
neighbors anyway."

Martin heard David shuffle toward his casket and stop.
He couldn't see David now, but his thoughts were clearer.
He was wondering if moving him wasn't going to make
him have a heart attack. *Well,* Martin thought, *you don't
know till you try.*

He felt the sensation of movement a few seconds later
and he thought about how a penguin walks, exactly how
David was trying to move the casket, he thought; left, right,
left, right, left, right. Slowly the Chrysler Building came
into view, and when he was only a few feet from the window, Martin heard David sigh and then sit down and catch
his breath. "I can't believe I did that!" David said.

By then, however, Martin could have cared less what
David had to say or think, and when David shuffled back
to bed, Martin didn't even notice.

Martin listened to the city like a kid watching Saturday
morning cartoons. Every once in a while he tapped into a
conversation, but for the most part, he was like a TV with
a bad antenna, everything jumbled and snowy, things leaping in and out and making no sense at all. But as the sun

started to brighten on the horizon, he finally picked up on something that sounded like it was happening right below him.

Follow the bitch, no one around. Follow her!

A man, Martin thought.

Christ, I'm such a jerk! Why the hell didn't I just stay in bed this morning?

A woman.

I didn't have to come in early, I didn't have—shit! He saw me. Goddamn it, he saw me!

Go'damn fever! Head feels like sh— She's going down an alley. Scared. Jesus, my head!

Where the hell's a cop? Where's a goddamn cop when you—

You're sick, man! You don't want her! You gotta get help, man! No way out, trapped. She's goin' nowhere.

Cops! Run! Oh, God, go away! Go away. Hide!

"Lady, where you at?"

Rape, death, hide, hide. There! Behind the garbage cans. Holy Mary, Mother of God, pray for us sinners . . .

Martin heard a metallic click, and he pictured a knife opening up.

"Look, lady, I don't want no trouble! I got this godawful fuckin' headache!"

Martin heard another voice then, lower pitched. "Hey, just what the hell you think you're doing?"

Silence.

"You'd better put that thing away! What the hell—I'm going for the cops! What're you doing?"

Footfalls then, fading fast.

Holy Mary, Mother of God, pray for us sinners, now and at the hour . . .

Fuckin' head!

Martin heard more footsteps, listened while they faded. More praying. Softer footsteps and the woman crying while she talked with the cops.

Martin kept listening to the city until daylight, because by then there were too many thoughts, too many conversations, and even he couldn't untangle the mess. But as tentacles of sunlight spread over the city, Martin began to worry. *What if David's overslept? What if he . . . died?* The top of the sun peeked over the Chrysler Building and Martin started to panic. *Get up, goddammit!* he thought. *You're killing me, human!*

Nothing.

A couple minutes later, he saw half of the sun, and he could feel it hot on his skin, reaching underneath, clawing at the bone. *Get up, David! Goddamn you, get up! Get up, human, damn you, get up! Get up! Get up! Get—*

"Sorry about that," David said.

Had he been able to, Martin would have caught his breath. He tried to move his eyes to see behind him, to see David. He couldn't.

"Guess I overslept."

My eyes, Martin thought. *Can't see. I can't see!*

Martin sensed David moving around in front of him. Martin saw him put on his glasses. "None the worse for wear," he mumbled, his face only inches from Martin's, studying him. He backed away and took off his glasses.

By now Martin realized that he wasn't blind, after all; that his vision was only blurred around the edges. He saw the sun peeking over David's shoulder like a shiny new hump and he remembered the boy holding the tent flap open.

"Be right back," David said. He walked past Martin, out of sight, and closed the door behind him.

Martin hadn't heard a word. *He's going to let me die!* he thought. He thought about a lot of things then, while the sun burrowed into him, about when he could move, mostly, when he could skulk about, and when he could drink to his heart's content. He thought about pain, too, because he knew something about pain, and he thought about when he was mortal and only wishing he was immortal. He was thinking about that when David came back, a green blanket thrown over his arm. He'd been gone for only about half a minute, but half a minute was plenty of time for a life to pass.

"Hope this helps," David said, and threw the blanket over the casket. "Sleep well."

Martin's relief was instant, like that of someone who'd just woken up from a bad dream. He heard the door shut behind him and he realized his senses had returned, too.

After a while, after he'd regained his composure, he started to really appreciate where he was. This wasn't some pissant little burg where nothing ever happened, this was New York City, in all its corruption and debauchery and vice, and it was calling to him like voices from a huge playground.

Sleep well. Yeah, sure. I'll probably never sleep again. Not here, at least.

Seven

David thought, *I wonder if he's comfortable?* and felt foolish for thinking it. Martin stood to his left, uncovered because it was dark out.

David moaned. He hadn't been feeling well. Nothing serious, he told himself, just a few aches and pains. Old age, probably. He kept those aches and pains to himself; no sense in alarming Emily unnecessarily.

He told Martin, though. He talked to Martin about almost everything. He had even moved a chair close by so he could be comfortable when they talked. Lately, he had been thinking about Martin the way most people thought about their pets. *And why not?* he asked himself. Martin lightened the stress load, just like a pet. And Martin even went one better—David didn't have to walk him or pick up after him.

He thought about what had happened that morning and the smile disappeared from his face. He had forgotten Martin's blanket the night before and the few hours of daylight—even on a cloudy morning—had taken a toll. Martin's lower lip had ballooned; it looked like a giant slug now, and the area beneath his eyes were slacker still. Looking at him now, David wondered if he couldn't rework the wax. If it *was* wax. Funny he hadn't opened the case and found that out by now.

He looked at Martin closely. *He sure is a sight. Heck, there was a time when he'd actually looked human; now he*

looks like a crazy man's taken a blowtorch to him. He
touched the case and tested the hasps and locks that had
been attached before they'd loaded Martin onto the truck
at the Lerners'. *Pretty solid*. He had the keys in the office.
David shrugged and went after the key, and when he returned, he stood in front of Martin and said, "Now, don't
you go running off."

After he unlocked the case, he swung the plastic cover
open, hesitating a moment before he reached in and dragged
his fingers across the back of Martin's hand.

"Hmph," he said, "still hard as a rock. Cold as steel, too.
I doubt you're made of wax, Martin. No wax is this hard.
You certainly are susceptible to heat, though. Strange. I
promise I'll be more careful. I mean, it wouldn't do to have
you get more ugly than you already are."

David reached up then and after a long look into Martin's
eyes, stroked his cheek. "Strange," he said, "your cheek's
just as hard as your hand. Some kind of special material,
I guess. What, though? And why in the world would some
second-rate carnival spend big money on a special alloy to
make something that no one gets to touch, something people just look at? You know, maybe I should have you analyzed, Martin. Maybe I should cut off a piece of you and—"

No, human!

David's scalp felt like it had turned to ice. He backed
away from Martin and gooseflesh rose on his arms.

"Martin?" he said finally, their gazes locked. "Was that
you?" He thought about it and couldn't help but smile. It
felt strange, though.

It was then that he noticed a small red bubble at the
corner of Martin's right eye. "My goodness, Martin, if I
didn't know better . . ." He touched the bubble and let it
gather on his finger. He looked at it closely, then sniffed
it. If it smelled like anything, David thought, it smelled like,
well, like a penny. "Part of the wax, probably," he said, and
held it away from his face. "Has to be." He sniffed it again

and then delicately placed the bubble on the tip of his tongue.

He smiled at Martin then, his mouth slightly open, and swallowed. "Can't have you melting all over the place, now, can we?" he said. "What would my guests say?"

He closed the cover and locked it. After looking at Martin a few moments longer, he left.

Martin heard David leave. He had heard some of what he had said, but he hadn't heard everything. His body was still screaming at him, still shot with unbelievable pain from having been left in the sunlight, so his concentration had been divided.

He had wanted to say something to David, to think something, but the only response he'd managed was the blood tear David had taken off his cheek and swallowed.

Eight

Ray Timmerson had been staring at his monitor for the better part of an hour, the longest case of writer's block he had ever had.

Like most writers, there were times when books like *Fathers and Sons* wouldn't let him alone, when they seemed to drain away every creative drop. And during their gestation, during the long hours of research and fine-tuning, he was on a constant high, in love with life and his craft and awaiting the arrival of his newborn with forced patience. But the thoughts and emotions that inspired books like *Fathers and Sons* had dark and sometimes disturbed cousins. One he called A. K. Shriber. It was Shriber's voice that called to him now, that demanded to be heard. Ray shrugged. "Gotta feed the lion to free the lamb," he said.

He tapped F10 to save his work, went back to the menu, and started a new file he called "Martin's Story." It didn't take long to write an opening. He rewrote Martin's physical description and then fine-tuned it. Of course, Martin's appearance, he knew, would only pique the reader's curiosity. It was how he'd gotten that way that would make them turn the pages.

He took a sip of apricot juice. He usually had a beer around noon, but he was on a health kick this week. He even had an exercise bike in the corner of the room. He'd thought about putting it in his bedroom, but at least in here it wouldn't turn into a clothesrack.

How Martin got that way, Ray thought. *How the hell* did *he get that way?* He sat back and stared at the screen. He could simply tap his imagination for the answer. It hadn't failed him yet. His other A. K. Shribers had been given a natural birth, unsullied by research. Straight imagination, no chaser. But this, well, this was something else again. Martin was real. Whether he was or not. And he certainly hadn't put himself in that swamp. Someone had put him there, and for a reason. Emily's explanation seemed too pat, though. Insurance fraud? No, he didn't think so. What could something like that be worth, anyway? Even if it drew a couple hundred people a night, it probably didn't support the Petry Brothers Carnival all by itself. And they could have gotten rid of him in a thousand other ways and places. They hadn't, though. They'd tossed him in a peat bog near Winchester, Massachusetts. Why there? Why the hell there and not in Topeka, Kansas, or Oshkosh, bygosh, Wisconsin?

Another sip of apricot juice, another thought, and then a rock-solid conclusion. *Solve the mystery, Ray,* he told himself. *Find out exactly what Martin was doing there, in that swamp. Find that out, embellish a little if the reason isn't spooky enough, and who knows, you may have a real story on your hands.*

He pushed himself away from his computer, saved what he had written, barely 500 words, got up, and called the airport to make reservations for the next flight to Boston. Then he called Hertz's 800 number to make sure there'd be a car waiting for him when he got there.

Ray's plane touched down at Logan at three that afternoon. It had looked like rain earlier, so he had a blue London Fog raincoat folded over his arm. Hopefully he wouldn't have to use it.

The trip to Winchester took about an hour. He knew he'd have to go out to Horn Pond, but the way he saw it, the Petry Brothers Carnivals had to have stopped in Winchester at one time or another. Winchester was the only town of any size close to where they'd found Martin. They probably hadn't strayed too far from the beaten path to get rid of him.

Carnivals, he knew, needed permits, and permits were normally filed at the town hall. He got directions at a gas station.

A few minutes later he bellied up to the counter at the Office of Titles and Deeds and looked around. There were four desks in the room, one occupied, a line of forms to his right, and a bank of windows beyond. The sun was off to the right, its rays slanting biblically into the room, at least for now. The wind had picked up in the last couple of minutes. Clouds had gathered.

A matronly woman with tight dark hair, tiny features, and thick glasses acknowledged him with a smile and then went back to reading her paperback. Ray glanced at the cover, wondering if it wasn't one of his. It wasn't. After a few minutes of being ignored, Ray cleared his throat to get her attention. The woman held her hand up and waved at him without taking her eyes off the page, while Ray choked back a tirade about public servants. A half minute later she looked at him like someone who'd just had sex. "What can I do for you, sir?" she asked.

Ray forced a smile. "I need some information about a carnival I have reason to believe stopped here within the last couple of years. The Petry Brothers Carnival. Ring a bell?"

The woman's brow creased. She glanced to the side as she thought, tapping her finger against her cheek. "Carnival, carnival . . ."

"Petry Brothers."

She pointed her finger at the ceiling and opened her eyes

wide. "Yes, I remember now. They were here . . . just about a year ago . . . last summer, in fact."

"Well, if it's possible, I'd like to know exactly where they set up. Would you—"

She pushed herself to her feet. "I can do better than that," she said. "Hang on just a sec." She opened a drawer under the counter and fished around. "Here it is." She pulled a poster out of the drawer and held it up. Across the top in big red letters were the words "Petry Brothers Carnivals." Below that were the requisite clowns and balloons and rides, all colorfully clustered.

"Let me get you a Winchester town map," she said.

She left the poster on the counter, went back to an adjoining room, and reappeared almost immediately. "Right here, at the bend in the river, near the old covered bridge," she said, pointing. "That's where they set up. Just take Route three out a few miles and you can't miss it. Here, take the map with you."

"Great," Ray said. "I appreciate it."

Well, he thought as he went back to his car, *step one was easy enough.*

Ray had no idea what he was looking for, but he'd know it when he found it. If he found anything.

He saw the covered bridge from about a half mile off. The Mystic River was off to his right, and the town of Winchester was still visible in his rearview mirror. He pulled over and got out. The clerk from Titles and Deeds had X'd the spot on the map.

There was a little league field a ways back and a few picnic tables beyond that, set up to overlook the river. *An idyllic spot,* Ray thought. He walked slowly through the tall grass, imagining the carnival encircling him, the aromas: cotton candy and sausages and hay and maybe greasepaint. Just getting the feel of things, how it had been back then, last summer. Immerse himself in the ambiance. Or the ghost of it.

He stopped at the riverbank and skipped a few stones while a car rumbled over the covered bridge and drove almost silently away. *Sure,* Ray thought, *get the feel of this book, let osmosis take over. Become part and parcel. . . .* He saw something at the grass's edge then, caught there, what looked like good old folding money. *My lucky day,* he thought, as he picked it up.

"Well, what do you know?" he said, smiling.

The dollar bill wasn't a dollar bill at all. It had the same markings as a dollar bill, but George Washington's face had been replaced with Martin's face, and in place of "In God We Trust" were the words "Immortality—One Dollar."

"Well, how about that?" Ray said.

Nine

David Kane sat next to Martin, doing what he could to understand what the hell was happening to him. His heart was racing like a scared jackrabbit's, and his thoughts were about as focused as snowflakes in a blizzard. He had to go somewhere, anywhere. Anywhere but here, because he sure wasn't going to find out what was wrong with him here.

Before he left, he managed to wade through his mental chaos long enough to make sure the sun couldn't get at Martin again, like before. God, he'd felt terrible about that. "Martin," he began, looking up at him, not knowing what to say next. He decided not to say anything and just left, leaving his destination up to God and fate, as if they weren't already connected. It was almost four, still quite a while before it got dark.

After he stepped out onto Thirty-fourth Street, he stopped and looked in both directions, trying to decide which way to go. The sun, filtered by high, thin cirrus clouds, felt hot on his face. He covered his eyes and looked away. At the same time, a woman hurrying out of a taxi bumped into him and spun him around, fueling his vision with a kaleidoscope of gray concrete and white faces and bright summer clothing. When he finally stopped spinning, he was facing right. For that reason alone he started walking in that direction.

He moved as if his muscles had turned to fat. He felt

drunk without the high. Funny, though, how the colors were so brilliant they made his eyes ache. And his hearing was remarkably acute, too. It was all so damned confusing! He looked into the faces of passersby for an answer, but no one looked back at him for longer than a glance until he got to Nineteenth Street.

A man had stopped for a light. Their gazes locked.

"Can you help me?" David pleaded.

The man looked David up and down as if wondering about the dichotomy between the way David looked and the way he sounded. "Help you what?" he finally asked.

David, who felt as lost as he looked, stammered, "I . . . I don't know." *Maybe a smile,* he thought. So he smiled and said, "Something's wrong with me . . . I don't know what, but . . . please, can you help me?"

David waited for a reply, and just when it seemed that he wasn't going to get one, the man took out his wallet and said, "You hungry? Is that it?"

David thought about that for a moment.

" 'Cause if you're hungry—"

"No, no, I'm not hungry . . ."

Suspicion clouded the man's face. He looked around, then looked back. "Lost, then . . . are you lost?"

"Yes, I'm lost," David said. "I think."

"Tourist, huh? Well, you know, it's not true what they say about New Yorkers."

David saw a woman then, waving to him from across the street. A black woman. He looked at her like someone studies a relative they haven't seen for a while. She was tall and thin, and she had straight white hair that came to a point on either side of her neck. *She looks like a photographic negative,* he thought. And dressed as she was, in faded and knee-torn jeans and red halter top, she looked very much out of place, too. But wasn't it funny—he hadn't gone to her, she had come to him. "Be right there," he said at a conversational level, as he started across the busy street.

"Hey!" the man yelled after him, "look out for the—"

David felt a hand on his arm. He stopped and turned and looked into the face of a middle-aged, impeccably dressed man. "You trying to get yourself killed?" the man said.

"No, I . . . I saw a woman." David turned again and looked across the street, in the direction of the woman. She was gone.

"Did you hear me?" the man said.

David pointed across the street. "Where'd she go?" he said.

The man rolled his eyes. *"Drunks,"* he muttered, and walked away.

David looked down Thirty-fourth Street at the thickening late-afternoon crowds. *Find her,* he thought. She was all he had.

He started looking, deciding that she had to have walked the other way because he would have seen her walk past him.

By the time the sun went down, David's search had taken him all the way to Brooklyn. Despite the fact that it was still very warm, he was cold—trembling, in fact, as if he were ill. He pulled his suitcoat tighter to him and kept walking, surprised that he had been able to walk so far without stopping.

"Where am I?" he mumbled. He'd long ago given up on the black woman, but he'd also lost his way. A cat glared at him from the top stoop of a tenement, and a little further down the street he said hello to a couple of guys drinking beer and playing cards.

A few blocks further on, sounds began to multiply and increase in amplitude. At the same time, everything around him took on an almost luminous glow. It was still night, but the streets and the cars and the buildings looked like brilliantly colored cutouts on black felt. He stopped and looked around him, turning in a circle. The two men he'd seen on the stoop were a few yards away, whispering. David turned away—they sure couldn't help him—and saw the black woman standing near a lamppost, spotlighted. All he could think about was some movie with Shirley MacLaine, something about hookers. The woman looked back at him and started laughing, great big roaring belly laughs that seemed to fill the whole neighborhood.

Fascinated, David moved toward her, and as he got closer, she stopped laughing and turned her forearms out. David stopped. She was bleeding. "You're bleeding," he mumbled, pointing at her wrists.

The woman raised her eyebrows and grinned. At the same time, blood began to flow out of her wounds at a remarkable pace, covering the brazenly colored sidewalk and gathering in large crimson pools at her feet. But still she kept smiling, and as David got closer, she looked dead into his eyes and said, *"Take, drink, for this is my blood, which I have shed for you."* Her grin broadened and she turned her head to the side. *"Take, eat,"* she said, touching her neck lightly, *"for this is my body, and I am the Life . . ."*

David stopped abruptly. The side of her neck had been torn away, leaving a gaping, oozing wound wherein maggots feasted, cleansing the flesh.

But David didn't run away, repulsed; instead, he moved closer, splashing through the river of blood and feeling it spatter onto his face and neck. Hungry, yes, he was hungry. And thirsty. As thirsty as he had ever been. As thirsty as anyone had ever been.

"Take, drink," the woman continued. *"For this is my blood, which I have shed for you."*

The coppery, pungent smell stung his eyes and his nose and made his eyes water. But she had the answers, and he damn sure wouldn't let a simple odor get in the way. He pressed on, getting closer and closer to his hideous meal, and the closer he got, the faster her blood flowed. It flowed from every body cavity now, splashing onto the sidewalk and onto a Chevy Caprice parked next to the streetlamp, creating a brilliant red blood wave that washed down the sewers with a mighty and deafening roar. She should have been completely drained a long time ago, David somehow understood, but still the blood kept flowing.

"Take, eat!" she bellowed, making herself heard above the gush of blood from her mouth, a vibrant red sea washing down the quiet street. "Don't stop now, David," she said, her voice deep and sexually demanding. "Come to me, David. I am your life, I alone am your salvation."

Feeling that he had no choice, his need as powerful as any addict's, David obeyed and started toward her. But as he moved to within just a few feet, more than ready to receive his meal, he felt a flash of incredible pain in the back of his head. He tried to turn, but all he could do was fall, and the last thing he saw before he hit the ground was the black woman fade and then disappear.

It was morning before he woke. His eyes fluttered as he groped for consciousness. After he found it, he looked around. There was a green 1950s-style sofa in front of him and an RCA television console with legs beside it. Beer cans and what appeared to be cocaine, three lines, two long and one short, littered the top of a coffee table. A big glass candy bowl sat next to the cocaine. Hershey kisses and wrappers. Glancing at the wall behind the sofa, he saw two bullet holes.

He got up, remembering the pain in his head. He'd been hit, probably robbed, too. Funny, though, he didn't have any pain. He checked his wallet, surprised he still had it. Two hundred ninety-five dollars and all his credit cards. He hadn't been robbed, after all. There was a window to his right, its shade drawn. David tugged on it and as soon as the shade popped up, the sun's rays flowed into the nasty little room. He raised his arm like someone who was about to be hit and backed away. Standing there looking at those cruel little shafts of sunlight, David wondered about how hot it was going to be today.

Home, he thought, looking around, he had to get home. Take a shower. Have his head wound checked out. He stepped on something, heard it break. Looked down. A syringe. He'd stepped on a goddamn syringe! "Christ," he said, "how the hell'd I end up in a place like this?"

Thinking about things, though, he couldn't help but grin. Relatively speaking, he was probably lucky to be alive, so it really didn't matter where he was. Alive here was better than dead at the Ritz.

Standing in the living room doorway, he looked into the dining room. The lights were off, the room bathed only in dark gray shapes. He reached to his right and flipped on the overhead light.

What he saw then should have repulsed him, but it didn't. All it did was arouse his curiosity.

There was a long dark wooden table in the dining room, piles of money, and bags of cocaine spread out over it. Some of the bags had split open, spilling cocaine onto the table. Four bodies filled out the scene, all more or less gathered around the table. Two young and naked Asian girls were slumped over the table like drunks. The other two bodies belonged to the two men he'd seen the night before. One was seated against a door that led to a stairway, and the other was pinned against the far wall like a moth under glass, a butcher knife stuck through his neck.

David took a closer look at the young Asian girls. *Caught in a crossfire,* he decided. One had been shot in the cheek, the other in the back. *Nothing unusual about them, except for the fact that they're naked.* He wondered about all the gunfire, remembering the holes in the living room wall. *Why hadn't anyone heard?* he wondered. *Silencer, probably,* he thought, *just like in the movies.* He went around the Asian girls and looked at the man pinned against the wall. His mouth was open as if he were about to receive communion. Blood tracked from the point of the blade and onto his chest as if the blade had leaked and not the man. David

turned the man's head to the right. Rigor mortis made it
snap and crackle. "Strange," David said. The side of the
man's neck had been torn away, leaving a fist-sized circular
wound not unlike the wound on the side of the black
woman's neck. David bent to the other man. Same thing.
He got up. "My God, David," he said. "How did you survive this?"

He wondered if he should call the cops and decided
against it. Being the only person left alive in here would
take a lot of explaining. No, the best thing to do would be
to go home and just forget about it. He'd obviously been
an innocent in all this, so why should he concern himself?
Sure, he felt terrible about the two young Asian girls . . .
or did he? Well, of course he did—anyone would . . .

"Go home, David," he said. "Go home and forget about
it. Something weird happened to you, sure, but you've been
sick. Strange things happen to people when they're sick."

The fact that he was sick, that he had been sick, went at
least a little way toward explaining things. Sick people had
hallucinations and bad dreams . . . sick people weren't responsible. . . . He looked around again, glad he had his
sickness to fall back on, then went home.

Ten

Ray sat at his kitchen table, poring over the material the clerk in Winchester had given him.

"I try to retain things for at least two years," she told him. "The Petry Brothers were especially generous with their materials."

She'd smiled at his coupon and pulled a couple more from her folder. "Cute little gimmick, don't you think?" she said.

Included with the coupons were an itinerary that covered the carnival's schedule for the next two years, some advertising circulars, and even a booklet describing Martin and how he had come into being. According to the itinerary, the carnival had swung south, stopping in Richmond before it had moved on to Georgia and then Florida. From there they hugged the Gulf Coast, stopping in New Orleans before moving on to Texas, California, and Washington State. Then it was on to the Southwest, the Midwest, and the Great Lakes. They were, coincidentally, going to be in a place called Hunt, in New York State, next week.

Ray got up and made a cup of tea, then sat down again. *Pretty interesting,* he thought. *Just eight short hours' drive away.* He picked up the advertising booklet and studied the cover. The booklet, eight pages long, described how Martin had been "made." Fiction, sure, Ray thought, but if he was going to fictionalize this whole incident, the booklet would probably be a good place to start.

It was red with black titles, surrounded by what could have been saber-toothed tiger teeth.

The Petry Brothers Carnivals and Fairs Presents

MARTIN

Beneath that, and in parentheses, was a qualification:

(Entrance to the tent is restricted to the Strong of Heart)

The coincidence struck Ray immediately. Out of the blue, David had named his vampire "Martin" . . . the same name the carnival had given him. *Maybe,* he thought, *it was time to buy that first lottery ticket.* He smiled and started reading.

Martin Crouper was a tall and large man, and while mortal he was considered somewhat of a ladies' man. That didn't change after he became immortal. If anything, it appreciated. He couldn't take all the credit, though, and he didn't. That kind of ability came with the territory, so to speak. When he tried to explain it, all he could come up with was a somewhat trite simile. Immortals were like caterpillars who had become butterflies. Trite, yes, but apt, Martin thought, considering the similarities between wing and cape, although he had never seen an immortal wearing a cape, other than at the movies.

His eyes were softly blue, not crisp and sharp, like Paul Newman's, but he still considered them to be his best feature. It puzzled him that their softness did not diminish after the change. He had dark hair—what he considered his worst feature—if hair can be considered a feature. He wore it to his shoulders, and every now and then, depending on his mood, he would tie it into a ponytail. He had dyed it honey blond once, but it didn't suit him. As an immortal, he was already something less than he had been. His features were large but pleasant, and he had bushy dark eyebrows. He guessed that he, unlike other immortals, longed for his mortal life more than was normal because he was still new, because he could still remember being mortal.

Martin's first taste of blood was not drunk from a beautiful starlet in town to promote a movie, nothing that glitzy. His first taste of blood came from a squirrel.

Okay, Ray thought, *I don't care about Martin's first taste of blood.* He scanned for a while, then came across something else that got his attention. How Martin had become a vampire, him and a friend, someone named Bobby All.

They were at a fair then, hoping to entice a few women to go home with them, to further Bobby's bumbling explorations of carnal pleasures. It was night and there was a storm on the horizon. They could hear the far-off thunder and they could see the lightning beyond the horizon as it strobed across the black sky. They were about to leave, having spent a great deal of money winning worthless prizes, when a tall, muscular man told them about an attraction that wouldn't open until everything else closed, where they could get back the money they'd lost and then some. They weren't given details. Back then, before their immortality, they didn't need much of an excuse to alter their daily and nightly regimens.

The storm drew closer as they wandered the quiet fairgrounds in search of the attraction; the wind began to howl and moan, and a chill had come into the air. By the time the rain started, they'd almost decided to leave, but they happened across a tent they hadn't seen. It was set back from the others, and there was a sign outside they absolutely knew hadn't been there earlier:

Immortality—One Dollar

The lettering could have been done by a five-year-old. They scoffed and pulled their collars to their necks. "We're gonna catch our deaths," Bobby said. *"And for what? For this?"*

Naturally, Martin agreed. *"What're they gonna do?"* he said, laughing. *"Carve your name in a rock or something?"*

Bobby laughed, too. They were going to go inside, though, they knew that. All they needed was an excuse, and the gathering storm gave them one. *"Maybe we'd better go in,"* Martin said. *"You know, wait out the rain."* Inside, as their eyes adjusted, they saw a gaily dressed dwarf seated behind a long table, the tent illuminated only by a string of chasing lights across the front of the dwarf's desk. The dwarf came around the desk and looked up at them. He was smiling. He had the smallest eyes they had ever seen on a human. *"A dollar, boys,"* he said in a gravelly tenor. *"That's all it takes. Tell me true, boys, you got one dollar for immortality?"*

He chuckled then, causing his old, old face to crack, and held out his chubby little hand. Martin took it into his own and asked him where the rock was.

"Rock?" the dwarf said in bewilderment. *"Why, there's no rock here, boys."* His eyes were like tiny sparkling jewels. *"Here you get what you pay for! You give me your dollar, you get immortality."*

They handed over a dollar each and were immediately directed to another room, the dwarf gesturing like a doorman at a fancy-dress ball. Beyond that they remembered little. The other room was as black as tar, but as soon as they entered, they knew instinctively that they were not alone.

After a minute of standing very still, Martin's anxiety got the better of him. He laughed a little and said, *"Jeez, Bobby, this is really . . ."* It was then that Martin felt a moment of extreme anxiety and then an explosion of pain on the side of his neck. He grabbed at it and felt the blood ooze between his fingers. *"What the—?"* he said, as he pulled his hand away and stared into the darkness, his blinded eyes scanning, but seeing nothing. There was laughter then, more a *derisive chuckle, actually, but only a moment's worth before silence prevailed once more.*

Seconds later, they staggered out of that dark room, past the smiling dwarf who mumbled something about getting their money's worth, and to their car, where they fell fast asleep, awakening only as the morning sun crested the horizon. Immediately they raised their arms over their faces to block its rays. Martin chuckled a little snort of denial. "Just like at the movies," he said, grinning and glancing at his squinting friend beside him. Bobby grinned back, but no amount of grinning would keep away the sun's rays, probing and groping and supplying them with endless unbelievable pain.

It was all they could do to drive home, a blanket over the side windows for protection.

Within a day things got worse—or better, depending on your outlook. Their senses were enormously heightened, their strength that of many men. Most of all, they discovered an increased intellectual capacity. Martin, who had just seen the movie Charley, *identified more now with Charley than with the rat Algernon. He stayed in his musty little room and tested his strength and his senses and his increased mental ability. Mostly that. Crosswords were a snap. He had a* Playboy *with "Questions for the Super Intelligent." He answered them all in just a few minutes.*

He called Bobby the next day. "It's true, isn't it, Bobby?" he said.

Bobby said yes, it probably was true, and Martin hung up and just stared at his ominously white skin, realizing then that he had indeed attained immortality for the bargain-basement price of only a dollar.

Of course, looking back, they supposed that immortality could have been theirs for a lot less, maybe even nothing. But, Martin waxed philosophically, something given freely was hardly as coveted.

Now, Martin was an impatient man who held a grudge

and kept it till it was satisfied. That didn't change when he did. His employer, a man named Stefan Unu, Father Unu, precisely, had, in Martin's mind, been less than charitable over the years. So one brightly starlit night long after the change, after he and Bobby had roamed much of the known world, Martin came back and visited his old employer, whose church had the distinction of being one of four churches, one on each corner. It was the only place in the whole world that could make that claim. Martin waited for Father Unu to leave his church—a place Martin knew instinctively he could not enter—and, having a choice, killed rather than alter him. Certainly it would have been enjoyable, watching a priest suffer the tug of evil, but death was far more final, and that night, Martin was much more interested in finality than in a long-range revenge.

Martin's satisfaction, sadly, was short lived. He began to age even before he disposed of Father Unu's body. In the ultimate irony, Martin, who had become a vampire to halt the aging process, would be subjected to an eternity of aging without the benefit of death, simply because he had despoiled a disciple of the Church.

Frantic for his good friend, Bobby tried everything, but mostly he kept Martin supplied with young boys and girls, hoping that the ingestion of youth would do the trick. It didn't. Bobby suspected at the time that it wouldn't. So rather than be subjected to what he feared the most, Martin killed himself. He set fire to the house wherein he had hidden, then retired to the front porch and waited for the morning sun.

But although that morning sun did return him to the ashes, it fell short of finishing him off.

A year later, having heard of a place near Tampa, Florida, where there lived a healer with the ability to restore Martin's ashes to life, Bobby came back and collected those ashes. The healer, a black woman of tremendous beauty, collected them from Bobby, and within a week the treatment was complete.

Sadly, she was able only to restore Martin to life. She was unable to restore any movement. And so Bobby, who loved Martin dearly, made a gift of him to the Petry Brothers Carnivals. "It is with you," a tearful Bobby All said, "where Martin will find the only happiness available to him."

In a way, that is true. Martin would have liked the label "entertainer," for that is what he is. Because fear, as everyone knows, is the ultimate entertainer.

Well, Ray thought, *Martin has obviously stopped being entertaining. Why else would they throw him into a swamp?*

But reading the booklet had fascinated him, and what better way to fill himself up with that story than to visit the Petry Brothers Carnivals? With luck, he might even find this Bobby All and maybe even the dwarf. Obviously, the fiction in the book was supposed to mirror fact, so maybe those two characters really did exist. And there was the black woman, too. A little voodoo, maybe? Vampires and reincarnation and voodoo. Interesting. Maybe even profitable.

Eleven

Emily waited for her father at his office because she was terribly concerned about him. A street vendor who knew both her and her father had seen him wander off the day before, looking dazed and frightened. "I would have gone after him," he told her, "but there wasn't no one to watch my stand. I hope he's all right, I mean, the way he looked . . ."

"Dad," she said when he came in, "where the hell have you been?"

He turned to her and she was immediately struck by how good he looked. Better than he had in a very long time. Never mind that the condition of his clothing made him look like he'd been in a street fight, she was more curious about his color. He actually looked healthy.

"Hello, Emily," he said, as if nothing had happened. "Good to see you." He gestured toward the windows. "Think you can draw the drapes for me? Awful bright out today."

Emily ignored him. "Dad, I asked you where you've been, and I expect an answer."

He came back to her and cupped her shoulders. "Emily, I'm fine, really. And if you must know, I spent the night . . . well, thinking."

"Thinking? All night? You spent all night thinking?"

"You think I'm incapable of that?"

Emily ignored his tone, one she had never heard before. "Where, Dad?"

"Sweetheart, you wouldn't believe me if I told you."

"Try me."

The look he gave her then was a look she had never seen. The warmth had leached from his face, leaving it cold and hard, *very similar,* she thought, *to Martin's.*

"It's none of your business, Emily," he said quietly. "Now, I'm gonna take a nap. And I'd appreciate it if you'd get the drapes on your way out, like I asked."

She watched him walk away and close the door softly behind him. "What do I do now?" she mumbled. "He looks fabulous, except for his clothes—*change your clothes!*" she yelled at him. "And stop acting like such a damn stranger, too! You hear me? Stop acting like we don't know each other!"

"Close the drapes, please," he yelled back.

Emily sucked in a calming breath and let it out. "Jesus," she said, "who's the shrink around here, anyway? You're acting more like the patient than the doctor, Emily Kane!"

"What?" her father yelled.

"I said I'm acting more like the patient than the doctor!"

A pause.

"Dad!"

"Get the drapes. Please!"

That tone again. "Yeah, okay."

She went over to close them but before she got there, she stopped and looked up at Martin's blanket-covered casket. Maybe her dad wouldn't listen to her, but this . . . thing had no choice. She tugged the blanket off him and let it fall to the floor.

Martin was almost a foot taller than Emily, which meant his blank stare had always been directed beyond her field of vision. But after she pulled the blanket off and looked up at him, she could have sworn that he looked down at her. Not for long, no more than maybe a half second, if that. But playing the moment back in her mind again and again as she looked up at him now, she clearly saw those baby blues staring back at her. Staring as if something actually lived beyond them. As if that living thing had something it wanted to say.

Ray picked up the phone and dialed David's number. David would definitely be interested in what he'd found. Three rings, then four.

"Emily, can you get that?" David yelled.

She went into the outer office and picked up the receiver. "Hello," she said, with a flicker of annoyance.

"Emily?"

"Yes, this is Emily—who's . . . Ray?"

"How are you?"

"I've been better. I take that back. On one hand, I feel pretty good; on the other, I'm a little confused."

"You want to elaborate?"

"It's Dad."

"What's wrong? Not a relapse, I hope."

"Ray, he was gone all night. I spent the night here waiting for him, thinking he'd be home at any second. He usually tells me when he's going somewhere overnight. Would you believe he got home not five minutes ago? And you know what else? The first thing I noticed about him was how great he looked. But did I say anything about that? No! I was so pissed at him for making me worry, I just blew up at him."

"The mother hen routine, huh?"

"Yeah, you'd think someone like me would know better." Ray chuckled.

"And you know what he did when I blew up at him? He told me to get lost. Well, not in those words, but the meaning was clear. And Ray . . . forget it. Forget I said—"

"What?"

"It's stupid."

"Hey, you're talking to an expert on stupid."

"He looked at me like some stranger who'd just had his seat taken on the bus."

"His seat taken—"

"Wild, cold indifference, Ray. He looked at me with cold indifference. I felt as if, well, if I said anything, he'd . . . Ray, I actually thought he might hit me or something."

"Hit you? David'd never—"

"Exactly."

"Emily, you know what I think? I think what's important here is how he looks, not how he looked at *you*. I think as far as reactions are concerned, you should probably examine your *own*."

He was right, of course. She'd acted like his mother. When you got right down to it, she probably should have expected his reaction. "Yeah, you're probably right," she said.

"I *know* I'm right. Now that we've got that settled, can I speak with him?"

"Well, I don't know, Ray. He's taking a nap. Maybe you'd better call back."

Ray chuckled again. "The tomcat comes home for a snooze, huh?"

"Ray, I'm sure—"

"Just kidding. Look, if I can't talk with him, maybe you'd be interested in what I found out."

"What?"

"I did some research into our stony friend Martin."

"Really?"

"Yeah, I went to Winchester and with the help of a very orderly town clerk, I was able to dig up some information about him."

"Dig up, Ray?"

"Sorry. Anyway, the Petry Brothers Carnival is going to be in New York State next week. I was calling to see if your dad wanted to go up there with me. Place called Hunt,

outside Rochester. The material I got is really quite interesting. I thought maybe we could find out exactly why they
tossed Martin into a swamp. Actually, I'd like to see the
looks on their faces when I tell them where he is now."

Where he is now, Emily thought.

"Emily?"

"Huh?"

"Have David give me a call, okay?"

"Sure. I'll leave him a note. Fascinating, really fascinating."

"Yeah, it is, isn't it? Take care."

Emily hung up, went back into the artifacts holding area,
and stared at her father's closed door. She hated the term
"woman's intuition," but she didn't deny it existed, and right
now her intuition was screaming at her. Something was very
right with her father, something that had to do with his
general health, but there was also something very wrong,
too. She was beginning to wonder if it didn't have something to do with that thing off to her right, with Martin.
She looked at the back of Martin's casket. She hadn't bothered to put the blanket back over him. "Burn baby, burn,"
she said, and immediately wondered why. The sun, she noticed, had inched ever closer to the casket. If Martin sus-
tained any more damage, her father would really be pissed.
And he'd blame it on her, too, for not closing the drapes
the way he'd asked her to.

Reluctantly, she crossed the room and picked up the blanket. But instead of throwing it over him, she hesitated like
a matador waiting for the bull. Hesitated because she again
felt as if Martin were looking at her. And although she
knew that couldn't possibly be true, she'd probably have a
coronary if her mind played a little trick on her and said
otherwise. *Silly,* she thought, smiling lightly. *Just look at
him, Emily. He's clay, not Claymation! Just lift your head
and look at him. Him, listen to me. At it!*

A few more seconds passed, then a few more. Emily drew

in an exasperated breath and let it out. *Emily, you're being awfully childish about this,* she thought. *You, of all people . . .*

Childish or not, she still couldn't look at him. She lifted her gaze to his legs and then to the huge, misshapen hands that hung almost to his knees, but she just couldn't bring herself to look any higher.

Finally, she raised the blanket over her eyes to block the view and flung it over the casket.

"God, Emily," she said, as she looked at the blanket, "you're a real wimp, you know that? A real first-class wimp!"

A few seconds later she wrote a note to her dad and left.

Twelve

It was almost dark when David got up and went into the artifacts holding area. He'd never felt better. Sure, he'd dreamt about what had happened, about everything that had happened, but that was only natural. He'd been through a very horrifying experience. Maybe he could've reacted differently than he had, like showing some remorse for the two young Asian girls, but adding shock to the equation, his reaction hadn't been too far from normal. If he went back there now, he'd probably react differently, probably show a little more remorse.

He saw a note taped to the back of the door into the reception area. "Dad, call Ray," it said.

He went into the outer office and dialed Ray's number. Ray picked up on the first ring and said hello.

"Emily said you called, Ray."

"David, yeah, thanks for calling back. Look, I found out some things about your vampire."

"Martin? What about him?"

"Too much to tell you over the phone, but there is one thing I thought I'd run past you. The Petry Brothers Carnival is going to be close by next week, just a few hours' drive away. I thought you might like to go up there with me—"

"Why would you think that, Ray?"

A pause, then, "Well, you seem so interested in him, I thought you might want to see—"

"Thanks, but I think I'll pass."

"Really? Frankly, I'm a little surprised. I thought you'd jump—"

"And I appreciate the invitation, but I'm going to be pretty busy from now on. What do you expect to find, anyway?"

"Well, that's just it, I don't know. File this trip under research—"

"You're going to write another horror novel?"

"They call them thrillers now. But yes, I'm thinking seriously about it."

David didn't say anything. For reasons he wasn't sure about, he didn't know if he wanted Martin's story told or not.

"You still there?" Ray asked.

"Yeah. Ray, you sure about this? He's just a conversation piece, that's all. Heck, I'm even getting a little tired of him. I can't see where he'd make much of a story."

"Now, that's where you're wrong. Sure, everything that revolves around him is fiction, but the circumstances themselves, when paired with one of the great imaginations of our time . . . anyway," Ray continued, when David didn't respond, "I'm going up there. If you change your mind, give me a call. I'll be leaving on Tuesday."

"Tuesday, huh? Well, have a nice trip, Ray."

"You're sure you don't—"

"Positive."

David hung up and went back into the artifacts holding area. He could see the twin towers, stark and ugly. His building at least had style. Those two monstrosities were about as stylish as oatmeal. He looked toward Brooklyn. Again he thought about what had happened the night before. The shootings would be on the news, and the news would be on in five minutes. He went back into his private rooms and turned on the TV. He was beginning to feel a little restless again, a little antsy.

Despite that, he watched the news right up to the weather. Nothing. Maybe, he thought, the story hadn't been big enough to make the news—and that was ridiculous—or better yet, maybe no one had found the bodies. That made a little more sense. He thought about the Asian girls again, conjuring up at least a low level of remorse. He didn't feel a thing for the men who had been following him—scum like that deserved whatever they got. A knife in the neck was probably too good. Being impaled like so much rancid meat was probably too good. Sons of bitches were going to rob him anyway, maybe even kill him. Good thing someone got in their way. He wished he knew who it was so he could shake their hand. Or maybe it was better he didn't know who it was. Rival gang, probably. They'd busted in while he was still unconscious and lead flew around like goddamn Frisbees. David smiled. Real Clint Eastwood stuff. Bang bang, you're dead!

But thinking hard about it again caused his restlessness to suddenly get out of hand. *Probably the Asian girls,* he decided, his gaze unsettled. He should probably notify someone about them, somehow. Do it anonymously, maybe. They were as innocent as he was. Well, maybe not *that* innocent. They *were* involved in the drug thing, after all, but then, what choice did they have? They probably had family. Family who should know that their kids weren't coming home anymore. Another smile. Yeah, not coming home.

David shut off the television and got up, and as he did, the route back to the tenement house played through his mind. He had an explanation, though. The incident, including how he got there, was bizarre enough to leave a burning image. And now he actually wanted to help out, to do something for those poor defenseless, dead, and naked Asian girls . . . slumped over the table.

Naked.

Blood splattered about like gallons of paint . . .

The phone rang.

Splattered like paint . . .

Rang a second time.

Like red paint . . .

He shook off the image and picked up on the third ring.

"Dad?"

"Hi."

"You okay, Dad? You sound, I don't know—preoccupied."

"What do you want, Emily?"

"I, uh, I wanted to apologize for the way I acted earlier, that's all."

For the life of him, he couldn't remember how she had acted. "That's all right. I understand. Look, I have to go somewhere."

He hung up, grabbed his umbrella and left.

On the other end, Emily could only stare at the phone and wonder.

Once outside, he opened the umbrella and hailed a taxi. "Take me to Brooklyn, please," he said to the driver, as he settled into the middle of the back seat.

The driver looked at him in the rearview mirror. "Any place in particular?" he asked. "I mean, Brooklyn's a big place."

"No, just Brooklyn. Drive around when you get there and I'll tell you when to stop."

"You'll tell me when to stop? This could get expensive, pal. I'm gonna have to have something up front."

David took out two hundred-dollar bills and handed them to the driver.

"Your money," the driver said with a shrug, as he pulled out into traffic.

They got to Brooklyn about half an hour later, and although the driver would have driven around enough to eat up two hundred dollars, he didn't have to. David had given him very precise directions. They even passed the cat that had glared at him the night before.

"Stop here, please," David said, when they got to the tenement.

The driver looked around. "You sure? I don't usually get involved, but you could get mugged—"

"Yeah, I'm sure."

With a shrug, the driver pulled over. David got out, opened up his umbrella, then walked into the tenement. Once inside he closed the umbrella. He paused a moment. The door was closed at the top of the stairs, and he distinctly remembered coming down those stairs earlier this morning. What he thought about now, what really got his attention, was his apparent lack of concern for his own well being this morning. He hadn't run down the stairs, tripping over himself to get away; he had acted more like, well, like he'd just left the dentist's office. Exactly the level of anxiety he felt now.

He climbed the stairs, and when he reached the top, pushed the door open. From here he could see into the living room. No coke on the coffee table, but the Hershey kisses were still there. There was a smell of blood in the air, too. Funny, he thought, how strong the smell was, as if the whole damn house were soaked in it.

He stepped into the living room, stopped, then went into the dining room and flipped on the light. The bodies were gone. He looked around, scanning, taking things in and re-membering. "Bodies gone, cocaine and money gone. Blood's been cleaned up, too. Only thing left behind is that knife hole." He walked over to it and ran his fingers through the slit. There was blood in there, he could see it. He pulled out a chair. *Maybe the cops are trying to set the killer up,* he thought. *Killers do return to the scene of the crime sometimes.* He didn't think that had happened here, though. No, the cops hadn't taken the bodies away, someone else had.

Out of the corner of his eye, David saw a shadow inch

slowly into the room from a doorway off to the left that led into the bedrooms. "Someone there?" he said at a conversational level, amazed at how calm he was.

The shadow grew, became a man. The man stepped into the room and grinned. He had long, dark, stringy hair that fell over the collar of his full-length dark wool coat. His short, dark beard contrasted dramatically with skin the color of milk. His full lips were cracked and parched. *Smells,* David thought. *Sweat, beer, blood.*

He glanced at the slit in the wall then back at the man. The connection made, he said, "Where are the others?"

The man didn't answer, but simply widened his grin, then left.

David didn't follow him. He just shrugged and went home.

Thirteen

It was only the middle of the day, but David didn't think he had a choice. He lay down and closed his eyes. Sleep arrived quickly, and a dream followed.

He was lying down in his dream, and there was a lit candle on a small table just to his right, lighting much of what he thought was probably a basement.

Caught in the flickering glow was a boy about ten, seated on a dirt floor near the door about twenty feet away. He had his head between his knees and he was crying. Another boy was to his right, dead, his head turned to the side, his eyes open, his head propped against the wall. He wore a pair of jeans, and it looked like his stomach had been ripped away. A young woman was to the left of the door, also dead, but unlike the boys, she was naked. She lay on her stomach, her right arm turned under. Part of her bicep was gone, the bone exposed. Rats had gathered around the wound; David wondered if they hadn't caused the wound in the first place.

Even in his dream, he detected an indescribably vile odor, a weighty melding of rot and mustiness that pervaded the room. *Strange,* David thought, *that I can make out an odor in a dream. But then, stranger things have been happening lately.*

He got up ever so slowly, as if rising were very difficult, and started toward the boy at a ponderous and lumbering pace. He could see his feet as he inched along. They were fat and hairy, the nails grotesquely long. *How old am I in this dream?* he wondered.

He turned his attention back to the boy, and as he drew closer, he mumbled one word: *"Food."* It was then that the boy looked up at him, terror in his eyes. His chin began to quiver and his eyes were flooded with tears. He shook his head wildly, saying, "No, no, no," over and over. David stopped and stood over him, watched while a huge and very old hand reached down to the boy. *I'm going to kill him,* David thought. *I'm going to cannibalize him, just like I did the others.* He thought about the rats again: they were blameless. He was wrong about cannibalizing the boy, though. He didn't kill him. Instead, he gently wiped away the boy's tears and lifted him, crying, into his arms. The boy kicked and screamed and wailed, but David easily took him to the door and opened it.

Standing in front of him was a middle-aged man in a cop's uniform, a surprised, even frightened look on his face. For a moment, they could only stare at each other, and although seeing the man caused David's anxiety to build, he didn't attack him. Instead, he handed the boy over to him, pushed past him, and went up the stairs.

It was the sun's rays that drew him, that made their way through a screen door and onto a dirty kitchen floor. He moved quickly toward those rays, toward that screen door, and once there, he pushed the door open and took a bold step into the morning sunshine. Ah, but the pain was too much, at least all at once, so he stepped to the side, out of the sun, and glared down at the sun-drenched porch. There was something to be understood here, David knew that, but there was so much to decipher right now, so much to understand. Better to just stand here a moment and get his bearings. Just gather his thoughts.

A little while later, he raised his gaze to the horizon and to the sun, appearing like a giant, glittering blade on the horizon, his attention drawn to it like a naughty child's attention is drawn to a belt. Funny, though—the relief he felt, the absolution . . . something began to shimmer into existence in the corner of his eye then, off to the right. He turned, expecting to see another boy, and in a way that was true. A bald and white-skinned dwarf with tiny, laughing eyes and a vulture's nose had materialized. Like David, the dwarf seemed to be admiring the rising sun, at least until they saw each other. The dwarf's laughing eyes turned to him and he grinned, baring a mouth full of rotted candy-corn teeth. With a tiny and chubby hand he pointed toward the rising sun, never taking his gaze off David. "It's gonna kill you quick," he said, his voice gravelly and old and mischievous. "Yes, sirree! Quick as silver!" He leaned in toward David. "Being what you are, the sun and you don't get along," he whispered. His attention seemed instantly drawn to the porch floor and to a tentacle of creeping sunlight. "There, see it?" he said, pointing. "It's looking for you, David. Looking real hard. And you can just bet it's good at what it does. Sizzle, sizzle, sizzle."

The dwarf, like the black woman, threw his too large head back then and wailed with delight. "Better hide, David," he said, his tiny eyes opening wider than seemed possible. "Or maybe . . . maybe get an umbrella!"

Umbrella? David thought.

The dwarf stopped laughing and gave David a conspiratorial wink. "Gotta go," he said. "Places to go and people to scare!" With that, he shimmered and disappeared, taking his maniacal laugh with him and leaving David alone.

Alone to await his death.

The pain, massive and debilitating, came as soon as the sun's rays found him. But he didn't hide from the sun or the pain. Instead, he moved to a rocker on the porch and sat down. The sun's rays followed him there, filling him with pain that coursed through his body, assaulting every nerve ending along the way; a million happy bubbles, all bursting in his bloodstream.

David tried to wake himself up, fearing that if he didn't, he would probably die. But he couldn't wake himself up, and as the pain grew, he began to wonder about his sanity.

But much to his surprise and relief, the pain gradually subsided and then disappeared altogether. Now he had something else to worry about. The pain had stopped, but the deterioration of his body hadn't. Smoke eddied from his arms and legs, circling toward the porch roof, and when his vision began to cloud over, he guessed correctly that his eyes had begun to melt. And as they melted, what he saw from the porch, the sun, and a few homes on the other side of the street slowly faded to gray and then blacked out altogether. But even in the darkness of his dream, David could still smell the odor of burning skin, could still feel the granite-hard bone in his arms begin to crumble and disintegrate.

After a while, though, even that faded, and for a short time the dream offered only darkness and a moment to reflect and even think about what had just happened. But as he started this mental rehash, darkness gave way to gray again, and as it did, he saw Orion, the Hunter, and he saw a parade of clouds march by.

Afterward, he heard people talking, a man and a woman, so he moved his eyes—discovering that he could move *only* his eyes—hoping to see who they were.

The black woman from Brooklyn looked back at him. Their faces were only inches apart. She had her head cocked to the side, and she was smiling.

"David," she said. "Welcome back, David." She seemed very pleased.

Back, David thought. *Back from where?* But as soon as she spoke, David's eyes rolled back to their previous position, again showing him only a starlit sky and Orion the Hunter.

"David?" she said, obviously puzzled.

David tried to move his eyes again, but this time they

wouldn't budge. The black woman bent over him again and looked into his eyes. She looked confused and then resigned. Then she looked away and said, "It's just as I feared. I'm sorry. He's alive, but . . ."

"Well, maybe you've got a suggestion about what I should do with him, then."

"That's your decision. I can kill him, if you like."

David waited for an answer, but for the longest time he didn't hear anything except the sounds of the night. Finally, the man said, "You can do that? Kill him, I mean."

"Easily. But I've got to do it now, while he's still vulnerable. It'll be too late when his body turns to stone. Even sunlight won't harm him then."

Circumstances, that's all, David decided. All he'd done was put the facts together in his mind and give birth to this really bizarre dream. What else? Just weird circumstances contributing to a crazy . . .

Dream.

Suddenly, he was awake, and there was someone knocking on his door.

"Dad?" he heard. "It's me, Dad, Emily. Let me in, please. We have to talk." The words echoed in the ruins of his dream.

David rolled out of bed. "Just a second," he yelled on the way to the bathroom. He flipped on the light, then looked at his reflection in the mirror. Horror washed through him in a torrent. Although someone else would be hard pressed to tell, he could easily see that the right side of his face, near the temple, had developed a concavity. His heart pounded as he ran his fingers lightly over the area. It was true: his face had altered its shape. *Lord in heaven, what is going on here?*

"Dad?" he heard again, louder this time.

He looked at the door's reflection in the mirror. *What if Emily sees me like this? How can I explain it?* He opened the medicine cabinet and took out his hairbrush. A short while later he looked at the side of his head again, now hidden by a fall of hair. The style was wildly different than anything he'd ever worn, but it was better that than having Emily notice what had happened. And explanations would probably be easy to come by, once he had time to think about it. Sure, a little rational thought would handle this situation. The mirror, probably. Something wrong with the mirror, something like that. A little imperfection in the glass . . .

"Dad? Are you all right?"

"Yeah, be right there."

He checked himself in the mirror one more time, then went into the other room and opened the door.

"Dad, I . . . what did you do to your hair?" she said. She reached out to touch it and he leaned away.

"Just a change. Like it?" he asked, smiling.

"Well, Dad, no, I don't. It doesn't suit you at all. You look, I don't know, you look like Hitler."

He shrugged it off. "What's the big deal? Can't a guy try something new? I like it, I really do, and I'll tell you what, I think I'm gonna keep it like this."

"Please tell me you're kidding."

He turned away from her. "Look, I was taking a nap. Did you want something?"

She hesitated, then put a hand on his shoulder. "As a matter of fact, I did. Look, Dad, is something wrong? You hung up on me and you've never done that before."

"Oh, that," he said with a chuckle. "Sorry. As I said, I'm pretty tired. It won't happen again."

Silence.

David turned to the left, his good side. "Did you hear me?"

She had a smile in her voice. "Apology accepted," she said.

David turned to face her and grinned.

"Oh," Emily said, "I left you a note from Ray."

"Ray? Oh, yeah, I got it. He wanted me to go to that carnival with him, you know, the one that dumped Martin into that swamp."

He saw bewilderment on her face.

"And you're not going?" she asked.

He tried to look surprised. "No, of course not. Why would I?"

"Did he say anything else? Why he wants to go, maybe?"

"Not really. He just said he'd found out some things about Martin. I really don't care. To tell the truth, I'm getting a little tired of him."

Emily didn't say anything, and David could imagine what she was thinking. She was trying to understand what was going on with him. He looked better than he had in a long time, and now he had gone and changed his hairstyle to something a little weird. And despite the fact that he looked rested, he had taken a nap in the middle of the day. Things just didn't add up.

"Dad," she said, "when's your next doctor's appointment?"

"I don't know, next week, I guess."

"You are going, aren't you?"

"Sure. Now, Emily, I'd really like to visit, but I've got things to do."

The look on her face said she didn't understand. He wondered if he should take her into his arms and apologize for dismissing her like this. He didn't.

"Sure, Dad," she said. "I'll see you soon. Don't forget about your doctor's appointment."

"Okay."

After she left, he went back into the bathroom and looked at himself again. It wasn't the mirror's fault. His face had actually caved in. How, though?

He went and stood in front of Martin, and looked up into his eyes, but Martin's gaze, locked on the New York skyline, didn't waver.

For the longest time, David didn't say a word. And when he did say something, the words left his mouth like he had a sour stomach. "Look at me, damn you!"

He actually waited for Martin to do as he was told, but Martin didn't oblige him.

"Dammit, Martin, something's happening to me. Something I can't explain. And somehow . . . somehow *you're the reason.*"

Still nothing.

"Christ," David mumbled, looking away, "what the hell's wrong with me? I'm talking to this . . . mountain of clay as if it can actually hear me!"

He looked back at Martin and he saw an image that left him totally confused. With his mind's eye he saw a smiling Martin seated on an elaborately jeweled throne, a crown propped on his misshapen head. Around him were people who had to be his subjects, although the way they were dressed didn't reflect the time or even the tone of the vision. They were just everyday working people, doctors and cops and people dressed in suits and people dressed in work uniforms with monogrammed business names: Northside Plumbing, Lois's Catering.

Out of the corner of this vision, David watched himself step out of the crowd. He had a sword in his hand, and as he approached Martin's throne, Martin rose and knelt before him, his head inclined, exposing the back of his neck. The ambiance was one of great sobriety, and David actually felt a moment of humility and a sense of purpose as he raised the sword and touched Martin's left shoulder and then the right, knighting him. Sir Martin. Sir Martin Crouper.

What David said then left him even more confused. "I dub thee King Martin, King of New York," his tone ponderous and thundering. Very fitting. He stepped back, and after an appropriate period of time, Martin rose and reclaimed his throne. Instantly, everyone clapped and whistled and generally gave raucous approval for the newly knighted King of New York. Sir Martin Crouper. Long live the king.

The vision faded then, and in its place the events of the last few days began to travel across David's mind just slowly enough for him to identify them. And although he felt a certain need to analyze the previous vision, a more pressing need took precedent. Somehow, he had to figure out what had happened to him—what was happening to him.

The blood tear had started it all . . . no, no, that wasn't quite true. Some powerful inner voice telling him to leave Martin alone when he thought about having him analyzed had actually started it. The blood tear had happened later. After that was when the old ball had started its metaphysical roll. The hallucinations, the dreams—which were probably related—the murders. All wildly inconsistent with the David he had come to know pretty well over the years. So if you added it all up, then threw in a catalyst, something that hadn't been there before, maybe you could find a link. Martin was that catalyst. The "something new" in his life. Okay, he reasoned, thinking more rationally than he had in a while, I've gotten from point A to point B. What next? What's the sum total of all these metaphysical parts?

"What if he really is a vampire?" his right brain said, the words volleying like a dozen tennis balls, too fast to stop.

"That's ridiculous," the left brain said.

"No, really. Think about it. If Martin really *is* one of the undead—"

"I told you, that's ridiculous. Now, shut up!"

"David, you're being stubborn. *You* started this whole thing when you pulled him out of that swamp and let him into your house. And since you started it, you've got to end it."

The right brain had a point, David knew that.

"If Martin really is a vampire," his right brain continued, "a lot would be explained, wouldn't it?"

"Then why doesn't he move?" the left brain asked, feeling pretty smug about the complexity of his question.

The right brain pondered that a second. It was, it had to admit, worth thinking about. But the right brain being what it was, the seat of creativity, answers were easy to come by. "David," it said, "if you accept the premise of the undead— vampires—then it should also hold that they probably exist in many forms, like every other species on earth."

The left brain grudgingly admitted that the right brain probably had a point.

The right brain, sensing weakness, said, "What you have to do, David, now that you accept somewhat all that has happened to you, is find out what you can about *why* it happened to you. Go to that carnival, David. That's as good a place to start as any."

That seemed reasonable, even logical, but ever since he'd started this little chat with himself, David couldn't get something else out of his mind, one of the last scenes to travel his synapsed highway—the man in the doorway, the man who just the night before had been impaled against the wall, a knife stuck through his neck. It seemed to him then and now that they should have talked—about what, he didn't know. They should have said something to each other, though.

So it got down to a choice. Go to the carnival with Ray, or find the dead man who—hopefully—had only been joking about being dead, because if he hadn't, well, if that guy really was walking around dead, it was going to be a very long, very hot summer.

Fourteen

Seated on the couch, sipping Wild Turkey on ice, Emily watched Ray hang up and look at her. *It's a little early, I know that,* she thought. *But I've got reason.*

"That was your dad," Ray said. "Now he wants to go. He didn't want to before. Go figure."

Emily chugged what was left of her drink, enjoying the burn, and picked up one of the pamphlets about Martin. She glanced at it, then looked back at Ray. "I'm going, too," she said.

Ray shrugged. "Sure," he said. "The more the merrier. Might be fun."

"Fun?" Emily said. "Ray, something's wrong with my father, and now he's added wishy-washy to whatever's wrong with him. When I spoke with him earlier, he was ready to throw Martin out the window! He wanted nothing to do with him or that . . . that carnival. I'll tell you, something's wrong with him. And I'm not about to let him out of my sight until we get this cleared up."

Ray sat down next to her. "Your dad's just under a lot of stress. Being ill like he is . . . well, I don't have to tell you. This trip'll probably do him a world of good. You'll see."

About then, Emily happened upon the fact that the carnival had also used the name "Martin." "Martin," she said, pointing at the pamphlet. "His real name is *Martin!*"

"Yeah, pretty wild, huh? Your dad names him Martin and it turns out that's his real name."

"Did you tell him?"

"No. Our conversation was brief."

Emily put the pamphlet down. "Ray," she said, "you've done a lot of research, I mean for your horror novels—"

"Not really. Some, but just enough to drive the story and fire up the reality. Why?"

"Your second book was about vampires, wasn't it?"

Ray smiled. "Wait a second, you're not suggesting—"

She really didn't know what she was suggesting, but she did have a mountain of strange facts to think about. And she knew a little about vampires, or the myth, so all she wanted Ray to do was validate what she already knew. "He's, uh, he's not himself, Ray. Oh, sure, I could wrap it all up nice and neat and say that he's identifying with Martin, with the idea of immortality that he sees every day, but that's just too damn pat, and for a number of reasons. First and foremost, he does look a lot better than he has, and I'll be damned if I know why."

"That's a good thing," Ray offered.

"Yeah, I know it is, but his personality's changed, too, Ray. And he's wearing his hair different and he's actually sleeping during the daytime—"

"Like a vampire?"

Emily paused, then, "Yeah, like a vampire." She looked away. "And boy do I feel stupid for saying it."

"But of course, he's not a vampire, he's simply identifying with a mockup of a vampire that he's taken into his home. Living vicariously through Martin, you might say."

Emily knew all that. She also knew it made a lot of sense, in a twisted and morbid kind of way. For all intents and purposes, her father had *become* Martin. Maybe a trip *would* do him some good. Maybe if he got away from his houseguest for a while, he'd lose that new and unwanted personality and get back to being the man she knew and loved.

"I know I sound ridiculous," she said, "but I've been under a lot of stress lately, too. I see the changes and I see Martin . . . I told you he changed his hairstyle, didn't I?"

"Yeah, I know. But I don't see—"

"Ray, he pushed it off to the side like he wants to hide that part of his head or something."

"And you equated that with Martin?"

"Reluctantly, yes."

Ray couldn't help but grin. "Talk about your sympathetic responses."

"You know, you might have something . . . if he *is* living vicariously through Martin, if he *is* sympathetic, then maybe he actually believes he's starting to look like him, too. I'm not saying his head really *is* concave, like Martin's, but maybe he actually believes it is and that's why he's changed his hair—to hide it. To hide something that isn't really there."

"Let me ask you something. Do you think the body is capable of healing itself, without medical treatment?"

She grinned a lopsided grin. "You bet I do. And if that's what's happening to my father, then I couldn't be happier."

"Yeah—me, too. But the problem, of course, is where does he draw the line? If we accept that he thinks he's a vampire, an immortal, then where does that stop?"

Emily got a mental image of her father dressed in Martin's vampire get-up, terrorizing a luscious young coed. There was, of course, a hint of humor in that image, but stripping away the comedy left her with an image that wasn't at all humorous—her father murdering someone to feed a bloodlust that he perceived as being critical to his continued existence. It was an image that wouldn't go away, and one she had to address immediately. She had to talk with her father about what she had learned. She wouldn't

allow this to go any further until she had. She picked up
the phone and dialed his number.

David answered on the second ring.

"Dad, Emily. Stay there. Just don't go anywhere, okay?
We need to talk—right now. I'll be there as soon as I can."

"I'll be waiting," he said.

After Emily hung up, she looked at Ray. He had to be
in on this, too. She couldn't keep him at a distance. If what
she suspected was true, he could only help. "Go with me,
Ray. I want you there while I talk with my father—okay?"

"Yeah, if that's what you want."

"That's what I want."

David gripped the phone hard and felt a surge of relief.
He had wanted to talk to her, too, but he hadn't known
what to say. Now maybe she could talk, and he could just
chime in where he thought appropriate. How would she respond to what he had to say though? How would anyone
respond?

Emily thought her father looked nervous as he opened
the door. He smiled anyway.

She stepped past him and turned. "Dad," she said, "I
don't know how or why or whether it was sheer coincidence
or what, but the name you picked for that thing out there
is the same name the carnival gave him. You named him
Martin and they named him Martin. Now, you know me,
I'm a scientist—well, I like to think I am—but there are
some things going on here that are very perplexing, to say
the least. Your demeanor, your pallor, why you chose that
name. God, even your hair. Ray and I, well, think that perhaps you're living vicariously through Martin, that because
of your illness . . ."

She stopped talking because her father had unceremoniously pushed the hair off the side of his head.

Emily brought her hand to her chest. "Oh, my dear God," she said.

"Good Lord, David, *how?*" Ray asked.

David smiled and let the hair drop over the spot again. "As far as I can tell, I have become, well, like Martin."

"Like Martin?" Emily said, "But how——"

"I have a suspicion as to how it happened, if you'll give me a chance to explain."

Emily looked at him, and not knowing what else to do under the circumstances, she hugged him. Something physical had definitely happened to him. Whether it was psychosomatic or not was questionable, but she certainly wanted to hear his explanation, because she sure didn't have one. She pushed him to arm's length and looked at him. "Tell us, Dad," she said. "Maybe we can help."

He saw the puzzlement on her face. "Help? How?" he said.

He had her there. "I just want to help, Dad, in any way I can."

David smiled and nodded, and Emily couldn't tell whether he was being patronizing or if he really understood what she was going through right now.

"Don't say anything until I'm done talking—agreed?"

Emily nodded.

"Sit down. You both look shaky."

Emily took his suggestion. Ray sat beside her.

David paced a moment, gathering his thoughts. "I stayed the night in Brooklyn the night I was gone. I stayed at one of those row houses . . . four people died that night . . ."

He took another fifteen minutes to tell his story, everything he remembered, from the blood tear to the dead Asian girls and the black woman, who, he said, had been only a hallucination.

"I think Martin's to blame for all this. I don't have any

reason to think otherwise. But please don't ask me to get rid of him, because I can't do that. I *won't* do that. You understand, don't you?"

Emily got up and took her father's hand into her own. "The truth? No, I don't understand, Dad, I don't. He's clay—just a goddamn carving!"

"No, he's not. Believe me."

"Okay then, he's papier-mâché, whatever, he's not human, he never was human, and you didn't . . . a blood tear didn't . . ."

"I'm going to the carnival, Emily. Are you going?"

What she really wanted was to have him admitted. She could do it, too; she had the authority. It wouldn't prove anything, though. There were answers other than the ones he had given; there had to be. And maybe that carnival would be a good place to start looking for them. Whatever the case, she damn sure wasn't going to let him out of her sight until she got those answers.

"Yeah, I'll go, but when we get back, Dad, there's something I'll want you to do—"

"Section eight, huh?"

"Dad, I just want you to get help."

David smiled. "You know," he said, "being a vampire has its benefits. It really does."

Fifteen

Over the weekend, David had to fight an overwhelming urge to go back to the scene of the murders. And once there, in that house and in the company of the man who'd been killed and reincarnated, he would, more than likely, be drawn into something insanely violent. There was, he had to admit, a certain appeal in that. He didn't go back, though, and he was glad he still had the courage to resist the urge.

They were taking his Cessna to Rochester. They were going to rent a car for the trip to Hunt. David took care of everything and asked Emily and Ray to meet him at his office at around nine on Tuesday morning.

That day arrived wet and gray, and David was glad. Wet and gray felt better than dry and sunny. Although he didn't think it would actually kill him, sunlight did make him uncomfortable.

They took a cab to JFK, and with David piloting, they took off around nine-thirty. They arrived at Rochester International about two and a half hours later.

Their rental car was a black and gray Lincoln that David asked Emily to drive. Ray sat beside her in the front seat, David in back.

"The itinerary just lists Hunt, so I guess we'll stop in town and ask directions," Ray said.

"It starts today, doesn't it?" Emily said.

"According to the itinerary."

Ray turned on the radio and got Bach. He left it on.

David still had the booklet Ray had picked up in Winchester. He'd read through it on the plane, and while he listened to the music, he read it again. Bach seemed somehow strangely appropriate as background music for Martin Crouper and Bobby All and the dwarf.

A mile or so from Route 31 East, the route into Hunt, the music ended and the news came on.

Ray reached over to find something else. He stopped when he heard the announcer say something about the town of Hunt and a priest. Like David and Emily, he had read the booklet detailing Martin's life. According to it, Martin had gone into hiding because he'd started to age after he'd murdered a priest.

"*. . . Last month. As yet, the police have no clues in what officials are calling a homicide. Father Wesley Higgins, pastor at St. Monica's Church in Hunt until his disappearance, was last seen alive three years ago yesterday. The body was found in the town of Macedon by two boys who had spent the night in the woods, camped beside it. In other news . . .*"

"You know what I think," Ray said. "I think we should get directions from the town sheriff. And while we're at it—"

"I heartily agree," Emily seconded.

"There's your turn," Ray said, pointing. "Hunt, twelve miles. Route thirty-one."

"Twelve miles, twelve minutes," Emily said, as she squealed the tires into the turn.

New business and a good time were equally hard to find in Hunt, New York, population about 20,000. Life trudged on here and nothing, save for the spread of city dwellers toward its borders, an army of yuppies and wannabes all looking for suburban stakes, would stop this march into anonymity. Everything else along the way was taken, leaving towns like Hunt, and further west, Victor and Canandaigua, the only places left for Rochestarians to escape the city dwellers' plight—high taxes and even higher crime rates.

Emily pulled up in front of the sheriff's office, a spanking new blood-red brick building across the street from a pet store called the Kritter Korner. Ray and Emily went inside while David stayed in the car and listened to music.

Judd Lucas, town sheriff and member of the school board, was hard at work on a crossword when the door opened and a set of bells announced that he had visitors.

"Help you folks?" he asked, as he laid his pencil down. His smile was genuine, his tan dark. His tiny eyes would have been difficult to see if not for the sun winking through a side window. He was bald save for a handful of hairs toward the front of his head that looked like antennae. He was dressed in the brown and black trimmed uniform of his office, his tie loose. His nightstick tapped against the wood floor when he moved.

"Sheriff," Ray said, "we were wondering if you could give us directions to the carnival that's setting up nearby. The Petry Brothers Carnival."

The friendly smile faded for a moment, but Judd reclaimed it before anyone noticed. "Carnival? I don't recall there being any carnival—"

Ray had the itinerary. He showed it to Lucas, who just glanced at it, then looked more closely at Ray and Emily. "Oh, yeah, I remember now. You folks are not from around here, are you?" He smiled like a used-car salesman.

"No, New York City," Ray said. "Shows, huh?"

Judd Lucas looked at them a moment longer, then went to the window and looked out. The sun bathed his face with a wash of harsh light. "Well, I think they're setting up on Fred Wilson's property again, just like last year," he said. "That's about a mile down from the Mormon Pageant grounds. You take Canandaigua Road right at the light, up there by Bert's Pharmacy—about four miles outside of town. If you go past the pageant grounds, you've gone too far. You'll see it, though. Hard to miss."

"Four miles. Thanks, Sheriff. Look, uh, there is one other thing."

Lucas turned and looked at Ray. "What might that be?"

He seemed put out. Ray looked at Emily, who could only shrug her ignorance. He looked back at Lucas. "Well, you know, I'm sure it's all just coincidence, but I've got this booklet." He pulled it out of his back pocket. "Anyway, it says in here that one of the carnival's main attractions was a vampire named Martin and that he killed a priest—"

"You're right," Lucas cut in with a static smile.

"Beg your pardon?"

Lucas sat down again and tented his fingers in front of him. "All coincidence. They found a dead priest in the woods east of here—"

"In Macedon, according to the news. I believe we passed through Macedon about four or five miles back."

"Yeah, that's about right. Father Higgins pastored at St. Monica's, down the road. And yes, I know all about that booklet. But you know, you folks look a lot more sensible than to believe there'd be a link. If there were, don't you think I'd be out there right now, asking questions?"

"We just thought it was, well, you know, fairly coincidental that this booklet should say something about the murder of a priest and then have that priest's body found nearby."

"As I said, there isn't any coincidence. That carnival's been here before—only last year, in fact. They just latched onto that story to beef up profits. Father Higgins's disappearance happened a few years back and they had it all set up when they pulled into town, that's all. Now, from the clothes you're wearing and the car you're driving, I'd say you folks know a lot about profits, so if you'll excuse me." He picked up his pen and started in on his crossword again.

As they turned to leave, the door chimes sounded again. "Taking a long time to get dir—"

David saw Judd Lucas then and immediately forgot what he was going to say. He knew this man; he had definitely seen him before.

"Dad?" Emily said.

"Yeah, I . . ." He looked at Emily only briefly, then looked back at Lucas. "Do I know you?" he asked.

Lucas looked up. "No, I don't think so."

David stepped closer. "You're sure? Your face is very familiar."

"Nope. Never seen you before in my life."

"C'mon, Dad," Emily said.

David grudgingly followed the others back to the car, looking behind him at a confused Judd Lucas while Emily pulled him by the arm. After they got back to the car, Emily asked him how he could possibly know the sheriff of Hunt, New York.

"Wish to hell I knew," he said.

The carnival was only about half up when they got to the site. Emily parked across the road, near a vegetable stand. A cardboard sign read, "We use the honor system. Please be honorable." She thought about putting this stand and its sign on a New York City street. "On my honor, judge, I only stole what I could carry on my person." Four semis parked with their back doors to them had been emptied of their contents and the carnival's skeleton was about ready for a layer of skin. The Ferris wheel, sans seats, was no great shakes. *Kind of puny,* Emily thought. And the merry-go-round, minus horses and swans, wasn't much better. While they watched, the PETRY BROTHERS CARNIVALS sign went up, flapping in a rising wind.

"Might get stormy," one of the men yelled, as he climbed down his ladder. The man helping him nodded and lit up a cigarette. There was a bustle of activity beyond the signs: booths being put together, tents going up—not the Barnum and Bailey kind, more like baby brothers to those. On the front of one at the top of a cul de sac, about fifty yards beyond the sign, were four large posters depicting women in various costumes, all skimpy: an ant farm where all the workers knew where to go and what they had to do to get ready for the evening crowds.

"I was hoping they'd be open for business," Emily said. "Looks like they won't be ready until tonight."

"I guess we'll just have to come back tonight, then," Ray said. "Tell you what we can do till then—pool our efforts and talk to some people around town. I think it's something we should do, especially since they discovered that priest's . . . what's his name?"

"Higgins," Emily said.

"Yeah, Father Wesley Higgins. I think we should take a walk around town and see what we can come up with. Maybe even check out his church."

Emily glanced at her father. He seemed distracted, his gaze fixed upon the rising carnival. Little did she realize that a sense of déjà vu had swept over him.

"Dad?" she said.

He didn't answer.

"Dad?" she said again.

"Huh?" David said, turning quickly.

"Where were you?" Emily said.

He looked at Ray. "Nowhere. I . . . sorry, Ray, guess I wasn't listening."

"No big deal. I just thought we'd nose around town a little. See what the townsfolk think about this carnival. Their impressions of Martin'll help, too."

"Sounds like a good idea," David said. He could still see the sign out of the corner of his eye.

"Well," Emily said, "I guess we should get a hotel room."

"Uh, you guys don't mind if I stay there while you two snoop around, do you?" David said. "I'm a little tired."

"No, I don't mind," Emily said. She actually preferred it.

David smiled.

Sixteen

They got rooms at Stouffer's West near the expressway, at a place called Bushnell's Basin. Its claim to fame was a thirty-year-old lovers' lane murder that had yet to be solved. The hotel was about 25 years the murder's junior and reminded them of New York, if only because of the ridiculously high room rates.

David lay down when he got into the room while Emily hovered nearby, her worry about him growing by the second.

"You going to be okay, Dad?" she asked.

"Sure. Never better."

It was false bravado, she knew. "Okay, Dad—look, if you need anything, just call room service. I guess we'll get something to eat out there after we're done with our sleuthing."

David smiled. She thought it looked almost natural.

She noticed as she left that her father had already closed his eyes.

She met Ray at the car. While they drove back to Hunt, they decided to split up when they got there. If anyone felt like he was being ganged up on by out-of-towners, he'd probably clam up quick.

Emily said she'd start in the pet store across the street from the sheriff's office because, first, she liked the name Kritter Korner, and second, people who liked animals were usually fairly talkative. Ray opted for a bar down the street; and if he struck out there, he said he'd try the CYO Building, next to the sheriff's office. Of course, he said, the same talkative nature was true of barflies and gym rats.

Emily parked one door down from Bert's Pharmacy. "In a half hour, we meet back here, okay?" she said, as she cut the engine.

"Sure," Ray replied.

She watched him walk in the opposite direction, then crossed the street and went into the pet store.

The smells in the Kritter Korner were as complex as the noise. As soon as Emily stepped inside, a blue-and-yellow parrot named Max—according to a sign that also listed his vocabulary—greeted her in a shrill soprano. "Customer, customer!" he shrieked. His talons clenched and unclenched his wooden perch as he shifted his balance from one foot to the other. Emily smiled at him, and Max rewarded her by asking her name.

"Trying to pick me up, huh? Well, my name's Emily, and you are obviously Max, the wonder parrot," she said.

"Customer, customer," Max said again, his eyes rolling like they were on ball bearings.

"You're not as smart as people think," Emily whispered. "All you can do is parrot."

Emily left Max to his job of announcing customers and moved down the "exotic pet" aisle past a giant tarantula and assorted lizards, toward the dogs—now all barking, thanks to Max.

There were four other people in the store, an older couple checking out the dogs and two teenage girls in front doing the same to the cats. Emily would have preferred talking to the girls, but they left before she could make her move. Max, as he had been trained to do, announced their departure. "Shoplifters, shoplifters," he screeched, which, Emily thought, might have been true, based on how fast the girls left after Max's announcement. But the clerk didn't even bother to look up. *He's accustomed to it,* Emily thought, as she watched the old woman tap on the glass outside the dogs' cages.

"Oh, isn't she just precious," Emily said, referring to a whining St. Bernard puppy that had made eye contact with the older couple.

The woman smiled at Emily. "Yes," she said, "but you know, the trouble with large breeds is they die so terribly young. Tragic. Such a shame, too, they're such a loving breed. Good with children. God works in strange ways."

The old woman's body suggested the conversation had ended. Emily thought otherwise. "I'm new in town," she said.

"Oh?"

As the conversation progressed past the polite, a man Emily thought was the old woman's husband glanced at her.

"My husband got transferred from Chicago and we just bought a place near Macedon," Emily said. "Our dog got hit by a car—"

"And that's why you're here? To replace him?"

"Oh, I could never replace him. I see you've got your eyes on the St. Bernard anyway."

"Goodness gracious, no. As much as I'd like to, we just couldn't afford him—"

The old woman caught her husband's gaze and stopped short, and again the conversation seemed doomed. But again Emily took another stab at keeping it going.

"Oh, did you hear the news? It was on the radio. They found a body just down the road from our new house. A priest, the radio said. Father Higgins?"

Suddenly the woman seemed as put out as Judd Lucas had earlier. "Yes, that's right, Father Higgins. You'll have to excuse us now, dear. I hope you enjoy it here."

The woman and her husband turned away, but Emily wouldn't be denied. "I see there's a carnival in town this week," she said.

The old couple stopped abruptly and turned. The old man whispered something to his wife, then walked back toward Emily. "A word of advice," he said. "Stay away from that carnival. Far away."

That said, he went back to his wife and walked her out the door. Seeing them, Max didn't miss a beat, his shoplifter alert again raising a few canine voices in response.

Emily felt a shudder rumble through her. This simple warning from an old man in a pet store had validated what she'd secretly feared all along. There was something extraordinarily wrong with her father. And Martin, just as her father had said, was the reason. She started out the door, intent on finding Ray, but she stopped short when the clerk said, "Crazy old coots."

Emily looked at him, confused. "Crazy old coots? *Them?*"

The clerk, about twenty, Emily thought, put a magazine down on the counter. "Well, I heard what the old guy said, and he just didn't have a right scaring you like that. New in town, huh?"

Emily thought she'd play along. "Yeah, we bought a place in Macedon. My husband—"

"I heard," the clerk said with a smile. "That old couple? That's Harry and Virginia Mulcahy. Their son got killed at a carnival some years back. His own fault. He was trying to set fire to a tent and lit himself up. That's why Harry doesn't want much to do with carnivals. Guess I can't blame him."

Emily studied the boy's face, looking for some indication that he wasn't telling her the truth. Of course, he had no reason to lie—at least, she didn't think so.

"So, you and your husband going out to the carnival, then?" the boy asked.

"We'd planned to."

"Well, you have a good time, now. And look, the boss is going to put the St. Bernard on sale next week, forty

percent off. I heard you say you lost your dog, so I thought
I'd give you first crack."

"Couldn't you get in trouble for telling me that?"

"Nah. The boss is my dad."

Emily thanked him and left. She decided that it wouldn't
take too long to get real tired of Max the wonder parrot.

While Emily made her way across the street, David sat
bolt upright in bed, dripping sweat. He'd had the dream
again, the one about the boys in the basement and the man
at the door. Now he knew where he had seen the sheriff
before: he was the man at the door . . . the man he had
given the boy to in his dream.

He picked up the phone and called the front desk. "This
is David Kane, room two-forty-five. Can you call a cab for
me, please?"

"Certainly, sir."

"Good, I'll be down in a just a few minutes."

Seventeen

Brooklyn, New York

Lesley Charleton, an associate at the law firm of Wade and Philips, specializing in real estate and tax law, put the finishing touches on her makeup, closed her compact, and left the building. She had about forty minutes to get to the Russian Tea Room—her fiancé would be waiting—and from here, on Flatbush Avenue in Brooklyn, she'd need a lot of luck to arrive on time. She prayed that traffic would be light, not only on the Manhattan Bridge, but all the way.

She finally managed to hail a taxi. "Russian Tea Room, and pronto," she told the driver.

"Yes, ma'am," the driver said smartly, as he tipped his old baseball cap to her.

He adjusted his rearview mirror and looked at her longer than she would have liked. "Okay, buster," she said, "now that you've added me to your fantasies, step on it. I'm in a hurry."

"Sorry," the driver said, as he pulled out into traffic.

A few minutes later, Lesley realized they were going the wrong way, away from the Manhattan Bridge. "Okay, pal," she said tiredly, "I'm not some tourist you can con into a big fare, so turn this rust bucket around."

The driver smiled into the rearview mirror. "I know," he said simply, "but there's a five-car smash-up on the bridge.

We're going to have to take the Williamsburg" He looked at her for a response.

"C'mon, you can do better than that," Lesley said.

"No, really, it's true. Bodies everywhere, legs ripped off, eyes gouged out, a real sick mess. One guy, Jesus, this is really morbid, one guy had his nuts ripped out and a coupla kids are playing marbles with them on the side of the goddamn road! Better that than hopscotch, though, right? Squish, squish! Never use those things again!"

A sense of alarm rushed through Lesley, but she clenched her jaw and put a stop to it. She'd met sickees before—hell, as a public defender she'd represented plenty of them. "And you expect me to believe that bullshit?" she said. "Stop the car, and I mean now!"

The driver raised his eyebrows and shrugged at her. "Well, you see, I don't know if I can do that, ma'am. No place to pull over yet, and if I stop here you might get your pretty little ass run over."

"Christ!" Lesley said. She reached for the door handle and grabbed empty air. She tried the other side; the same. "All right, what the hell's going on here?" she said, still angry enough to sound that way. Fear stood patiently by, waiting for a chance. "What is this, a cop car or something? Stop the goddamn car and let me out. I demand that you let me out *this instant!*"

Again the driver smiled. "Or something," he said, with absurd nonchalance.

"What, dammit? What did you say?"

"In answer to your question, it's not a cop car, it's an 'or something' car."

"And I'm supposed to know what the hell that means?"

It was then that Lesley noticed the strange shape of the driver's head. The right side appeared to be concave. But again, you met all kinds in New York City, mental and physical wrecks both. And she still had her self-defense class experience to draw on, if it came to that. A knee in the groin would drop this turkey. For now, though, with no way to get out, she thought she'd try to reason with him. "Look, I've got, I don't know, about three hundred bucks. It's yours. Just let me out of the car and you can have it."

"Really?" the driver said, feigning delight. "Now I can buy that electric train set I've always wanted! Suggestion, lady—just sit back and relax. You won't be in the car much longer."

He took a right turn and on both sides now Lesley saw some of the row houses for which Brooklyn was famous. She leaned against the door. Maybe he hadn't closed it tight. Maybe if she leaned hard enough it would just pop open. It didn't budge, and she could see the driver smiling in the rearview mirror at her futile efforts. Maybe she could flag down a cop, if she saw one. Then she realized something else: the windows in this cab were darkly tinted. She looked more closely at the driver than she had before. "I demand to know where you're taking me!" she cried, trying to sound threatening and realizing it wouldn't do much good because this guy held all the cards.

The driver rolled his eyes. *"I demand to know where you're taking me, I demand to know where you're taking me! Well, lady, I demand to know why you won't shut the fuck up!"*

Lesley slumped in her seat. Suddenly she began to view the rest of her life as a matter of minutes instead of years. That was about half true.

Hunt, New York

Emily stepped into a bar called the Tiger's Paw, where light was provided by three domes hung from a high tin ceiling. After her eyes adjusted, she saw only an old woman seated at the bar hunched over something with a foamy head. A quick glance around the room, at dark vinyl booths, confirmed that Ray wasn't here, that hardly anyone was here. *He's probably at the CYO,* she thought.

Ray had been watching a game of three-on-three at the CYO, wishing like crazy that he'd been six-foot-four and skinny. Sure, life as a writer was full of surprises, and giving your brain a proper workout was at least as important as giving your body one, but there was a side to him that wished he'd had a normal upbringing, that wished he'd been the first selected for pickup games, that longed for the physical satisfaction of a sport. He jogged, but he'd started jogging because he'd heard so much about the runner's high, about how the body produced a set of substances that perfectly simulated illegal drug highs. That hadn't happened to him yet. *Probably never will,* he thought, *unless I push the envelope.*

He'd talked with a couple of kids earlier, before the game had started, asking them if they were going to the carnival and if they'd gone last year. "Yeah, sounds like fun," one of them said. "Didn't go last year, but I hear they got some real nasty freaks, man!"

The other kid said he'd heard they had a vampire, a real honest-to-goodness, bite-you-in-the-neck-and-suck-your-blood vampire.

"Martin," Ray said.

"Yeah, that's him. Big ugly sucker."

Ray didn't bother to tell them what had happened to Martin. They'd been the only kids in the place then; the other four had shown up since. They'd started their game right away, before Ray had had a chance to talk with them. The score, in a game to ten, was nine-to-eight; you had to win by two. Ray thought the game would be over in a couple of minutes.

Emily showed up when the score was ten-to-nine.

"What did you get?" he asked.

"A warning."

"What are you talking about?"

She told him what had happened and said she still didn't know what to think. Hearing that, Ray decided maybe he was wasting his time here.

"Let's take a walk," he said.

"Where to?"

"Church. I suddenly feel religious."

David, seated in the middle of the back seat, felt like a dog on a scent. He'd had the taxi driver stop outside the sheriff's office, wondering if he should actually go inside and talk with Judd Lucas. But he didn't go inside, primarily because he'd felt an urge to go someplace else in town. Where exactly, he didn't know, but like last time, money talked and the driver quickly consented to driving him around until he could make up his mind.

They took a right at the four corners churches, where David had a sudden panic attack, as if he'd caught a glimpse of a gun pointed at his head, and crossed a bridge that spanned the Barge Canal. "Turn around," David told the driver, when they got to the other side.

The driver did as he'd been told.

"Take a right here," David said, as soon as they'd gone back over the bridge.

They took a road that paralleled the canal for about a quarter mile, until David told the driver to take a left. After they turned they went up a slight incline, passing houses built at the turn of the century, until they reached a dead end. There was an open field of scrub grass on the left, and beyond that a half mile or so, a stand of trees. An Amtrak train roared past, the tracks hidden by the scrub brush. On the right was what David at first thought was a vacant lot. But the more he stared at it, the more he realized what he had stumbled upon.

The driver volunteered some information. "Had a big fire

here a couple years back," he said. "Scuttlebutt had it that there were a couple of murders in the house and that the guy set fire to the place and burned himself up. 'Course, you can't believe everything you hear."

That was all the catalyst David needed. His mind slipped quickly from one point of view to another. First he was in the taxi, staring at that vacant lot, then he was on the porch of the house that had burned down, just as in his dream . . . then he was in the car again, then back on the porch. He actually started to get dizzy. It didn't take him long to understand that his dream had probably actually happened. That somehow he had shared that experience in a dream with the man who really had sat on that porch and killed himself. The big question now was why had he killed himself? He was very old, sure, God only knew how old—those grotesque hands and feet leading the way in his dream were hard to forget. Maybe that was why . . . but Martin was very old, too, if the booklet about his life could be believed, so maybe . . . no, no way. Martin hadn't been in that cellar. That was ridiculous. And as far as Martin having murdered that priest . . .

Think about it, though, David. If it's true, if Martin really *did* kill Father Wesley Higgins, then maybe the aging was simply his penance for killing a priest.

"Yeah, there's a lot of bullshit comes with what happened here," the driver continued, breaking David's train of thought. "There's some who say that one of the undead, you know, a Dracula, lived here. Me, I don't believe in that shit. 'Course, a lot of weird shit went on in this town a couple years back."

David ignored him and got out of the car. It was overcast now, but a weak sun shone through thin clouds. He pulled his collar around his neck and walked into the weeds. The house in front of him, beyond this vacant lot, a two-story older colonial, was vacant, too, as was the house to its right.

David stopped where he was, positive his dream porch

had been here before, right where he was standing. He looked back at the taxi as the driver lit up a cigarette, content to sit back and collect his fare.

David wanted something more to happen—what, he didn't know, but there had to be something. He didn't wait long. Suddenly, his point of view shifted again to a spot just a few feet from where he stood, from the left side of where the porch had been. And while he watched, a man came running out of the house—Judd Lucas, he was sure of that—carrying a boy in his arms, the same boy he had handed over to him in the cellar. The boy appeared to be unconscious. He watched while Lucas ran to the road, yelling.

What now? David wondered hopefully. But although it seemed that something else should have happened, nothing did. Lucas and the boy simply shimmered and disappeared, and David's point of view shifted back to where it should have been, to the present. Certain that he wouldn't see anything else, he went back to the car and told the driver to take him to the sheriff's office.

St. Monica's Catholic Church was on the southeast corner of Main and Gifford, just a couple hundred yards from the CYO.

"Boy, if you can't find religion here, you're just not gonna find it," Ray said, referring to the four corners churches.

Ray led the way and rang the doorbell at the rectory behind the church. The door opened almost immediately. A short, dark-haired woman invited them inside. "Father O'Brien is taking a nap," she said, as she closed the door. "He should be up shortly, though. Who may I say is calling, and what is the nature of your visit?" *Both official and friendly at the same time. Perfect for a rectory,* Emily thought.

"We'd like to make a contribution to the church," Emily said.

The woman smiled and clenched her hands prayer-like in front of her. "Please wait here. I'll see if Father O'Brien is up."

The woman came back a minute later. "Father will be with you shortly," she said, releasing a hint of sausage into the air when she disappeared into a room off a connecting hallway.

"Contributions?" Ray said.

"Let me handle this, Ray."

Father Kevin O'Brien came down the stairs about five minutes later. He towered over Ray and Emily and spoke in a voice deep enough to rattle the floorboards. "My housekeeper mentioned you were here about contributions," he said.

"That's right," Emily said. "But there is something else . . ."

Father O'Brien's hands dangled in front of him, the fingers entwined. "If this is about Father Higgins—"

"Well, as a matter of fact . . . I was hoping you could tell me about the last time you saw him, Father? I mean, did you talk, and if you did . . ." She stopped there. That about covered it.

Father O'Brien tried to look gracious and fell short. "I don't want to appear ungrateful," he said, "but if your contribution is predicated upon getting information about Father Higgins . . ."

Emily looked at him a moment. She got a tight little smile for her efforts.

"Consider this a bribe," she said. She took out her checkbook and wrote a check for a thousand dollars while Father O'Brien watched, then handed it to him.

Father O'Brien looked at the check, then back at Emily. "I appreciate it when someone gets right to the point," he said. He smiled. "The roof leaks anyway. I'm afraid, however, that nothing I can tell you about Father Higgins would be helpful to you. His last day, or rather, the last day we spoke, was no different from any other. And he certainly had no enemies. He was a priest, after all. So if you'd like your money—"

"Father," Ray said, "there's a carnival setting up outside of town, the Petry Brothers Carnival. What do you know about their operation?"

"Not much. I don't attend such things. They were here last year, I know that."

Ray hesitated, wondering if the line of questioning he had in mind was proper. They were in the rectory of a Catholic Church, after all. But who would know more about evil than someone like Father O'Brien? And the booklet had used Father Higgins's disappearance to their advantage. For that he thought Father O'Brien should be at least a little upset."

"And you know about the attraction, the vampire?"

Father O'Brien's face tensed noticeably. "Yes, of course. I know about the fantasy."

"The fantasy?"

"Come into the living room," he said. "It's more comfortable there."

They went into the room, just off to the left. There was a threadbare Oriental carpet on the hardwood floor and dark wood antique furniture scattered about. The smell of sausage cooking was stronger here. Lighting was muted, giving the room a rustic but comfortable feel.

They sat down on a mahogany settee, a freshly dusted potted fern behind them. Father O'Brien sat down across from them in what was obviously his favorite chair, a wingback with a cream-colored pillow. He crossed his legs and dangled his hands over the arms of the chair as he settled in. "As you may know," he said, "ours is one of the four corners churches. Some years back, the powers that be got together and hired one man as custodian and general handyman for all four. His name was Martin." Father O'Brien saw their surprise. He raised his hand. He had to get this out, then he could finally close the door on this whole thing.

"I know about the advertising circular. I know they named their vampire Martin. I also know that he's remarkably similar in appearance to the man we employed. I also know that the coincidence, Martin's disappearance and then Father Higgins, as well as a number of other strange occurrences, make for a wonderful and fantastic story. But that's all it is, a story. The carnival, I'm told, has a different advertising circular for each town they visit. And that, I am also told, is good for business."

"Do you know where Martin lived?" Emily said.

Father O'Brien's face tensed. "He lived here. Upstairs. He had a small room on the third floor."

"Today must be our lucky day," Ray said "May we see it?"

"Why would you want to see his room?" Father O'Brien asked.

"Father," Emily said, "I'd hoped that my donation might buy something more than what you've given us. I'm afraid that our reasons for wanting to see the room are our own. I hope you understand."

Father O'Brien hesitated, then said, "Very well. Follow me."

They used a dismal, cramped servants' stairway. Martin's room was on the third floor, toward the back of the rectory. Father O'Brien took a master key out of his pocket when they got there. "Forgive the appearance," he said. "It hasn't been touched in years."

"Oh? Why's that?" Emily said.

Father O'Brien thought a moment and said, "Frankly, I can't get the housekeeper to stay in here long enough to clean it." He smiled tightly, then unlocked the door.

The room was spotless, save the dust on everything. Emily thought about the first shovelful of dirt on a casket.

"Feel free to look around," Father O'Brien said. "I have some things I have to attend to."

"Father," Emily said, "is this the way he left it?"

"Exactly the way he left it," he answered from the top of the stairs. "Now, if you'll excuse me."

They waited until his footfalls faded, then went inside.

The room was small and spartan. The bed was beneath the only window, the blanket drawn tight, military style. There was a dark wood dresser with a dusty doily and mirror next to the bed. The wood floor was bare. A lone window looked onto the back of the church. They watched a couple go inside, through white double doors.

Anxiety crawled into them within a minute after they'd entered the room. At first they denied it, casting confused glances at each other and smiling, but the more they denied, the more anxious they got. They both fought it and wondered how long they could before they followed in Father O'Brien's footsteps and went back downstairs.

"The walls," Ray said, "what the hell do you suppose that's all about?"

The walls were papered with photographs and postcards, all of New York City and its attractions: the Statue of Liberty, Radio City Music Hall, the Empire State Building, Broadway.

"He liked New York, I guess," Emily said.

She opened a dresser drawer. In it were neatly folded underwear, a hairbrush. She closed it and opened the drawer beside it. In the bottom was a photograph of two men, one a priest—he wore a Roman collar—the other, Martin. They were standing near the front of the church, by the street. Martin had his arm draped around the priest, a man she guessed had to be Father Higgins. Martin's head was twice the size of Father Higgins's and he stood at least a foot taller. *Like father and son* . . . She put the photograph in her purse and said, "C'mon, Ray, let's get outta here. This place . . . I guess I just don't like being here."

Ray smiled. "Me neither," he said. "Why do you suppose that is?"

"I don't know, Ray, but I don't feel like talking about it, at least, not in here."

"Neither do I, but I find it rather remarkable, don't you? Here we are, two educated, supposedly intelligent people, and we're scared silly just being in this room." Ray looked around and shook his head. "Psychological. Gotta be. What do you think, Doc?"

Emily looked at him, fighting a demon she couldn't see, trying to control emotions she'd rarely felt. They could hash this out somewhere else. They could laugh at themselves in that cozy death room good Father O'Brien called a living room. *Come to think of it, this whole damn building* . . . "Come on, Ray, I've seen enough."

Ray looked around again like someone trying to pick a fight. "Yeah, me too, I guess," he said. "Maybe they'll serve tea."

Father O'Brien was waiting for them downstairs.

"I apologize for being so rude up there," he said.

"No need to apologize," Emily said. "Look, I . . ." She took the photo out of her purse. "Do you mind if I take this?"

Father O'Brien shrugged. "No. May I ask why you're so interested in Father Higgins and Martin?"

"Father, I doubt you'd believe me if I told you."

Eighteen

Brooklyn

The driver turned to Lesley Charleton and said, "See that window over there?"

Lesley looked at a first-floor window in a gaudy purple row house. It was open a couple of inches.

"There's going to be a gun pointed at you from the moment you get out of the car until you get inside," he said. "Probably an unnecessary precaution around here, but one we took anyway."

"You'd shoot me?" Lesley said. Her tone had slipped to whiny.

"Not me, the person in the window. I'd just shove a knife into you. I hate loud noises."

The driver got out then and went around and opened Lesley's door. She got out, her eyes fixed on that open first-floor window. She didn't see a muzzle, but she didn't know if she should take a chance, not yet. Once she got inside, though, what then? Gang rape, maybe—or worse? She looked down the street. There were a couple of kids playing hopscotch about fifty feet away. She remembered what the driver had said about those kids on the bridge playing with someone's balls. *Probably all for effect, though,* she thought. *The gun in the window, maybe that's for effect, too.*

"C'mon, dammit," the driver said, as he glanced at the sky.

Getting nervous, Lesley thought. *Maybe he really is in this alone.*

The driver pulled his collar around his neck and yanked his cap farther down on his head. *Could be winter, the way he's dressed,* Lesley thought.

"No," she said simply.

The driver's eyes tightened into slits. He was sweating. "No? What is it with you, lady? You wanna get shot, or what? C'mon!"

"No!" Lesley said again. She liked to see him sweat. Out of the corner of her eye she saw one of the kids down the street glance in her direction.

The driver smiled. "Proof, huh," he mumbled. "Okay, there's your proof." He nodded at the window.

Lesley saw something glint in the sunlight. It could've been anything, but somehow, she knew what it was.

"Satisfied?" the driver said. "Now c'mon, dammit!"

Die now or die later, Lesley thought. *Not much of a choice.* At least she still had a choice. She walked up the steps and went into the house.

The hallway that stretched out before her was darkly lit, but it smelled clean. Light spilled onto a tile floor from two rooms on the left, about ten feet apart. There was a stairway on the right and a photograph of a toddler wearing a fireman's hat on the wall at the bottom of the stairs. The photograph lifted her spirits.

"This way," the driver said. Lesley thought he sounded less threatening now. She didn't know if that was good or bad.

When they got to the first room on the left, she saw a fat, dark-haired woman stirring food in a large pot on the stove; the smell reminded her of how hungry she was. But that was the least of her troubles. She looked at the woman. *All this normalcy, all this everyday stuff going on.* The two women just looked at each other, and while they did, Lesley swore she saw the beginnings of a smile work onto the woman's large face. Lesley smiled back, hopeful. But as the woman shifted her weight, Lesley saw a rifle propped against the wall behind her. She felt as if she'd been dipped in ice water. It wasn't possible. *How could someone like that . . . murderers don't come prepackaged, Lesley. You know that. They're young and old and nice looking and not so nice looking. Remember that lady from Scarsdale? Looked a lot like this lady, didn't she, Lesley? She killed three people.*

Something moved behind her, on the stairs. She turned and saw the kid in the photograph, older, larger, but still the same kid. He smiled at her, and Lesley smiled back. Yet her spirits did an about-face. Nothing jibed, nothing at all. Kids, and a woman cooking, and guns, and windows blacked out . . . no door handles . . . *Okay,* she thought, *get a hold of yourself, Lesley, get a grip. You're a survivor, remember? And you're going to survive this, too. Play along. Do what they want. Wait for your chance. Just keep your wits about you and you'll be okay.*

"C'mon," the driver said again.

"Where we going?"

"You'll see."

He took her by the arm and Lesley looked behind her at the woman cooking. She just looked away, and as she glanced back at the stairs, Lesley saw that the child was gone, too.

They passed the second lit room, a living room. The television was on, but no one was watching and the sound was turned way down. Lesley caught a fleeting glimpse of Tom Selleck on the screen, a group of women in bikinis lolling around him.

A few steps later, she saw a door on the right open up. A tall man stepped into the hall.

"Hello, Lesley," he said with a smile, his voice a pleasant and lyrical baritone.

Her spirits suddenly rose again. *A smile, he'd actually smiled at her. Maybe they didn't want to kill her after all; maybe—*

"I don't know you," she said.

"I know *you*, though," the man said.

The only light came from the man's right. It was weak enough to make his features get lost in shadow. He was tall and thin, his hair longer than was fashionable. Even in this light, she could see how dirty it was. It hung in long, greasy ringlets on either side of his head.

Lesley felt the driver's grip tighten on her arm. He led her toward the doorway. The other man didn't move and they passed within a few inches of each other. Despite herself, Lesley thought he had a nice smile.

She saw an enclosed flight of stairs before her. The driver was behind her.

"Go on," he said. "Don't be afraid."

She turned and looked up at the thin, long-haired man. "Please, what are you going to do to me? Please, tell me what's going to happen to me!"

The man shrugged. "Well, if you really wanna know, we're gonna give you a choice: life or death."

Lesley thought about that and felt a sudden wash of relief. Finally, someone had said what she'd been thinking. And she had a choice, too. But then again, what kind of choice was that? Anyone in her right mind would choose life. *Anyone!* Then why would he say something like that? Why would he even *suggest* that she might prefer death over life?

By now her eyes had adjusted to the light, and as she looked more closely at the tall, thin man, she could plainly see that his face had a concavity on one side, just like that on the cab driver's face.

The man turned his head slightly and Lesley suddenly saw herself like him, with part of her head caved in, looking into a mirror and trying vainly to hide the deformity. Was this what she had to look forward to? Was this what could make death preferable to life? *No,* she decided, *impossible. These people'd been born like this. Mutants, they were all a bunch of goddamn . . . brothers, probably. She was normal, she'd been born normal. Nothing could make her look like this. Nothing.*

But hearing what she had heard and seeing what she had seen only made her that much more confused; and the more confused she got, the more frightened she became. *Maybe it was time to think about—*

"Lesley," the thin man said, as if he'd read her thoughts, "you can't get away. Believe me. And I'm afraid that if you try . . . just *don't,* okay? The way it is, you've still got a choice, but if you make a run for it . . ."

If she tried to run, they'd kill her. That's what he meant. But if she went down there, into that cellar, they'd probably kill her, too. She'd always been a survivor, though, and somehow, in some way, she was going to survive this, too. She turned and started down the stairs. The two men followed.

Hunt, New York

The taxi pulled up outside the sheriff's office. David got out and went inside.

A woman in a brown and black uniform, her hair clipped short, smiled at him. She carried a manila folder, and placed it on the desk. "Hello," she said. "May I help you?"

David looked around the office. There was a door behind the woman that led into the cells, and there was an administration area off to her right. Apparently the sheriff wasn't here. "Sheriff Lucas, can you tell me where he is, please?"

The woman hesitated, then, "And what business do you have with Sheriff Lucas?"

She didn't trust him, David could see it on her face. Did he look that bad? "I was his English teacher. I was just passing through, and I thought—"

The woman smiled. "He's at lunch, Mr. . . ."

"Kane."

"Mr. Kane."

"And where—?"

"At the diner next to Bert's Pharmacy."

"Thanks."

David left in a hurry and looked both ways. Bert's Pharmacy was about a hundred yards down the street. He opened the taxi door. "Wait for me, okay?" he said to the driver.

"Sure, pal."

David crossed the street, walked past Bert's Pharmacy, then stopped in front of Ed's Diner. He pushed on a screen door and went inside. Booths stretched out on either side and there was counter on the right. A waitress in a pink and white uniform was pouring coffee into an old man's cup. She glanced up at him. "Kathy'll be with you in a minute," she said.

David nodded and looked around. The booths stretched beyond a counter to the right. He stepped away to get a better look. Judd Lucas was back there, in a booth. He was facing him, talking with someone. Someone short, David decided, because he couldn't see his head and the tops of the booths came up to the sheriff's shoulders.

He had been mentally reworking what he wanted to say to Lucas, but every time he went over it, he didn't like it. However he structured his sentences, he sounded crazy. He had finally decided that the only thing he could do was tell him the truth. There was a reason he had dreamt about this man, and that reason had a lot do with what had been happening to him.

A woman suddenly appeared in front of him. Her name tag said, "Hi, I'm Kathy."

"Follow me, sir," she said.

David nodded toward the back. "I just came in to see the sheriff," he said.

Kathy smiled. "Sure," she said, and reclaimed her seat next to the cash register.

David started back toward Lucas. About halfway there, Lucas saw him and looked at him. It was about then that the person Lucas had been talking with stuck his tiny head out from behind the booth. David stopped and looked at him and realized right away who it was. This was the kid he had given to Lucas in his dream, a little older, a little larger, but still the same kid.

Lesley had expected something very much removed from the sixties-style attempt at middle-class decorating that she saw when she got to the bottom of the stairs: birch paneling, a red shag wall-to-wall carpet, and a very old beige sofa with spindly legs against the wall. Three women sat on the sofa, regarding her the way people look at strangers on a bus. An eight-track tape player played Neil Diamond at low volume. A bar in the corner had two barstools pulled up to it. A boy sat on one, the other was empty. There were five more people in the room, the light low enough to conceal their ages, but she didn't think any of them were over forty. Three men, three women. The boy. *There should be kids necking in the corners,* she thought.

She felt a hand on the small of her back and looked into the face of the thin man. From his smile, this could have been a neighborhood social.

"Hey, I want you to meet some people," he said.

Lesley stopped in front of each person and the thin man told her their names, although she barely heard them. They all smiled at her and shook her hand, and when the introductions were done, the tall, thin man said, "I'm Louis. You can call me Lou."

The ambiance was anything but threatening, and when

she thought about it, she decided she felt very relaxed, even comfortable. They were just a bunch of everyday working class people, not a murderer in the bunch. She even wondered if this wasn't just some stupid practical joke. *Maybe Konchak—he'd always had the hots for her. Asked her to lunch all the time, even did some research for her . . .*

"Now, can you tell me what the hell's going on here?" she said to Louis.

He gestured to a chair beside the tape player and she sat down.

"Where the hell can I start?" he said. "Probably the beginning, huh? 'Cause if I start at the end, I won't have nothin' to say. Sorry, just tryin' to lighten things up a little. See, Lesley, you work on Flatbush and I live on Flatbush, and every day I see you sitting at the fountain and eating your lunch, and every day I say to myself, 'Go talk with her, Lou. Be a man. Go tell her how you feel.' But Jesus, you're so goddamn beautiful, Lesley! How can I do that? What if you told me to go fuck myself? What then?"

She squirmed a little.

"Anyway, until now I haven't had the nerve to *tell* you how I feel. But now, I don't know why, now I don't give a shit. I say to myself, if she tells me to go fuck myself, I'll just kill her."

Lesley swore she could feel the blood gathering behind her eyes. She tried to smile and something static happened to her mouth. "That's what this is all about?" she said. "You just wanted to ask me out? Well, why didn't—"

"Well, as I said, my nerves—"

"Then all this stuff about life and death—"

"Ah, you know, that's, that's where it gets a little sticky, Lesley. You see, thing is, you know about us now, so we ain't got much of a choice."

"What do you mean, know about you?"

Louis grinned. "Come on, Lesley, we're not stupid. You saw Tony and me. The others are just like us. See—what we want, Lesley, what *I* want, is for *you* to be like *us*. Like *me*. And when that happens, then there's no way you can tell me to go fuck myself. And if you don't tell me to go fuck myself, then I don't have to kill you."

"Oh, shit!" Lesley mumbled.

Louis knelt and looked at her like he was going to propose. "You know, Lesley, I hate to admit it, but this thing is bigger than me. Bigger than you. There's somethin' else goin' on here, Lesley. I'm just kinda keepin' things in control, know what I mean? Kinda like the little boy with his finger in the dike. Shit, Lesley, look at these people! I can't control 'em for long. Won't be much longer they'll tell me to go fuck myself; then what you got is anarchy, know what I mean? A fuckin' uprising! I told them the only way we're gonna get through this is together, but it's damn hard to make other people believe that, especially the ones who ain't got no patience. Thing is, I didn't want you killed, I wanted to give you a chance to, well, to . . . be changed, instead."

Changed, Lesley thought. *What the hell does that mean?* "Jesus," she mumbled, "I can't believe what I'm hearing. You're all lunatics, you know that? You're all a bunch of goddamn lunatics! What is this, anyway, some kind of cult, or something?"

"A cult? No, Lesley, this ain't no cult. It's something, but it ain't no cult. We got rules, though. You gotta have rules. You got anarchy without rules."

Louis got up and nodded to the taxi driver who bounded up the stairs and returned a minute or so later with the woman Lesley had seen earlier.

Louis put his arm around her. "This is Lucinda," he said. "Lucinda, this is Lesley. Remember, you saw her in the kitchen making supper?"

Lucinda looked at her while Louis smiled at Lucinda.

Yet another sweet, nonthreatening moment. Louis and this kindly looking woman. Family was sacred. As portents went, this wasn't one, so when Louis bent to the short, fat woman, opened his mouth wide, and sank his teeth slowly yet deeply into her neck, Lesley just lost control. She screamed and her world became a horrifying union of sickening sounds and brilliant colors—and a not-so-bright future. Lucinda, her blood all over Louis's face now, her eyes wide with terror as she thought about how close she was to dying, also tried to scream. But she couldn't; the best she could do was open her mouth wide and beat the air with her arms and legs like a flipped-over beetle in the sun. She was dead within seconds and after she died, Louis dropped her onto the red shag carpet, spat out a square of flesh, and waited for her to regain her composure. He waited for quite a while.

"Disgusting, isn't it?" he said finally, as Lesley looked up at him, her face red and shiny with tears. "Had to be done, though. I mean, I asked her, I said, 'Lucy, you've got a choice. You're my wife, the mother of my son, so I gotta give you a choice.' Know what? She says, 'Lou, I don't wanna look like that. I'd rather be dead than look like that.' Well, she knew she couldn't run. She *knew* that. Only thing she *didn't* know was *when* she was going to die. Today was when. Lesley, we don't know how this shit happened. We don't know how we got this way. I've got suspicions, sure, I've got my suspicions.

"There was this guy who Tony and I did a number on, well, we took him home, you know, to finish him off, but the guy turns out to be the god-damnedest fighter you ever saw. Last thing I remember is—now, this is gonna sound weird—but the last thing I remember is pullin' a knife out of my throat and thinkin' that I should be dead. But I wasn't dead; I was as alive as you are now."

Louis looked at one of the men. "Tom here, he was my first, and after I did him, he said, 'Hey, Lou, you don't s'pose we're vampires, do you?' 'Shit,' I said, 'I don't think so, Tom. Least, not the movie kind.' I could tell Tom was thinking about that. 'But the blood, Louis,' he said. 'What about the blood? How come we like it so much?' See, he'd done his first by then, too. But you know, Lesley, that made sense. Why do we like it so much? I thought. Why've we gotta have it? And here's another thing, vampires are s'pose to have fangs, right? And shit, Lesley, fangs would help, too. Look at poor Lucinda."

Lesley looked at Lucinda again, prone, dead, her neck torn away. Had her husband's teeth been sharper, that wouldn't have happened. She would have died more cleanly.

"It's really weird, Lesley. But we're starting to get this thing figured out. We all have dreams, see, I told you that before. We dream we're in this basement and all around us are these bodies, all chewed up. Like Lucinda there. But the dream doesn't stop there. We all dream that we save someone that hasn't been eaten yet, some kid. We just hand him over to some guy in a cop's uniform and after we do that, we go outside and die in the sun, like a real vampire. And that's weird, too. We're all sensitive to sunlight. Janet there got roasted good the other day, but shit, no one's disappeared in a puff of smoke yet, not even her. There's more, too—something to do with some black chick. No one's figured that one out yet, though.

"So now you've got it, Lesley. Now you know why I want to give you a chance. So it's up to you now. Die like Lucy, or become one of us: your choice."

Lesley thought back to other important moments in her life—her engagement, her marriage; her divorce; her miscarriage. The death of her father. All moments that stopped time, moments that had become indelibly etched on her subconscious. They, as well as other parts of her life, paraded before her now, as the people in this odd cellar room gathered closer to her, waiting for her answer. She looked into each face, and as she did, she remembered how many times she'd thought about the moment of her death and how it would arrive. Would she die slowly, violently, happily?

Would she die in her sleep? And if she did, would she think
she was only dreaming? She never thought she'd die like
this, certainly not like this. She grinned a lopsided grin,
amazed at her own sudden resilience. She was a survivor,
dammit, and she'd survive this, too. Let them do what they
wanted to her; as long as there was still breath in her lungs,
she had a chance.

She pulled down the collar of her blouse. "Will it hurt?"
she asked Louis.

Louis grinned. "You bet it will," he said. "That's part of
the fun."

At about the same time, in a bar in the Bronx, a man
named Keaton stood over a urinal, relieving himself. Lost
in the ecstasy of a good long pee, he didn't hear another
man come into the bathroom. And when he did finally realize that someone else was in here, he didn't much care.

Out of the corner of his eye, he watched the well-dressed
man step toward him, past the third urinal. *Jesus,* he
thought, *get away from me, you gay bastard!* Disgusted, he
looked away and begged his bladder to hurry it up. His
bladder obeyed, but just as he shook off and began to stuff
himself back in, he felt a massive pain in his neck, a pain
so sudden and so deep, he pulled his zipper up before he
should have, snagging himself and drawing a liberal amount
of blood out of his penis. But that, of course, wasn't what
he was really worried about. The man at his neck had gotten
his full attention. He tried to get away, but he couldn't.

After the killer finished draining Bruce Keaton of his
blood, he checked his clothing over for bloodstains. There
were none that he could see. It was a good thing he'd had
on a dark suit today. He'd have to be more careful from
now on. Couldn't let this thing get the better of him. He
looked down at his victim—his second—and smiled. Poor

bastard got his dick caught in his zipper. "Jesus," he said, "that must have really smarted."

After he had fixed his tie and wiped the blood off his mouth, he opened the door slowly, saw that no one was around, and left.

Nineteen

"Got a minute?" David said to Judd Lucas.

Lucas looked at him like someone looking for a gun, trying to decide whether it was loaded or not. "That's about all I got," he said finally.

"Mind if I sit down, then?" Lucas and the boy seated across from him were in the middle of their respective seats.

Lucas reluctantly scooted over and David sat down next to him, looking more closely now at the dark-haired boy.

"This is my son, Steven," Lucas said, nodding.

"Hello," David said, "my name's David Kane."

"Hi," Steven said, and stuck his small hand across the table. David took it into his own and gave it a shake. Cold, huh? he thought. He let it go. It wouldn't do to alarm the boy. He had alarmed him, though, he could see it in the boy's eyes as he let go of his hand. Steven glanced quickly at his father before he looked back at David, a studious and cautious glaze settling onto his thin and tanned face. Looking into his eyes, David decided that this dark-haired, handsome boy knew a lot more about life than a kid his age should. Or maybe anyone. A search for innocence in those eyes would probably come up empty.

"I gotta go to the bathroom," Steven said.

Probably an excuse, David thought. He didn't like being here. Not now, not with him.

Steven looked at his father for permission. Lucas nodded

and Steven got up, casting a long look at David before he left.

Is that fear in his eyes? David wondered.

Both men watched Steven disappear into the men's room. He wouldn't be back, David thought, not while he was still here.

David turned and looked at Judd Lucas.

Something passed between father and son. Some understanding. David forced a smile; it felt silly.

"As I said, I haven't got much time," Lucas said.

David glanced across from him, where Steven had been sitting, then looked back at Lucas. "Nice-looking boy," he said.

Lucas just looked at him.

David got up and moved to the other side of the booth. Lucas didn't object. "Truth is, though," David whispered, "I could have told you exactly what he looked like without having seen him."

He waited for that very enticing statement to take effect. He didn't wait long. The words, if not the tone, had sounded threatening.

"Look, I don't know who you are—"

"Something happened here, didn't it, Sheriff? To you and to your son. People died, didn't they?"

Lucas looked at him, eyes lowered, his breathing labored.

Hit some nerve, didn't I? David thought. *Rubbed it raw.* "And it had something to do with that vacant lot near the canal, didn't it?" David continued. He was on a roll now; there was no stopping him. Sure, he sounded crazy, but maybe they had that in common.

Lucas stood up too quickly; Steven's Coke tipped over, flooding the table. Neither man noticed.

Lucas glanced around, saw people looking at him, sat down again. "Look, friend, I don't know who you are—but that has got to be the most ridiculous bullshit I've ever heard. Now as far as I'm concerned, this conversation is over."

Lucas pushed himself up, glared down at David, then walked away. Steven had just left the bathroom. Lucas took him by the hand and led him out the door. On the way out, Steven looked back. On his face David saw a blend of fear and fascination, with just a hint of recognition.

"I'm staying at Stouffer's West," David yelled after them. "Room 214."

Lucas heard him plainly, David was sure of it, but he didn't say a word.

David got back to the hotel about the same time as Ray and Emily. He had just closed the door behind him when he heard a knock, followed by Emily's voice.

"Dad? You still asleep?"

He didn't answer. Let her think he really was still asleep.

"Dad?" she said again, louder this time. Then, a few seconds later and a little more softly, "Must have been really tired, huh?"

Ray's with her, David thought.

"Think he's hungry?" Ray said.

There was a pause, and David wondered if Emily wasn't thinking about the word "hungry" and the various allusions. "Maybe," she said finally, "I'd rather see him get some rest. I don't think he'd mind if we got something to eat and came back for him later."

"Sounds good to me."

David listened to their footfalls as they walked away, then lay down and stared up at the ceiling. *Still treating me like a convalescent,* he thought. She didn't believe him, despite what he'd showed her. Ray neither. They'd find explanations in some technical manual, not some advertising brochure about a carnival vampire. He thought about how he felt about that and decided that he was a little miffed. Hell, "miffed" might even be stretched to "mad" if he tried hard enough. He fidgeted, suddenly uncomfortable. Mad—what the hell was that all about? Mad at his only daughter because she didn't think he was a vampire? What next? A little nibble on her neck for punishment? That thought made him even more uncomfortable. Better to change topics than dwell on something like that. He thought about the carnival, about what they'd find or wouldn't find there.

He didn't dwell on the carnival long because his thoughts started to drift. No matter where they went, though, there was always a vulture-nosed dwarf in the wings, waiting, wanting to get noticed.

At exactly eight-thirty, David heard another knock on his door. He reached over and turned on the light. "Yeah?" he said.

"Dad, it's me, Emily."

He got up and opened the door. Ray was with her.

"How do you feel?" she said.

David forced a smile. "Like Rip Van Winkle. You're going out there now, huh?"

"Yeah, you ready?"

"All set," he said eagerly.

The sun had wedged into the horizon by the time they got to the carnival, glossing the sky with shades of red. An open field crammed with cars served as a parking lot. The closest spot they could find was about a quarter mile away, but even from here they could hear the steam-whistled notes of a calliope and the dull roar of the crowd; the laughter of children. The PETRY BROTHERS CARNIVAL sign flapped lazily in a growing wind.

"Looks typical," Ray said. "You can even smell the cotton candy, maybe even sausage and onions, if you work your nose hard enough."

They got into a lazy line. Just before they got inside, the calliope stopped playing. People strolled past, eating and laughing, good times everywhere. The carousel had ground to a stop; new passengers were getting on.

"What now?" Emily said.

Ray shrugged. "Good question. Just look around, I guess."

"Maybe we should stick together," Emily suggested.

The calliope started up again. "Definitely," Ray yelled, trying to be heard above the noise.

Allowing for browsing time, it took them only ten minutes to get around the entire carnival, and by the time they got back to where they'd started, beneath the entrance sign, they all felt a little frustrated.

"I don't know about this," Emily said. "We haven't seen a thing that might even begin to suggest—"

"It's early," David said. "Way too early." Slowly, while Emily and Ray watched, David looked around. "They're here," he said. "I know it. I can *feel* it. They're definitely here."

Emily touched his arm. "How can you possibly know that, Dad?" she asked.

The sounds of the carnival had become only background noise. Her father's gaze settled on her, but only for a second. He smiled. "Let's take a ride on the merry-go-round," he said. "I think we're going to have to wait a while anyway. How about it?"

"Yeah, why not?"

David sat on a horse while Ray and Emily sat in the belly of a swan. They watched David—who looked like he was lost in thought, absorbed by it, wondering what he was thinking about, where his thoughts had taken him.

They strolled around the fairgrounds for the next three hours, testing their luck at games of chance; the odds were that they'd lose. They didn't always, though; Ray actually won a stuffed bear for Emily by throwing softballs at milk cans. David wasn't so lucky. He lost a couple of dollars pitching quarters onto saucers and tossing darts at under-inflated balloons.

"You know," Ray said, "this is kinda fun."

"Summer of eighty-two," Emily said.

"Eighty-two?"

She just smiled at him and Ray remembered something about how she'd lost her virginity at a carnival. She'd shared that with him over a bottle of Kendall Jackson Merlot. Summer of eighty-two. She never did tell him who the guy was.

With all this fun, they almost forgot why they were here, the best test of a good time. They were very clearly reminded of it when Emily saw the dwarf.

They were in what was in fact a strip joint, a tent that featured "Women of the World," when it happened. Four women had been paraded onto a stage, their bodies spotlit from the back by primary colors while music blared from both sides. He'd been standing in the wings and Emily had seen him only because a very chubby stripper dressed as Cleopatra had accidentally kicked the curtain during her act and pushed it aside. She saw him for only a second, but when she saw him, she nudged Ray.

"Where?" Ray said.

"Behind the curtains," Emily said. "On the left. I don't know, I think he's gone now."

Ray didn't see him, but he had no reason not to believe her. "Okay," he said, "there's a dwarf. You've seen him. What do we do now?"

Emily thought and said, "We wait until everyone leaves, then we have a look around again." She looked at her watch, pushed the button that lit the dial. "It's almost midnight. They should closeup around one. You game?"

"Why? You gonna shoot me?"

"C'mon, Ray, get serious."

"Sorry. Yeah, let's do it."

"Dad?"

David leaned in. "Now we're getting somewhere."

He looked back at the stage, at a woman in a military uniform that would never pass inspection, pleased something had finally happened. He saw her and he didn't; his thoughts had drifted again, taking him back to the row house in Brooklyn and the man impaled against the wall. While he watched, the dead man casually removed the knife from his throat and opened his eyes.

Twenty

They waited behind the "Women of the World" tent, listening to the sounds of the carnival slowly fade until all that was left was the occasional greeting from one carny to another.

At about one-thirty, after about ten minutes of stillness, they left their hiding place, crouching low, and looked around. Nothing moved, save for a few candy wrappers batted around by a capricious wind. Staying off the beaten paths, near the attractions, they moved down the midway toward the front of the carnival. About halfway from front to back, a line of game booth tents jutted off to the right for about fifty yards. It was there, toward the end of the line, where they saw a man and a woman holding hands, their bodies—youthful bodies, Emily decided—lit by soft colored lights.

"C'mon," David whispered.

Ray and Emily followed, careful not to trip over the guy wires, while David went around to the back of the tents. The couple came into and out of their sight as they passed tents and then openings, but when they got to within twenty feet or so, the couple vanished. "They're in there," David whispered, pointing at a tent, its interior awash in a multicolored static glow.

"I think we should go in," Emily whispered. She looked at her father.

"I don't think we have a choice," he said.

Looking at him, Emily felt gooseflesh rise on her arms. This light didn't suit him, not at all. His skin was the color of buttermilk. She looked at Ray, hoping he looked the same. He didn't. She wished she'd worn a coat.

"What do we do now?" Ray said. "We can't just walk right in there, can we?"

"That's exactly what we should do, just like we're supposed to be here," Emily said.

"Follow me," David said. "And don't do anything hasty." He put his hand on Emily's and Emily almost pulled it away. *Just reflex,* she thought. *You stick your hand in icewater, you pull it out. Reflex.*

He looked at her. "I know what you think," he said. "I know you think this is all pure fantasy, that whatever's happened to me has a valid explanation. Well, Emily, you may be right, but for now, for the next few minutes, let me take charge. There's danger here, very real danger, for both of you."

"Danger?"

David looked at the tent, back at Emily. "For that couple, too. Emily, listen, listen good. Something's wrong with me—"

"I know, Dad." *That's why we're here, isn't it?*

"No, you don't. You haven't got a clue about what's wrong with me," he said.

"I think I do, Dad," she said.

"Dammit, Emily . . . I'm a vampire!"

Emily smiled, then lost it. "C'mon, Dad!"

"I've become a goddamned vampire! Now, don't ask me how—"

"Dad, please don't. Look, I really think we should—"

"Will you just *listen* to me for once in your life! I'm your *father! Listen* to me!"

She could only look at him. She'd never seen him like this, so animated. So . . . obsessed.

He pulled the hair away from his head, from the concavity. "Psychosomatic, right? That's what you think, isn't it? Both of you? It's not, Emily! I've had dreams, fantastic dreams. I've seen things . . . I wish I had time to tell you about them. But we don't have time, not now. I'm thinking about that couple, Emily. I'm worried about them—and about you guys, too. Do me a favor, can you do that?"

Emily nodded lightly.

"Just let me do things my way for a while. Please."

No way did she want to let him do things his way; all she really wanted to do was get him home and into the hospital, where he belonged.

When she didn't answer right away, he said, "Fine," and went around to the front of the tent by himself.

"Dad, dammit, Dad, you come back here!"

He was already inside.

Emily and Ray looked at each other, then went after him.

There was a string of multicolored chasing lights along the front of the tent and a sign out front jammed crookedly into the ground. "Immortality—One Dollar," it said.

"Jesus," Emily mumbled.

They hurried inside and what they saw then was right out of the advertising booklet. David was there, and in front of him, seated behind a long desk decorated by chasing lights, was the dwarf Emily had seen earlier. When he saw them, he got up in a hurry and glared with tiny jewel-like eyes. "Who are you?" he said in a crackling alto. "What do you want?"

David didn't bother to turn. He knew this tiny man, knew him very well. They'd talked at length in his dreams. He stepped up to the desk. "What happened to them?" he said. "Where are they? What did you do with them?"

There was a room to his right, hidden by tent flaps. David looked at it, looked back at the dwarf. "Or is it too late for them now?"

By now the dwarf had regained his composure and his

smile. "I'll need to see a coupon before I can let you go in there," he said. "No pay, no play. Gotta have rules. Without rules, you've got anarchy."

David grinned at him. "Coupon? C'mon, little man, that doesn't wash anymore. We know all about this little setup.

"Stay here, you two," he said to Ray and Emily without turning.

"No way, Dad!"

David ignored her and started toward the other room. Behind him he heard Emily say, "Don't, Dad! You come back . . ." But as the tent flaps closed behind him, her words were cut off as effectively as if a brick wall had gone up between them, and a veil of cloying darkness fell. He took a few steps into that darkness and stopped.

He wasn't alone; he knew that. The air smelled of blood.

Seconds later, he heard a man's voice; "Martin? Is that you?"

David almost blurted out a response, surprised as he was by the question. But he fought that urge and didn't say a word. Let him think what he wanted. See what he had to say, and then say something.

Neither man said anything for the next minute or so. Finally, the other man said, "No, no, you're not Martin. Who are you?"

David didn't answer.

"Where were you made, and what are you doing here?"

Where was he made? How could he know . . . where was he? David wondered. Hard to tell. One second he was in front of him, the next behind. "Why did you think I was Martin?"

David felt something brush his arm. He jumped back. The smell of blood intensified. "Answer my question. Why are you here?"

"Why?" He thought about that a moment. Then, "Because I don't want to be this . . . thing, that's why! I want to be human again. Why else—"

The man laughed, not with rip-roaring belly laughs, just light chuckles, like someone remembering an old joke. "You're new, aren't you?" he said. "Have you even tasted blood yet?"

David didn't answer. He didn't have an answer anyway. He didn't know if he'd tasted blood or not. If he had, he didn't know it consciously.

"As I thought," the man continued, "you're still a virgin, a virgin in denial. Spare me."

He was very close, inches away, probably.

"But I'm intrigued," the man continued, circling now. David could feel his breath on the back of his neck, then fingers caressing the same spot. He didn't move. "What contact have you had with Martin? I know you've had contact, why else would I have sensed his thoughts, his memories?"

The man moved around to the front of David.

"I have Martin," David said. "He belongs to *me* now."

The man laughed again, more loudly this time. "You actually found him in the swamp? Incredible, absolutely incredible! And now you say he belongs to you! Ha, don't delude yourself. Martin belongs to no man. He may be afflicted, but that doesn't mean very much. Tell me, just how did he make you? He was paralyzed, so how could he possibly . . . wait, wait. Your thoughts betray you, my friend. A blood tear . . . *you dined upon a blood tear.* That's how it happened, isn't it? A blood tear?"

Tell me more, David thought.

"Where is he now? What have you done with my old friend Martin?"

"You're Bobby All, aren't you?"

The man clapped twice, loudly. "Yes, I am Bobby All. Let me see, you are Daniel—no, not Daniel. David . . . your name is David. And there's a woman with you . . . and a man with her. They're out there in the waiting room. I know, all I had to do was look, but I didn't, you have my word. That would be cheating. I can see them in your thoughts. Tell me, are they here to help you become human again?"

"Leave them out of this, dammit!"

The man was very close again. David could feel him like static electricity. "Is she pretty?" he whispered. Hot breath blew over David's ear like a summer wind. "Is she awfully pretty?"

"Damn you, damn you to hell."

The man backed away, laughing. "Hell? Damn me to hell? David, hell would be a step *up.*"

The power of this vampire was palpable, the air in here infused with it. If he himself were a vampire, David thought, he wasn't like this one. His power, which he barely understood, paled in comparison.

"Tell me," David said. "Tell me what you do, how to become human again. I demand that you tell me."

A weak shaft of light suddenly shot through the room and then died. The vampire had pulled a tent flap aside, only for a moment, but long enough to leave his profile as an after-image. For only one reason, he remembered what Ray had said about Martin, that he didn't have any fangs. He remembered that because this vampire did—at least the fang he could see in profile. And the one hand he saw, which held the tent flap open, was very long, the nails like daggers. He also saw the vampire look at him out of the corner of his eye, before he let the flap fall back into place, again throwing the room into darkness.

"Yes, she is pretty," Bobby All said. "Favors her mother, I would suspect. Excuse me now, I have some matters to attend to. You do understand, don't you? Say hello to your daughter for me. Oh, one last thing . . . you would do well to return Martin to where you found him. And as far as returning to human form, well, that, I'm afraid, has never been accomplished. Should you die, however, maybe Lenora can do for you what she did for Martin."

"Wait, those two people, the couple. What—"

"David, we are brethren now. I leave them for you. All for you. You can't remain a virgin forever, you know. *Bon appetit!*"

David was alone again. He knew that because the air had suddenly become less oppressive. But he didn't leave. Instead, he stayed in the room, wondering about what Bobby All had said about the young couple. They were out there somewhere—close by, probably. Maybe he could save them if he was quick enough.

He moved to the other side of the tent and found the way out rather quickly. He peeked outside first, wondering about how Bobby All had left without being seen, and stopped when he got outside. He was on the far side of the tent. The parking lot was in front of him; two cars there, his and . . . the couple's. Had to be. The cars were fairly close. Even from here, he swore he could see two people in the front seat. *It's not too late,* he thought.

"He's been in there for at least five minutes," Emily said.

"Yeah, I know," Ray said, looking as frustrated and anxious as she was.

They looked at each other.

"He'll be out in a jiffy," the dwarf said with a chuckle. "Then it'll be your turn."

Emily glared at him. "Screw you," she said. In a heartbeat she crossed the room and pulled the tent flaps back. Lambent light pierced the gloom. The room was empty.

"C'mon, Ray," she said.

They hurried outside, stopped near the sign, and listened. All they heard was a few insects and the low, chiding laughter of the dwarf.

* * *

David felt it when he got to within thirty feet or so of the car. "No," he said. "No, dammit, no!"

He felt like he was on fire, one of those stunt men running around like a human candle. He could see the couple, seated in the front seat of their Dodge Spirit, and his perception of them now was entirely different from what it had been. They were a source of energy now, a little something to hold him till dinner.

He looked back at the carnival. "Emily," he said, gesturing. He started back. "Emily?" he said frantically.

He stopped. What could Emily do for him now? What could anyone do? He looked back at the car, then at the carnival again, back at the car, at the two people in there. Why had he called for Emily? To inject a little humanity, maybe? His alter ego, making a nuisance of itself again. You see, David, you really want to kill that nice young couple in their shiny new car, but on the other hand, you're having a little trouble convincing yourself that you should, that it's what's best for you. It's time though, you know that. Just as Bobby All said. *Virgins, spare me . . .* wasn't that what he'd said?

You've got to fight this thing, he told himself; you've *got* to!

But his strength had begun a slow decline. The virus was stronger than he was now, and getting stronger. It wasn't as though he hadn't known about the stirrings within him, either. He'd sensed his needs for quite a while now, ever since the incident at the row house. He'd blocked those stirrings, though, calling on a strength of will that years of battling leukemia had only fortified. Like his leukemia, the stirrings had also been in remission. Now though, whatever protective veneer he had covered them with had pretty much dissolved, leaving a hunger and a desire unlike anything he'd ever felt. Denial wasn't the alternative it had once been.

He mopped his suddenly sweaty brow and looked at the car. The couple hadn't budged. Maybe . . . maybe they were already dead. He went around to the driver's side. Their eyes were open, but . . . hypnotized, maybe?

He looked around. No one nearby that he could see. He looked back inside the car, at the keys dangling from the ignition. Seeing them, he thought a little about symbolism. He got in, pushing the man over next to the woman. They were still breathing, still warm. He started the engine.

It was all he could do to control himself on the way, only a distance of a couple of miles. But he did control himself and damn the tiny voice that actually had the nerve to attempt battle with his desire. While he drove, what had really happened at the row house took shape in his mind. He saw faces contorted in agony and he saw the two Asian girls only seconds before they'd died. Through these images, his desire rose like a blood-red tide.

He could see the vacant lot now. He looked at his reflection in the rearview mirror. No dream could prepare him for what looked back. His image had become transparent. Through his head he could see the road behind him and through his chest he could see the back of the seat. He pulled back his lips and looked at the man beside him, at the throbbing vein in his neck . . .

And lunged at him, his mouth gaping wide. It wasn't the sharpness of David's teeth that did the trick, it was the power of his bite—a circle of skin attached to the roof of his mouth. He could feel the wash of blood through the man's system, and he could plainly feel that his own strength had been bolstered and renewed.

He squeezed his eyes tightly shut, embraced by luxurious pleasure, allowing it to fill him up completely, to drain him more than any sex act ever had or could.

When he was done, he leaned back. It took him a very long time to look at the man. When he did, though, something else happened; the passenger door opened, lighting up the inside of the car. A huge hand reached in and wrapped the girl's waist. "I get leftovers—is that it, David?"

Bobby All grinned in at him, then whisked the girl out of the car and ran off to the woods on the other side of the tracks, laughing all the while.

David pushed the man aside, got behind the wheel, and drove to a spot that overlooked the Barge Canal. There was a canal lock to his right. The water level was at its crest, as it always was in summer. It would be a long time before they found the car or the body.

He got out and tested the ground the car would pass over. *Seems solid enough.* The grass would be laid over for the rest of the night, but it would be back to normal by morning.

As good a place as any . . .

The window was all the way down. He rolled it up halfway—it wouldn't do to have the body float to the surface through an open window—then got out.

He reached into the car and put it into neutral. While it rolled almost soundlessly toward the canal, David wondered about tomorrow night. And the next night, and the next . . .

Twenty-one

Emily and Ray had looked everywhere, but David was nowhere to be found. Ray had returned from the car seconds earlier; he wasn't there, either.

"Back to the tent," Emily said. "We're going to drill that little bastard until he tells us where my father is."

But even before they got to the tent they knew something was wrong. The lights out front were off, and when they got there, the tent was gone, too.

Emily cupped her hands around her mouth. She felt helpless, alone, defeated, "Dad!" she yelled. "Dad, where are you?"

Ray took her by the arm. "C'mon, Emily," he said. "We'll get the sheriff."

She yanked away. "Dad? Dammit, answer me!"

An echo traveled around the empty carnival like an alien probe.

"C'mon," Ray said. "We'll find him, but we're not going to find him by ourselves."

"Where is he, Ray?"

"I don't know; I wish I did . . . Emily, we might get into trouble if we stay here."

She looked at him. He was right, of course. Her father had disappeared and standing here in the middle of this deserted carnival, yelling, wasn't going to do him or anyone any good. Even if he could still hear them.

"Let's get to a phone," she said frantically. "We'll call nine-one-one."

"Emily, no. Think about it: the state cops'll never believe us. The only shot we've got is that town sheriff. He knows more than he's letting on. I say if we drill anyone, we drill him. Whether he'll crack or not . . . it's all we've got, at least for now."

Emily looked around; chances were they were in a lot more danger than she'd first thought. "You're probably right. C'mon, let's find a phone book. I hope that sheriff's a light sleeper."

Judd Lucas had been dreaming about his wife, Cynthia, as he had every night since she'd died. He didn't much welcome a ringing phone.

"For God's sake, who the hell . . ."

He leaned over and picked up, Cynthia loitering in the periphery of his subconscious. "This had better be life or death . . ."

"It is, Sheriff."

He knew the voice, vaguely. "Who is this?"

"Emily Kane. We talked earlier, at your office. You gave us directions to the carnival."

"Directions? What the . . . look, Miss Kane, it's very late."

"My father's missing, Sheriff. He went into a tent at the carnival and never came out. There was a sign in front of that tent. 'Immortality, One Dollar.' Maybe you've seen it before."

Judd Lucas dropped the receiver to his neck and stared at the back wall. He'd known this was going to happen. He should have talked these people out of going out there. He damn sure— "Your father—David Kane, right?"

"Yes."

A conversation he'd had with his son earlier, soon after

he and David Kane had talked, came back to him. "He's one of them, Uncle Judd," Steven had said.

There were oddities, yes—what he was doing out in the sunlight, for one—but given Steven's background, Lucas trusted the boy's judgment. How could he tell these people that their friend and father was more than likely a vampire?

"Meet me at my office in a half hour," he said. He'd think of something on the way.

"We'll be there."

After she hung up, Emily said to Ray, "There was something in his voice, Ray. *He knows*. He knows everything."

David had been wandering aimlessly since he'd dumped the car into the canal, letting the night coddle him like a gentle lover and feeling an affinity to it that he hadn't felt before. The pleasure derived from his kill lingered, making it very difficult to deny the possibility that he wouldn't do it again.

His wandering had taken him back to the vacant lot, and as he realized where he was, he also realized that Bobby All most definitely knew a lot more than what he'd said. He looked across the field, toward the stand of trees where Bobby had taken his victim. Was he still there? Resting, or maybe idling over his . . . dinner? More important, though, did he dare go into those woods to find out? Sure. Why not? he decided. They were brethren, after all, and if Bobby All wanted to hurt him, he could have done that earlier in the tent, or in the car. Here. But then again, maybe he hadn't tried anything because he knew they were equals . . . no, they weren't equals. *Just brethren.*

He started toward the stand of trees, and as he got closer, the heaviness he'd felt in the tent slowly returned. Silence was king in these woods. *Bobby All's in there, somewhere.* He hesitated a moment, then stepped into the woods, and as he did, the air again seemed as weighty as it had been before,

casting a funereal pall over everything. *Someone died here,*
David thought. Dead leaves crunched underfoot as he moved
slowly along a well-worn path, glancing to both sides and
expecting that Bobby All would appear in front of him at
any moment, or maybe brush against him again, as he had
in the tent. He was immune to that now, though. In his "condition" he really didn't have a lot to be afraid of, especially
parlor tricks designed to frighten him. He smiled. "Where
are you?" he said. The woods echoed his question, but he
didn't get an answer. "More games, Bobby? Look, we have
to talk, so you might as well . . ." A small structure suddenly
came into view. David stopped and looked at it. "Some kind
of kid's fort," he mumbled. He moved closer and the impres-
sion that someone had died here grew stronger. There was
a makeshift sign on the front of the fort, the letters "MTD"
scrawled onto it. David ran his finger over the paint and as
he did, he swore he could see the paint begin to run like . . .

"Midnight Till Dawn," he heard from behind him.

He wheeled. Bobby All, looking much less menacing
than he had earlier, stood a few feet away.

"That's what MTD stands for. 'Midnight Till Dawn.' It
was the nickname the boys gave this place. They had a pact,
see. If you spent the night here alone, you could become a
member of the Midnight Till Dawn Club."

David saw someone standing behind Bobby, far behind.
A woman.

"Her name's Karen," Bobby said. "Tell me, David, did
you get the man's name first?"

David fought off a flush of embarrassment.

"Thought not. Come on in to MTD Headquarters, David.
As you said, we have to talk."

Bobby All bent at the waist and went into the fort. When
David didn't follow him in, Bobby stuck a long-fingered
hand out the door and gestured to him. By now, Karen had
moved to within ten yards of the fort. She looked at David,
her head cocked to one side, curious. David felt a sudden

urge to apologize to her about her husband, but he didn't. Instead, he went inside.

A lit candle sat on a short leg table in the middle of the fort, immersing the interior with an inconstant glow. There were posters on the walls, all members of World Wrestling Federation. Hulk Hogan led the way—there were three posters of him. On the back wall, behind Bobby All, sitting Indian-style on the floor, was a poster of Rowdy Roddy Piper, playing bagpipes with one hand and squeezing the life out of another wrestler with the other. A few empty beer bottles completed the look.

"Typical, isn't it? Of kids, I mean," Bobby said. "Martin and I had a fort like this when we were kids. We called ours 'The Sad Café.' My idea. We weren't exactly social butterflies, so we started the café. I know, it was kind of brooding and self-absorbed, but hell, someone had to feel sorry for us, didn't they?"

David shrugged.

"There were four of us, and sometimes we'd sit around and see who could tell the saddest story. I'm not talking about being picked last for softball, David, I'm talking about cliques playing tricks on you. But what the hell, David, that's all in the past, and most of the people who belonged to those cliques have paid a dear price anyway. Come on, sit down."

David sat down across from him wondering if his face looked as malevolent as Bobby All's in the inconstant glow of the candle.

"What is this place?" David said.

Bobby All looked around, then looked back at David. "A final resting place, a boy's final resting place, if you must know. You took my advice, I see. Tell me, how was he?"

David felt terribly uncomfortable, and he'd be damned if he'd tell this creature about the experience. "What did you do to the girl?" he said.

"Do to her? Why, what every caring immortal would do.

I made her. I extended her life after I took it. I was lonely, and she is beautiful, isn't she? So why not? You killed her husband, after all, you left her all alone in the cold, cruel world." Bobby grinned, exposing slightly retracted fangs.

"You said something about Martin, that I should get rid of him."

Bobby's grin vanished. "After we parted company earlier, I gave that a lot of thought. I think Martin is a topic we should discuss at length. His continued existence, you see, is contrary to our own."

"What do you mean, our own?"

"A vampire's existence. Karen's, mine. Yours, though? I don't know. Your growth has been abbreviated, as was Martin's in his rebirth. It appears that like Martin, you reached a certain point in your evolution and then stopped."

David felt a moment of hope. "Then there's still a chance for me?"

Bobby smiled. "I don't know. Perhaps," he lied.

With this morsel, David's thirst for knowledge suddenly grew. He wanted to know everything about Martin and Bobby All, about vampires in general. The more he knew, the better he could fight this thing.

"Then the booklet was true, everything was true," he said.

"Yes, everything. You see, both Martin and I were made at the carnival a number of years ago. Afterward we traveled extensively, eventually returning here, to Hunt. It was when we returned that Martin broke one of the laws that guide immortals: he killed a holy person. Ate his flesh. The flesh of such a person, you see, is permeated with divine grace.

"Anyway, it's, well, it's like the virus within you and me. Once Martin had ingested that divine grace, he had to pay the consequences."

"He began to age."

"Precisely. Now, please don't misunderstand me—he didn't become human again, he didn't lose his immortality; he simply began to age. And if ever an immortal lived through hell, he did. You see, Martin chose immortality because he didn't want to suffer the fate his dear grandmother had—a life that had lost all viability. Seeing her in her bed, oblivious to anything and anyone around her, Martin vowed that if he ever found a way to avoid that end, he would take it. And he did. But ironically, he suffered an even worse fate. Even Martin's grandmother eventually died. Well, Martin killed her, but that's another . . . She had a way out, though. For her, death was a way out. But Martin would never die because he was immortal. It would be a contradiction in terms. I mean, how can you be immortal . . . sorry. At any rate, Martin was exiled to a lifetime of aging without relief."

"So he killed himself. Over there, in that house."

"Yes, where that house used to be. It's a vacant lot now. I found it fascinating that you should take your victim there. Obviously, you felt compelled—"

"I saw it in a dream. I was drawn to it."

"That makes sense, I guess. Anyway, when Martin began to age, I took it upon myself to find a cure. We made a pact at a meeting of The Sad Café. We would do whatever was necessary to see that neither of us died alone or lonely. And living as Martin would have lived was even worse than dying alone or lonely. Don't you agree, David? The obvious cure, of course, was the ingestion of youth to counteract the aging. I brought him children and young people while he was in the basement of that house, and he ate their flesh and drank their blood. God, Martin was insatiable! Anyway, in the end, it didn't help, it just got him fat and he just kept on aging. Two boys stayed here one night, in this clubhouse. Or at least, they tried to. I found them wandering on the railroad tracks in the wee hours. Chickened out, I guess. One I took to Martin, the other I took for myself. But Martin killed himself before he could kill the last boy. He simply—"

"Handed the boy over to the sheriff, went onto the porch, and let the sun finish him off."

"That's about it."

"And you came back and found his ashes—"

"I took them to a woman in Florida—"

"Lenora!"

"That's right, Lenora. Anyway, Lenora restored him, but unfortunately, she could do only so much. His mind, however, as we later found out, was fully restored. Very powerful. In fact, his will would eventually surpass my own . . . let me back up a little. Martin had a dream, a lifelong dream. I remember he told me about it when we were kids, during a meeting of The Sad Café. He said he wanted to be somebody someday, and the biggest thing he could think of was to be the King of New York—"

"King of New York? Is that what you said?"

"I know it sounds ridiculous, but Martin was a very simple man before he was made. Custodian of the four corners churches was all he could attain, all he *did* attain, before he was changed."

"I had a vision . . ." David looked away, remembering every moment of that vision, then looked back at Bobby. "Martin was seated on a throne and around him were crowds of people, working class people—"

"And you stepped out of the crowd, sword in hand, and knighted him, right?"

"Yes, yes, but I didn't really knight him—"

"You made him King of New York."

"And everyone applauded, but how—"

"Did I know?" Bobby All grinned. "The same thing happened to me. I think you're beginning to understand the extent of Martin's power. In his paralyzed state, with his mind so powerful, he tried to 'talk' us into making that same dream come true for him. While we slept, he filled our heads with thoughts of vampires running amok in New York City, killing every human in sight. I even dreamt about giving Martin an oath of office. I had a King Arthur sword in my hand, just like you, and while he knelt before me, I also dubbed him

'King of New York.' Even as a powerful immortal, with a wonderful intellect, he wasn't immune to silly thoughts. We were on our way to New York when I found the courage and the will to get rid of him. The dwarf and I. It was the hardest thing I've ever done. But the farther I got from him, the safer I felt, until, finally, I felt totally safe.

"What I fear now is that you and your people have inadvertently given him the chance to become what he had wanted to become—King of New York—and if we allow him to do that, or even try, the whole world will be alerted to our kind, not just the believers. Even the strongest skeptics will join in the hunt, and although there are more of us than people realize, humans far outnumber us. Many humans would die, yes, that's true, but in the end, a whole race would be wiped off the face of the earth. And Martin, in his haste to become King of New York, would have achieved the genocide of his own race."

Instantly, David understood the ramifications of what Bobby All had said. But it struck him that even now, they might be too late. Martin's childish yet viable plans of conquest might have already begun. "Something happened," David said. "After I drank the blood tear, something happened to me."

A concerned look passed over Bobby All's face. "You're not the virgin I thought you were, are you?"

David shrugged. "That's just it, I don't know, not really. I have some memories, I saw some things—"

Bobby leaned forward. "Right at this moment, where is Martin?"

"In my artifacts holding area, in his casket."

Bobby All stood up. "We've got to destroy him. If we get rid of Martin, maybe the others will lose interest and just leave the city. But with Martin alive and leading them . . ."

"When do we leave?"

"Now, you idiot! We've got to go now."

Twenty-two

Emily glanced at her watch, then looked back down the deserted highway. "Where the hell is he?" she said.

"Give him a chance," Ray said. "You're not always right on time, either, you know."

Emily looked at him. "Ray, being prompt for the opera is not a life-or-death concern. This is."

But what if he's already dead? Ray thought, as he looked into eyes that glittered with frustration and anger.

"What time is it?" Emily asked again a short time later.

"A minute later than the last—"

"There he is," Emily said. "I see a car."

Ray stepped into the road and saw a car coming toward him. It slowed down at a flashing yellow, then continued on, stopping after it pulled past and into a parking spot that said, "Reserved for Sheriff, Town of Hunt."

Judd Lucas opened the driver's door and got out while his nephew, Steven, got out the passenger side and opened the back door. He had a grocery bag in his hand. A large German shepherd jumped out and stood beside him.

"Come on inside," Lucas said companionably.

They went inside and Lucas said he was going to make a pot of coffee. "Oh, make sure you get that door, too, miss," he said, as he opened a cupboard.

Emily closed the door, which hadn't closed properly when she'd pushed on it. *Funny,* she thought, *that Lucas wants the*

*door closed. Has to be in the seventies, and the air's like a
used dishrag.*

"I'll have a cup," Ray said. "And I like mine strong."

"One cup of strong coffee, coming up. Have a seat."
There was only one available. He nodded to his nephew.
"Steven, bring Ann's chair in here, will you, please?"

Steven put the paper bag on his uncle's desk, went into
the administration area, and came back pushing a padded
chair. "Here you go," he said to Emily, smiling.

"Thanks."

"Sorry," Lucas said, "forgot my manners. This is my
nephew, Steven."

"And this is my dog, Sam," Steven said, as he rubbed
the dog's massive head.

Sam chuffed and held out his paw. Despite the nervous
energy raging inside of her, Emily shook Sam's paw and
introduced herself. It dawned on her then that Lucas had
brought the boy and the dog with him for a reason. "Sheriff," she said, "is Steven with you for his own protection?
The dog, too?"

Lucas had just poured coffee crystals into a measuring
cup. "Matter-of-fact, he is," he said. "Good and strong, that
what you said?"

No answer.

Lucas turned. "Good and strong, right?"

"Oh, yeah, yeah. Good and strong," Ray said.

Ray looked at Emily and she at him. Their suspicions
had been confirmed, she thought. What next?

"This brews fast," Lucas said. He poured the contents of
the measuring cup into the mouth of the coffeemaker. "I
don't want you to think I'm doing this just for you," he
added, his back to them. "I'm definitely gonna need a cup
or two. Once I'm up, there's no way I can get back to sleep
again. Steven, tell you what, why don't you show these folks
what you've got in that bag while I'm doing this."

"Okay."

Watching him, Emily imagined Pandora letting loose the sins of the world, her face gleaming with satisfaction, rebutting the popular belief that she had been only an innocent in all that wickedness.

Steven removed the contents of the bag, pushing a few three by five photos aside to make room. Ray and Emily watched, and although they recognized each item, their significance didn't quite register.

Lucas cleaned his hands by clapping them together and picked up a two-foot wooden stake sharp enough to pierce anything. About the same time, the coffeemaker started percolating behind him. "Okay, this to a vampire is like a bullet to us. And when you couple it with this," he picked up a simple claw hammer, "it's like a fired bullet." He put the hammer and stake down and picked up a string of garlic cloves. "I know it sounds ridiculous, but it's true. Put it up around your door and you won't have a thing to worry about."

He put the garlic down, picked up a small vial, and held it close to his eye. "I'm sure you know what this is," he said. He smiled like a man with a secret. "This particular holy water came from St. Monica's. I hear you paid them a visit. Anyway, it's been blessed by Father O'Brien himself, one of Martin's former employers." He shook his head. "Goddamn world's so full of skeptics." He glanced at Emily. "Sorry, got off track a little. Anyway, if you throw some of this into a vampire's face, it acts just like an acid. Believe me, it's not pretty. Now, getting back to Steven and Sam."

He glanced at Steven and looked back at Emily and Ray. "As I said, I brought them here for protection. I'm sure they'd have been okay at the cabin, it's protected; but vampires aren't exactly trustworthy. They're born liars. I just thought it best that I bring them along tonight. Especially with the carnival in town. You see, Bobby All assured me that none of us would be harmed, not even Sam. If you read the circular, you know who Bobby All is."

Lucas stopped talking and smiled lightly. "You know, before I got into the car, I told myself that I'd take it slow. I said, Judd, if you ramble on like you sometimes do, you'll just confuse the hell out of those folks. Well, I think I've rambled a little, so lemme start over. But first things first."

The coffee was ready. Lucas poured two cups, asked Ray what he wanted in his, obliged him, then started over, a steaming cup of coffee beside him.

"You know, without Bobby All, none of this would have happened. Let me tell you a little more about him.

"Would you believe Bobby and I went to high school together back in the sixties? We weren't friends or nothin' . . . it was Martin and Bobby who got together, even though Martin was a lot older than Bobby. A few chapters later, and unfortunately for me and mine, I stole Bobby's high school sweetheart. I married her. Her name's Cynthia, or maybe was Cynthia, I don't know which tense . . . sorry." Lucas sipped his coffee, then put it down.

"Well, Bobby never forgave me that. In fact, he didn't take it well at all. After he got chan . . . after he became a vampire, he transformed Cynthia, made her a vampire, and took her with him. Well, he came back to town many years later, he and Martin, and when they found out about Steven, Bobby kidnapped him. I guess he was gonna be some kind of, I don't know, gift or sacrifice. And Martin would have killed him, too, but the strangest thing happened.

"One night I got a line on where Steven was, so I went there, a place on the other side of town, near the canal. Well, I went inside, and when I didn't find him upstairs, I went down to the basement. I tried a closed door—nothing. Tried another—it was locked. What do you suppose that told me? It told me that Steven was probably inside. I panicked. I knew Steven was in there, had to be in there, so I started beating on the door, doing what I could to get inside, at least, until I smelled smoke. Right after that, the door opened.

"Who do you suppose I saw standing there, with Steven in his arms? Martin, or at least, it looked a hell of a lot *like* Martin. Except this guy was old—I mean indescribably old. All I could do was stare at him. I expected to die right there. I thought Martin'd just reach out and take my head off somehow. You know what he did instead? The son of a bitch just handed Steven over and walked right past me. The fire was really goin' by then. I saw some other people in that room and I think some were alive. Some weren't, though. But I wasn't about to stick around and find out why they were dead. No way. I ran up those stairs with Steven in my arms, leaped the steps, and didn't stop runnin' till I got to my car.

"When I looked back, I saw Martin on the porch, in that rocking chair. God, he looked like some old-timer just . . . he grinned at me, you believe that? Well, the fire got to him about then, just roasted the shit out of him. See, what's really weird here . . . why the hell would he just hand Steven over to me like that? And why he killed himself, well, I got no idea about that, either. But he did. I saw the whole goddamn thing. Sam here, well, Sam'll always have a special place in my heart—in Steven's, too. Cynthia attacked him, see, after she got changed, and old Sam here did what he could to protect him. Almost cost him his life. Well, that's my story. What do you think?"

"That's incredible," Emily muttered.

"Yeah, I guess. Insane, too. Totally outside the laws of nature. One day I've got a loving wife, and the next, she's a goddamn bloodsucker. One day my in-laws are alive, the next they're ripped apart. One day, kids are having a swell time, the next, they're turning up missing. I went to a town in the southern tier, there was a girl there, in bed. She was dead. She didn't look dead; in fact, she looked fantastic.

But she was dead—no pulse, no respiration. But she got out of her cage at the morgue and killed an attendant! She just pushed the door open and tore him limb . . ."

He noticed then that he was yelling, and he hadn't wanted to do that. "Sorry—I, uh, get carried away sometimes." He looked at Steven for a long time, then looked back at Emily. "Miss, what I've got to say may be hurtful, you may want to call me every name in the book . . . because of Steven's experiences—he spent a long time in the company of those things—he came to know them pretty well, their touch, their smell. Well, the other day when your father—"

"My father says he's a vampire, and you're gonna tell me that Steven thinks so, too. Right?" Emily was considerably more calm than she thought she'd be.

Lucas felt a great weight lift from him. "He told you?"

"Yes, he did. We're here to find a cure, Sheriff. We don't think he's totally . . . evolved yet." She was one step ahead of him, ahead of herself, saying things that had only flirted with her consciousness until now. "You see, when you mentioned Martin, we drew an instant connection. He's my father's property now, in New York City."

"The same Martin—"

"Gotta be. My brother Hal found him in a peat bog in Massachusetts. My father thinks he's still alive. He can't move, but . . . my father thinks he was transformed by drinking a blood tear. Somehow, Martin . . . God, this is really incredible!"

"Then it's true. Somehow, Bobby All brought him back to life. Martin didn't die in that fire after all!"

"You know, there are theories. I've read a lot about vampires, I mean considering what's happened . . . heck, I thought it'd help us stay alive. Anyway, from what I've read, evil can't really be destroyed, and some people have the ability to . . . what did it say?" He shook his head, trying to bring back the paragraph. " 'Restore the evil entity from the most humble of remains,' that's what it said. Well, obviously, Bobby All knew that, too. You say your father's missing?"

"He went into the tent, into another room in the tent, actually, and he never came out. You know anything about that?"

Lucas gathered his thoughts. "I know that Bobby All is part of that carnival." Again a huge weight seemed to lift from him. "He told me he'd kill Steven if I told anyone. I'm sure there're other people in town who know—"

"I think I met a couple of them at the pet store," Emily said.

A knock at the door then startled everyone.

Lucas got up. "Who is it?" he said.

Sam growled low in his chest and bared his teeth.

Another knock. Then. "May we come in?"

Emily started for the door. "It's my father," she said.

Lucas wrapped his hand around her arm. She looked at him. "He said we. *We!*"

"But who? Who can—"

"May we come in?"

Someone else this time.

Sam's growl deepened. "Bobby All," Lucas whispered, attempting but failing to keep the fear out of his tone. "Your father's got Bobby All with him!"

Twenty-three

From his casket overlooking the city, Martin dredged up memories long buried, of Bobby and himself and their club, The Sad Café. He wished Bobby hadn't betrayed him as he had, by tossing him into that peat bog. Their old friendship didn't mean a thing. Now, if he saw him again, he'd have to destroy him. There was no way around it.

He suddenly got tired of old memories, so he let his mind fill up with the carnage taking place throughout the city.

With his mind's eye he saw one scene after another: a nurse in a hospital approached from behind while she saw to a patient's needs; a young boy, unable to sleep, probably, opening a door that led to an unlit yard and being lifted high into the air; a beat cop with the Verrazano Narrows Bridge as a backdrop, attacked while taking a sip of coffee.

He found that he could pick through these images, dwelling only on those he found stimulating and interesting.

After a parade of these bizarre and very satisfying visuals, he eventually concluded that something fantastic was happening in this city, and although he wasn't sure how or why, it definitely involved him. Certainly his mental ability was astonishing, and his ability to influence human thoughts, especially those of someone sleeping, was stunning. And he did love to play around in the dreams of humans, manipulating their reflections and assembling for them what he wanted them to see. But what was happening now was not the end product of mind manipulation. It just couldn't be. These creatures, he sensed, were very much like him. Well, almost. There was one obvious exception: they could move. But the widespread devastation brought something else to mind. If these creatures were like him, if he had somehow fathered these beings, did they also have his dreams and his desires? Did they know about The Sad Café, and that he had always wanted to be King of New York? No, he thought, probably not. They didn't realize they were his dreams; they probably thought they were their own. They were killing and transforming to promote their own selfish desires. And that just wouldn't do. There could only be one King. Only one.

Despite herself, Emily felt like she was going to faint. For the longest time, she had denied what had happened to her father, and now, with corroboration from the man glaring at the door, the truth stood bold and powerful and rock hard.

"Dad?" she said weakly.

"Emily? Let us in, Emily."

Again she started for the door, but again Lucas stopped her. "My God, don't you see?" He was angry now. "Dammit, it's all true, haven't I convinced you of that yet? They can't come in here unless we invite them in. That's the only way! Those are the rules! Even these creatures have to have rules!"

"And what do you think they're gonna do when they get in here, Sheriff? What are they gonna do? Are they gonna ravage us? Are they gonna suck our blood? What?"

Lucas smiled out of one side and shook his head. "You still don't get it, do you? Ravage us? Suck our blood? Sounds ridiculous, doesn't it? Real Gothic bullshit! Tell you the truth, I don't know what the hell they're gonna do, but I wouldn't put those things at the bottom of the list. That's what their kind do, you know. That's exactly why they exist.

If we open that door, I can't promise you that any of us will live to see the sun rise. If we don't open that door, we will. Positively. Now, you think about that. Digest that for a while, then see how fast you run to that door."

She looked at Ray. "Help me, Ray. Please help me."

Until now, Ray had only played in the fields of the supernatural. But with thundering abruptness he realized that he wasn't playing anymore. There were still realities, though; there were still rules that these creatures had to follow, just as Lucas had said. His first thought involved their safety—*don't open that door for whatever reasons*—but his second involved the residue of human spirit left inside David. But there was more than David to consider. There was Bobby All, too. And they knew what he was capable of. "I'm sorry," he said. "We can't be sure. It's not your father I'm worried—"

"Damn you," Emily said. "Come on in if you want," she said to the creatures beyond the door. "The door's not locked."

Emily heard Lucas curse, and as the door opened, she saw him uncap the vial of holy water.

She glanced at Sam—he didn't like this, not one bit. He snarled as if he were surrounded by rabid Dobermans.

Seconds later, Bobby All and David Kane stepped inside.

In a heartbeat, Sam broke free of Steven's grip. With his leash trailing behind him, he took two steps and flew through the air, teeth bared. With one hand, Bobby All caught the dog by the neck and held him out in front of him.

"No!" Steven screamed. *"No!"*

Sam wiggled like a fish on a line, strangled sounds of fear and anger pressing through what little opening was left in his windpipe.

Bobby All was obviously furious, his face crimson with anger, but Sam just kept on growling and snarling, even though his life could end at any second.

"Sam!" Steven yelled, the word trailing behind him as he raced across the room and threw a shoulder into Bobby All's stomach.

Bobby didn't budge, and Steven slammed onto his back like a toppled tombstone. He wouldn't give up yet, though; he scrambled to his feet, ready to have at it again. By then, Bobby had released his death grip. "Take him," he said to Lucas. He held the dog out in front of him. "And be thankful. Again."

Lucas took the dog's leash and wrapped a beefy arm around Sam's middle. Sam, dazed and winded, staggered when Lucas set him down. For his own protection Lucas led him to one of the cells and put him inside.

Bobby All waited for Lucas to get back. After he had, he said, "I didn't come here to harm you or the dog. As a matter of fact, if it were up to me, we wouldn't have come here at all. David, however, didn't want to leave his daughter."

"Leave me?" Emily said. "Where—"

"Emily," David said, "we have to go back to New York. We have to destroy Martin. Before it's too late."

"Sooner, if possible," Bobby said. "Although David may not be totally susceptible to the sun's rays, I am. The trip to New York will take about an hour and a half. In two and a half hours we might make it to his offices. Another hour and a half to get rid of Martin will bring us close to sunrise. Now, we don't have time to discuss this; we have to go now. If we don't go now, I will kill you all and go myself. We can talk about what has happened on the plane."

This was ludicrous, Emily thought. If they didn't go now, they'd be killed, but if they did go, they'd be on a very small private plane with two vampires.

Still, if he had wanted to kill them, he'd have done it by now. And he wouldn't have spared Sam, either. But what good would it do to destroy Martin?

She asked Bobby that very question.

"I don't know," he said, "maybe no good. But don't you

see? He's the head of the serpent, and if we cut off the head, maybe the body will die, too—maybe not. There are no guarantees. We have to do something, though."

"Let's go, then," she said.

Judd and Steven watched them get into their car and drive away. After Judd went back and got Sam, they did the same.

They were quiet on the way home. *At least for them the danger has passed,* Lucas thought. *But what about the people in New York City?*

He looked over at Steven. Sam had rested his head on the back of the seat. He wouldn't worry about the people in New York; they had themselves to worry about.

Twenty-four

Mayor Ed Lawrence hated to be disturbed and middle-of-the-night disturbances always meant something was really wrong. The caller was the chief-of-police, Bill Kranepool.

"Ed, we've got a situation here," Bill said. "I think you should take a look."

Ed put on his trousers while his wife got a freshly laundered shirt out of his dresser drawer. "What kind of situation?"

"Well, there's probably a coupla hundred people here, and they're all gathered around the Empire State Building. They don't have a permit to demonstrate, but they haven't given any indication that they might get violent, either. Truth is, they're not really demonstrating."

Ed's wife gave him his shirt and he slipped it on. "Then what's the problem, Bill? If they're not demonstrating—"

"That'd be kind of hard to explain over the phone. This is something you should see for yourself."

The mayor hated to beat around the bush. "For God's sake, man, is this a gang thing, or what?"

"No, no, these . . . I've never . . . sir, I'd really rather you saw this for yourself."

The mayor exhaled, frustrated. Two in the morning and he gets called out of bed for something that can't be explained over the phone. Maybe he should get a chief who could verbalize properly.

His wife knotted his tie for him. "What the hell, I'm up," he said. "For the life of me, I can't understand why a crowd gathered around the Empire State Building should be so . . . dramatic. Be there in twenty minutes."

Bill Kranepool hung up and went back into the crowd, looking into faces and then at the building, then back into faces. Occasionally someone would look at him, but only if they got bumped.

Bill thought the obvious when he got there. A jumper or some rock climber thought he'd use the building for practice. There was no one up there he could see. Asking these people what the hell they were looking at had gotten him nowhere. They just ignored him. He even tried asserting a little authority, but that didn't work.

Bill stepped past a young woman and stopped. Was that Dr. Ficus standing alongside that Mercedes? He moved closer to get a better look. *Sure is. Probably caught up in all this, just like me.*

Dr. Andrew Ficus was his wife's gynecologist, and Bill thought there probably wasn't a more sober, down-to-earth guy in the whole damn city. His apartment was close by.

"Dr. Ficus," Bill said, a smile in his voice.

Andrew Ficus, tall and bald and dressed in his pajamas and bathrobe, didn't respond.

"Dr. Ficus?" Bill said again. He was within ten feet now. He had to have heard him.

Bill moved alongside Ficus and wrapped his hand gently around the doctor's arm to get his attention. "Dr. Ficus?"

Ficus still didn't respond, and given such strange behavior from a man like him, Bill started to get a little uncomfortable. A smile worked onto his face. "Look, Dr. Ficus, I don't know what's going on here, but I'm going to have to insist—"

Suddenly Ficus altered his gaze and the passive, even,

submissive expression on his face changed, too. His eyes opened wider than seemed possible and his lips curled back, baring a set of perfect white teeth.

Bill felt like ice-cold darning needles had chased up his spine, and in some dusty childhood memory, tucked nicely away for the last thirty years, he saw a bat fly through the darkest recesses of a giant cave.

Slowly, though, Ficus looked back at the Empire State Building, and the intense and menacing expression on his face disappeared. *From Dr. Ficus to Mr. Hyde and then back again in the time it took to notice,* Bill thought. He didn't like that at all.

Still, he didn't feel like trying Ficus again, and as he backed away, bumping into one person and then another, he felt suddenly claustrophobic. He had even lost a little of the professional calm he was so proud of. He looked into the faces of the people around him, the men and the women, the children, very much expecting from them what he'd gotten from Andrew Ficus. *Don't touch them,* he told himself, *for God's sake, don't touch them!* He did his level best not to, but they were so tightly bunched and he was so large, not touching them proved impossible.

Eventually, he nudged a powerful-looking man dressed in a T-shirt. He stopped cold and sucked in a breath as the huge man looked down at him. Then he wrapped his hand around the butt of his service revolver and waited for something to happen. For almost a minute, the two men simply looked at each other, and during that minute, Bill actually held his breath, waiting for the inevitable. Nothing happened, though. Like Dr. Ficus, the man simply looked back at the building, his face again passive, even trance-like.

Good Lord, Bill thought, *what the hell's going on here? What's happened to all these people?* He made his way through the crowd, slinking between and around people until he finally made it back to the safety of his car.

He flipped on his walkie-talkie and instructed a lieutenant

to have his men pull back. "Do it carefully," he said. "Very carefully. And for God's sake, no confrontations. No matter how they react, just keep pulling back, understand? We don't want this thing to escalate."

He looked back at the crowd, thinking he'd made the right decision by calling His Honor. *Let him make a decision.*

Ed Lawrence saw the crowds as he cruised south on Thirty-fourth Street. Even from a distance he could tell something was wrong.

"What do you make of this?" he asked his driver.

"Protest, maybe?" his driver said. "They got some strange businesses in that building. Maybe Greenpeace?"

"But where are the protest signs? They're all just standing there, looking at the goddamn building! This is awfully strange, Terry. Pull over."

The driver pulled over next to Bill Kranepool's car and the mayor got out. Even from a distance the passivity of the crowd had gotten his attention. Was that why they'd called him? Because these people were behaving so illogically?

"Ed," Bill said, and stuck out his hand.

"Chief."

They shook hands and Bill handed Ed a pair of night-scope binoculars.

"Sight in on that guy in the middle," he said. "The tall guy with the military cut."

"What am I looking for?" Ed said, as he raised the glasses to his eyes. "And what the hell's that rancid odor, anyway?"

"I think you'll know it when you see it, and as for the odor, well, it's coming from them, from those people."

"Christ! Smells like ruined meat!"

"Yeah, that's what I thought."

Ed looked for the tall man, found him easily enough, and

focused the binoculars on him. "What the?" he mumbled. He lowered the binoculars. Seconds later, he sighted in on another man, shorter and closer. "Chief, tell me there's something wrong with these damn things," he said.

"Brand new, fresh out of the box."

Ed lowered the binoculars again and looked at his chief. "Are they all like that?"

"The ones we can make out. Some of them got a lot of hair . . . well, you can see that. So, you know, we don't know about them, not for sure, and I really hate to draw conclusions—"

"Draw conclusions? What else can we conclude? They're all like that, they gotta be! Why else would they be here, doing what they're doing? Or what they're *not* doing. Jesus, this is fucking weird!"

"Yeah . . . but Mr. Mayor, what are they doing?"

"I wish to Christ I knew."

"Any suggestions?"

"On what?"

"On whether we disperse them."

"You tell me."

"I don't think we should—not yet."

Bill hadn't decided whether to tell his boss what had happened to him. Hizzoner might conclude—logically—that he had only been reading something into a highly volatile situation. He'd done that before. He really didn't know if he had the words to describe what he'd seen, anyway. Better to just let it slide. "So we just wait, is that it, Ed?"

"I don't see that we have a choice, Bill."

Lesley Charleton stood toward the back of the crowd. Out of the corner of her eye she saw a uniformed cop, looking very closely at her. How long he had been staring she didn't know, because until that moment, her grip on reality had been tenuous at best. Her mind had been work-

ing with memories. The most vivid was her transformation in
the cellar of the row house. Lou had done it . . . Louis. She
reached up and touched her neck. A huge scab had formed.
She'd covered it with a red scarf. She remembered little after
that, although she did remember being laid on the couch and
everyone leaving. From there, things had progressed at an
alarmingly quick pace. She had waited until nightfall before
she'd gone home. At first, she didn't notice any difference in
her behavior or her way of thinking, so she went about her
life as if nothing had happened. Wishful thinking, she knew
now. Hungry, she had begun to prepare one of her favorite
meals, spaghetti and meat balls and homemade sauce. For a
long time she stared down into the pan of red, thick sauce,
stirring it with a wooden spoon and occasionally adding this
spice or that. But of course, a dash of oregano and a pinch
of garlic wouldn't produce the desired results. Not even close.
And after about fifteen minutes of staring down into the bub-
bling mixture, she realized that all too well, so she dutifully
turned down the heat on her sauce—it wouldn't do to have it
burn—and left her apartment in search of the missing ingredient. She found it on the third floor of her building.

Lesley, her attractive mouth now filled with the proper
ingredient, went back downstairs and into her kitchen. Once
there she introduced the missing ingredient into her sauce
and blended it in with her wooden spoon. But although she
went as far as preparing pasta and setting out the wine, she
didn't actually eat anything. And looking back, she realized
that she hadn't eaten because she had already been sated,
and beyond that, she also knew that nothing short of the
missing ingredient, no amount of pasta or Italian seasoning,
would ever satisfy her again. She had become like Louis
and the others, a vampire of sorts. Realizing that, she com-
mended herself on not giving up, on the fact that she was
actually still viable—if not actually alive. She wondered if
she should go to work in the morning.

She did go, although she didn't stay. Her office had a

wonderful easterly view, but there weren't any drapes on the windows and the rising sun had made her very uncomfortable. She went home, heard from a neighbor about the murder of poor Mr. Estes on the third floor, and locked herself in her apartment.

She had felt the puppet-like tug about two hours earlier, and when she'd left her apartment and gotten into her car, she'd really had no idea where she was going. She simply went in the direction that felt most like home.

The closer she drew to the Empire State Building, the more she realized she was going in the right direction. Lots of others were going there, too. Far more cars were out than should have been at that hour.

She had parked a couple of blocks away, in the closest spot she could get. She didn't speak to anyone after she fell into line. She hadn't felt the need. She simply took her position near the Empire State Building and waited.

While she waited, a new sense of purpose and direction seemed to permeate into her. She felt like she belonged now, more so than she had ever felt as a mortal. Looking up into the red and green lights of the giant building, she had felt a sense of comradeship and protectiveness that she hadn't thought she was capable of feeling. She had always been a solitary person—if you wanted to succeed in this city, you had to have a strong sense of self-worth—but now she had become what she'd always loathed, a team player. One of the masses. And it felt pretty damn good.

She began looking around at those who weren't like her, and her rage grew. But she sensed that now was not the time for a confrontation. She—they—probably weren't strong enough yet, anyway. But being here, close to this building, had revitalized her so much. . . . She could wait. They could all wait. Their time would come.

That was the implication.

* * *

"Something's happening," Bill said.

"They're leaving," Ed said, giving private thanks.

"What now?"

Ed watched the dispersing crowd for a moment and said, "Now I go back home and see if I can't get back to sleep. The city council meets tomorrow, and I want to be fresh."

"What about—?"

"And I'd suggest you do the same, Bill. What we've just seen is some kind of . . . aberration, that's all. No harm done. Thank goodness the media didn't see this. They'd have a field day."

Bill watched Hizzoner get into his car and wondered whether they should keep this thing quiet. If he wanted to keep his job, he'd do as he was told, and he'd direct his men to do the same, because in this economy, jobs like his were definitely at a premium.

Twenty-five

David called his driver from Rochester and asked him to meet them at the airport. "We need the stretch limo," he said.

Larry didn't ask why; he just did as he was told. He arrived at the airport well ahead of time.

Forty-five minutes after the plane landed, the Lincoln pulled up to the curb outside the Empire State Building. Larry cut the engine and sat dutifully behind the wheel.

Bobby, seated by the door, got out. "Smell it?" he said. He looked at David.

David looked at him and sniffed the air. "Blood."

Bobby glanced around at the empty streets. A couple of cop cars cruised leisurely down Sixth Avenue, then disappeared. Seeing the cars, Bobby said, "Something's happened here."

Emily glanced at Ray. For the last two hours she'd been in very close quarters with a being who could end their lives as quickly and as efficiently as they might kill a beetle. To say she was apprehensive would be a wild understatement. And now that Bobby and David were both exhibiting preternatural talents—they could smell blood in the air, for God's sake—her anxiety was almost debilitating.

"Mugger, probably," Ray said.

Bobby smiled joylessly. "No, nothing that mundane."

His attention was drawn to the buildings. "Funny," he

said, "how these giant slabs of concrete and steel could just as easily be a forest of giant sequoias. Probably just as many wild things here as there, maybe more."

His gaze locked on the Empire State Building, and for a moment he thought he saw something hovering in the night sky, looking down at him. For a very long time, he stared back at what he finally decided had to be an illusion.

"What is it?" David asked. "What did you see?"

Bobby looked at David and tried to smile. "I'd know he was in there even if you hadn't told me," he said.

His smile grew. "He's even more powerful than before."

The crowd had totally dispersed over the last hour or so, leaving no clue that anything had ever happened, other than the lingering odor of blood. A light rain was falling, freckling the sidewalks and streets.

"Would you rather we brought him down?" David said. "Ray and I can handle it."

On the plane they'd decided to take Martin out of his casket because the casket wouldn't fit inside the car. Bobby looked at David curiously. "You don't feel it?" he said.

"Feel it?"

"Fear, dammit! Aren't you afraid?"

"Afraid? Yes, of course, but . . ." He looked hard at Bobby. "Yes, yes I am," he lied.

Bobby was trying valiantly to maintain his composure, and he knew this pseudo-immortal standing beside him was lying. "You're not, are you?" he said. "You're not really afraid, you're just patronizing me. Dammit, why aren't you afraid? Why the hell . . ." Bobby looked at the building again, then looked back at David. "Because he doesn't hate you, that's why. He doesn't want to destroy you. He knows I'm here, he knows I'm close, and he's directed his anger at me." Again he looked at the building, high up the building, and as he did, an enfeebled expression passed over his face and his chin began to quiver.

What struck Emily then was the physical manifestation of

Bobby's fear. Here was what she had assumed to be the most powerful and evil entity on the face of the earth, appearing as frightened as a schoolboy in a midnight graveyard. But as she—and Ray, she believed—took that thought to the next level, she finally began to understand Martin's power.

"I'll go," Bobby said. "I've got to confront him sometime. It might as well be now."

The elevator ride to the seventy-fifth floor was spent in silence, and when David unlocked the door to his office and pushed it open, Bobby immediately felt as if he had been struck. He recoiled and a dozen thoughts spiraled through his head, all of them hideous, all having to do with his gruesome and not very speedy death. Moving into this room was like slogging through neck-deep quicksand.

"Cover him!" he snapped, when they got into the artifacts holding area. Martin was still twenty feet away, facing the window. Bobby glared at Ray. "Didn't you hear me? I said *cover him!*"

Ray looked at Emily, and she at him. Then he crossed the room, picked up the old army blanket that lay in a heap beside the casket, and did as he was told.

Bobby instantly felt some relief, but at the same time he felt more than a little humiliated. Martin had won this round too easily. He hadn't even had the nerve to go around the casket and look him in the eye. He looked at the others, at David and Emily and Ray. He could see them laughing at him. Damn them. He could see them having one fantastic time at his expense.

Feeling a surge of courage, he moved quickly to the back of the casket and yanked the blanket off, and despite the fact that he instantly felt physically and intellectually weaker, his will was at least intact. He went around the casket, moving slowly—really having no choice—and when he got to the other side, he looked into his old friend's eyes.

Bastard!

Bobby lost his balance, his knees buckled.

You wanted to kill me, bastard! You filthy bastard!

Suddenly Bobby felt like a small boy again, looking up into the eyes of his tyrannical and ruthless father. What large and misshapen hands he had, what a gruesome and equally misshapen face, hair like old straw, eyes like diamonds in the sun, the black skull buttons on Martin's white shirt throwing back the lights of the city. Tears gathered in the corners of Bobby's eyes and his chin began to quiver again. He backed away from Martin, his hand held out defensively in front of him. He'd been a bad boy, a bad, bad boy, and now he would pay the price.

"Martin, I—"

He swore he could see Martin leaving his casket as if they'd already opened the plastic cover.

"Please, Martin, please, no!"

He was stepping toward him now, his father's strap replaced by fangs the size of bear teeth. Teeth or strap, the effect was the same. He felt so humbled, so weak, so insignificant . . . as submissive as a yelping pup.

"Martin, I'm sorry."

Coward!

"Please, please, don't!"

"Bobby," David yelled.

Bobby hadn't heard.

In Bobby's mind, Martin moved closer and closer, growing in size with each step while Bobby himself grew smaller and smaller, less and less significant.

"My God, David, what's wrong with him?" Ray said.

"Cover him," David ordered.

Ray hesitated.

"Do it, damn you!"

Emily beat him to it. She snapped up the blanket and threw it over the casket like a fishing net.

Cowering in a far corner, Bobby saw her look at him.

He felt humiliated and defeated, and suddenly he knew that she was not the least bit afraid of him, that she probably even pitied him.

Lesley Charleton got out of bed and went to the window. Rain speckled the glass, altering her view of the empty street. She thought of what a bee might see. Something had happened inside of her while she lay in bed, something beyond simple bloodlust. She smiled. *So that's it,* she thought. *That's what I have to look forward to.* She felt a lather rise between her thighs.

A man stepped out of the shadows and moved under a streetlamp, and looked up at her. "Louis," she purred. Her smile grew and the thing inside her that had spoken almost tentatively earlier spoke with much stronger resolve now. As she looked down at him, the heat began to rise from her calves, continuing into her knees and then into her thighs. She was moistening quickly. She felt her hips begin to move. Louis started across the street. *He can smell it,* Lesley thought. She thought about a wolf charging instinctively through a forest and her hands began to probe, to explore, while she looked down at him. She passed her hands over her breasts as Louis disappeared, then dropped them onto her thighs as she heard his footfalls on the stairs. A low moan worked out of her. *Gently,* she told herself, smiling demurely. *Always gentle.* That's what she'd told her past lovers. *Slow and gentle wins the race.* Ah, but things had changed, things had definitely changed. "Slow and gentle" had somehow lost its appeal.

She cupped her pubic area, and as her eyes rolled back into their sockets, she rammed a finger deep inside. She was breathing furiously now and she could feel her lips peel back from her teeth. "Louis," she mumbled. She could hear him bounding up the stairs, lumbering, impassioned Louis. An image of spittle glistening fangs flashed into her thoughts and another finger joined the first; three went in soon after, then another, and finally the whole hand. Her head lolled back with the exquisiteness of her pain and she heard the door fly open. She turned. Louis stood naked and spotlit near the door. But he didn't rush into the room. Instead, he stayed at the door. It appeared that he was allowing his fire to build, stoking it with patience. But of course, Lesley hadn't yet learned patience. She tore off her clothing and crossed quickly to him, entwining her legs and arms around him and humping wildly, madly. She heard Louis grunt his satisfaction. "Louis," she said huskily, as she licked the scar on his neck. *"Louisss!"* she said again, so enjoying the bloody residue.

"No!" Louis screamed, and threw her to the floor. He stood over her, watching her body gyrate. He grinned. "Oh, your ass beats a merry rhythm," he said. "Thump, thump, thump! Careful, now, you'll wake the dead. Careful!"

He climbed aboard then and instantly the building vibrated with the sounds of their passion. But Louis and Lesley didn't care much about the noises they were making or who they might be disturbing. There was something at work here that was far stronger than civility and prying eyes.

With each thrust they cried out; no need for fantasy here, no need to replace this lover with someone better-looking or younger or more adept. And when Louis exploded inside her, the building shook with his cries.

A few of Lesley's neighbors went into the hallway to see what had happened. But all they could do was gaze with curiosity and wait for the noise to happen again.

They didn't hear it again, though, and eventually everyone went back to bed. But no one slept.

In Lesley's living room, Louis looked at her and ran his hand over the concavity on the side of her head. Then he went to the window and looked at the Empire State Building.

"Something's happening," he said.

"What?"

"Death, maybe." He turned. "Lots of death."

Lesley smiled and opened her arms to him, and minutes later Louis exploded inside of her again.

Ah, she thought, *the benefits of immortality.*

Twenty-six

While everyone was trying to figure out what to do—their rock to lean on had apparently crumbled—Bobby got out of his crouch and moved slowly toward Martin. "Damn you!" he said. "I won't let you do this—not to me, not to our kind. I won't *let* you!"

But that, apparently, wasn't up to him. He stopped suddenly, an expression of pain on his face. He looked like a man experiencing drug withdrawal, his face stretched and contorted. His eyes opened wider than seemed possible, then closed tightly. But just when it appeared that Bobby would lose this battle, too, a look of great relief passed over his face.

"Hurry," he said, as he realized what had happened. "We have to hurry. He's too tired to continue." The realization that Martin's power was limited filled Bobby with renewed vigor and intensity. "David, where're the shovels? You said you had a couple of shovels."

"In back. I'll get them in a second, just let me get him free." He took the key out of his pocket and unlocked the plastic cover, but as soon as the cover swung open, David looked as unsteady as a kid who'd just gotten off a merry-go-round. He stepped back and almost fell down, his hands out in front of him for balance.

"Dad?" Emily yelled as she rushed to him. "What's wrong, Dad? My God . . ."

He looked at her. "I don't know, all of a sudden I feel . . . sluggish."

"It's Martin," Bobby said. "Get out of the way."

Emily helped her father move out of the way and Bobby undid the straps. He looked at Martin a second; he liked what he saw. "You're a sight," he said. "Head sunken in, mouth like a prize fighter's. What's happened to you, Martin?"

He laughed. Martin couldn't retaliate, so why not? These were the kind of moments he could really enjoy. He leaned Martin forward and cradled him under his arm like a suitcase without a handle, Martin's head facing the front.

"I'll get his legs," Ray said.

David could only watch while Ray and Bobby took Martin out the door and into the outer office.

"Help me," David said to Emily.

"The shovels," he said, after he got up, "let's get the shovels."

They went into his private rooms, found the shovels, then hurried to the elevator. They arrived just in time.

"What about security?" Emily asked on the way down. Martin was beside her. Bobby had a hand on his chest to keep him from falling down.

"What about security?" David said, as he looked up into Martin's face. "He's just a wax statue. And he's my property. All we're doing is moving him. Nothing wrong with that."

The guard stopped them on their way out, asked the necessary questions, then allowed them to pass. *Somehow,* Emily thought, *there should have been more to it.*

They put Martin in the stretch limo first—which was a lot like bending a box spring around a corner—then had a discussion about who should go with him. David and Bobby had been appointed that job. That didn't seem advisable right now, although they both thought the danger had passed.

Ray didn't think it had. "I'll do it," he said. "There's no telling when he'll get his strength back."

Bobby didn't argue. "Remember," he said, "take him far away from the city and make sure you bury him someplace where no one will find him. Remember!"

"There's a gorge in New Jersey," Ray said. "About fifty miles from here."

"I'm going, too," Emily suddenly announced.

Ray looked at her curiously. "Larry and I can handle this, Emily. I think you should stay here."

She looked into his eyes. Did she tell him the truth? Did she tell him she'd rather be with a paralyzed vampire than two that weren't, even though one of them was her father?

Bobby, it seemed, had read her thoughts. "You have nothing to fear from me," he said.

Emily felt silly. She looked at her father.

"I'd rather you didn't go," he said. "As Ray said, they can handle this. I'd feel better if you stayed here."

"I appreciate that, Dad, but I'm going to go."

"You'd just be in the way."

"I'm going."

"If she wants to come, let her," Ray said.

David's head snapped toward Ray. He looked back at Emily. "Go then, dammit!"

In spite of herself, Emily hugged him while Ray got into the car. She smiled at her father, then went around to the street side and sat on Martin's left. Once inside, she rolled down the window. "I love you, Dad," she said.

"I love you, Emily," her father said. He waved to her as the car pulled away.

Martin was in the middle, his head lying on the back-facing seat, his feet propped onto the back of the forward-facing seat. The almost seven-foot expanse was just large enough to accommodate him.

"New Jersey," Ray said to Larry over the intercom. It was raining harder now, making it difficult to see. The wipers slashed the rain away furiously.

"Yes, sir," Larry said. "Then where?"

"Just get us to Jersey."

They went up Thirty-fourth Street toward the Lincoln Tunnel.

"Symbols," Ray said while the car clipped along just below the speed limit.

Emily looked across Martin's chest at Ray. "Symbols?"

"I was thinking about symbols of evil. Seemed appropriate."

He glanced at Martin's face and discovered that he couldn't do that for very long. He looked back at Emily, a better choice. "Swastikas, burning crosses, things like that. All inanimate objects symbolic of pure evil."

"Like Martin, you mean?"

"Exactly. And if what Bobby All says is true, then Martin is just as inspirational as a swastika or a burning cross. Hell, he's more than that, if he's actually alive, if he can actually control his kind with his thoughts. This may be a wild stab in the dark, but you know what I think happened back there? I think there was a kind of meeting. To talk things over, you know?"

"Plan strategy, you mean? Beings like him—like my father—got together and telepathically discussed strategy?"

Ray couldn't hold back a grin. "Okay, it's pretty farfetched, but so are vampires. You know, I wonder about your father, Emily. I wonder what really goes on inside him." He lost his grin.

"You wonder if he's killed anyone yet, don't you?"

Ray looked sad. "I don't know. Why not say, 'did what he had to do to survive'?"

Emily looked out the side window at a couple of kids on a street corner. One glanced around cautiously, having just handed something to the other. "You know what I wonder about, Ray? How I'd react if I were in his situation. Would I do what I had to do to survive, or would I try to end it?"

She looked at him.

"Is that what you want?" he said. "You want your father to kill himself?"

Her first thought was just reaction—of course she didn't. Death was so final. But what if he didn't? What kind of life . . .

"I suppose I could live with whatever decision he made," she said. "Truthfully, though, I guess suicide would be the better choice."

She looked out the window again, not wanting him to see the tears in her eyes.

It happened on the corner of Eighth Avenue. The car stopped at a red light, but when it turned green, they just sat there.

"Larry, is there a problem?" Ray said into the intercom.

Larry didn't answer.

"Larry?"

"Ray!" Emily said.

"What? What's wrong?"

"Out there, Ray. Those people."

They were moving from the alleys and the shadows like spilled ink—men, women, children, at least twenty people, all walking slowly toward the car, the rain hammering down around them.

"Did they have something at the Garden tonight?" Emily asked.

"Not this late! Dammit, Larry, get this thing moving!" Ray yelled. He checked the doors—locked. He touched the switch, just to make sure.

"Who are they?" Emily said, her gaze flitting from one person to another. "They look so . . . impassive. They look like a bunch of—"

"Zombies?"

Emily could only stare at him.

Ray shook his head, groping for some kind of explanation. Looking at Martin, he found one. "They *want* him, Emily. They want *Martin*. Jesus, what else can it be?"

Looking at Larry, Emily felt her face go blank with horror. "He's one of them," she said in a monotone. "My God, Ray, Larry's one of *them!*"

Ray looked hard at Larry. He hadn't moved. "Of course! How else—"

"If it were up to me," Larry said, "I'd get rid of both of you. Unfortunately, I still work for your father—"

"My father?"

"All you have to do, miss, is get out of the car and walk away. Just walk away. No one'll harm you."

The crowd drew closer.

Emily tugged on Ray's arm. "C'mon, Ray, let's get outta here. We haven't got a choice. Let's just go while we still can!"

Larry turned slightly. "I'm afraid you misunderstood me. Just you, Miss Kane, just you. Mr. Timmerson will have to stay."

"Stay?" Emily said. "And be turned into one of them?"

Larry smiled. "That depends."

"On what?"

"On whether the vampire that gets to him first is, well, in the mood."

Emily smiled. "This is crazy," she said. She looked at Ray. How the hell could anyone make a decision . . .

"In the mood, huh?" Ray murmured. He stuck his hand into his front pocket. "We'll just see about that!"

Emily watched while Ray folded back the cover on a book of matches, took one out, and struck it. Nothing.

"Damn!" he said, and took out another.

"Hey, what the hell's going on back there?" Larry yelled.

The crowd was only a few steps away now. Emily glanced at the closest vampire, a young woman, then watched as Ray struck the match. He got a spark. "C'mon, baby!" He struck it again. This time the match lit, giving off a plume of smoke and the pungent odor of sulfur.

"Hey, what the hell?" Larry said, as he opened his door.

"He'll go up like a tinderbox," Ray said, as he stuck the flaming match under Martin's sleeve.

Larry and the woman were at the door, yelling and beating on the glass.

"Get out, Emily, get the hell out!" Ray yelled.

The fire was spreading fast; she had only seconds. A shove on her door caught one of the vampires in the stomach and sent him sprawling backward. At about the same time, Ray caught Larry square in the chin with the top edge of his door and sent him reeling.

"Emily!" Ray yelled frantically, as he sidestepped the woman and an old man.

"Over here," she yelled back.

While the fire raged, Emily saw Ray focus his gaze on one of the portable toilets across the street and at her, standing next to it. By the time they saw each other, the inside of the limo was like a huge candle. There were three vampires on one side of the car and four on the other, some beating furiously at the flames, others trying to pull Martin out.

It worked! Emily thought. They'd been so intent on saving Martin they'd forgotten about Ray and her.

Ray ran across the street and stood beside her while they dragged Martin's burning body out of the car, sparks leaping off of him, the crackling heard even above the screeching of the vampires.

Emily thought—hoped—they were witnessing Martin's death. Not so. She watched Larry hurry back into the burning limo, exposing himself to the fire. The tires squealed then and didn't stop squealing until the car slammed into a fire hydrant, sending a fountain of water twenty feet high. The flames were extinguished within seconds, leaving only a gentle hissing in the air. Even Larry escaped.

"Good Lord!" Ray said.

"I don't believe it, Ray," Emily said. "He was willing to sacrifice himself for Martin. My God, Ray, do you realize the implications?"

They heard sirens wailing in the distance then, but by the time the trucks arrived, Martin had been taken away and the streets, save for a few people who had been witness to the whole thing, were empty. But those witnesses, frightened and confused, left before the authorities arrived. And although Ray and Emily wanted to tell someone what had happened, they didn't feel that now was the time to tell their story. They started for Emily's apartment on foot, moving fast.

Twenty-seven

They accomplished the forty-eight-block walk in small, shadow-to-shadow bursts, hustling through the light-drenched areas by the Port Authority Bus Terminal, heading uptown. When they were at Columbus Circle, at the southern tip of Central Park, they heard a series of muffled screams, the timbre of which suggested an agony more intense than they could imagine.

"My God, Ray," Emily whispered after they'd heard the first scream, "what the hell was that? That wasn't any mugging."

They were on the Central Park side of the street, the wrong side, Ray decided. "Come on," he said, "I think we'd be wise to stay away from the park."

But simply moving across the street didn't stop the screams; they didn't stop until they'd passed Tavern on the Green. They walked up Central Park West, past the American Museum of Natural History, and finally, just a block from her apartment, the Hayden Planetarium.

They arrived at Emily's around three in the morning, but they didn't go in right away.

"You don't suppose he's in there, do you?" Ray whispered.

"You mean my father?"

Ray nodded.

"Maybe, I don't know. But I know Bobby's not there.

They're on different teams now, so . . . Ray, you don't think . . ."

"What?"

"You don't think my father would actually kill me, do you?"

"No. He let you go at the car, didn't he?"

"Yeah, but that was before we tried to kill Martin. I think that offer's probably null and void by now."

"Before *I* tried to kill Martin, not *we,* Emily."

"I don't know, Ray, somehow I can't see two of those things rationalizing something like that. Somehow I see instinct being stronger than intellect with them."

A light was on in her apartment. She always left one on, hoping it would keep burglars away.

"What's your intuition tell you?" Ray said.

"Not to trust anyone."

"I mean about your dad."

She shrugged. "I don't know. If push came to shove, I'd have to say he isn't here, Ray."

"Okay. Give me your key and I'll check."

"And what if he is in there? You were the expendable one, remember? No, you stay here. I'll go. I'll flip the light on and off if it's all right."

"Be careful, Emily. Okay?"

She looked both ways, no cars, save for one on Eighty-First Street. "Remember, watch for the lights," she said, and started across, moving as quickly as she could.

She fumbled with the key for a moment, cursing under her breath before she finally got the door open. She slipped inside and waited, bracing herself. Alpha and Gamma were asleep on the white leather sofa, facing each other like bookends. She heard another cat jump down from her bed. *Beta,* she thought. He lounged on her bed whenever he got the chance. Then it dawned on her: her father wasn't here because no one had been around to extend an invitation.

With a sigh of relief, she crossed to the living room, arriving there just as Beta sauntered in from the bedroom, purring. Emily scratched his ears, then flipped the light on and off.

She watched as Ray ran across the street, then met him at the front door a half minute later.

"Make sure you lock it," he said, as he stepped inside.

"Ray, how could we be so stupid? We forgot something. One of the rules."

He looked pensive a moment, then smiled. "An invitation, right? They need an invitation, they can't just barge . . . how could we be so dumb?"

"At least we know we're safe as long as we don't invite them in. I think we've got something else to worry about, though." She crossed to the window and looked out at Central Park.

"What?"

"C'mon, Ray! There's something monstrous happening to the people in this city." She turned to face him. "I hate to even think . . ."

"What, dammit?"

"I think it's only just begun, Ray. It's gonna get a lot worse before it gets better."

He knew she was right. The crowds of people that looked and acted like her father, the terrible screams in the park. . . . There was a virus at work in this city, probably just hitting its stride even as they spoke, and somehow, in some way, it would have to be stopped. Her father would have to be stopped.

"I'm open to suggestions," he said. "I haven't got a clue about what we should do."

"Suggestions? I wish I had some. I was hoping you—"

"I think Bobby's our only hope."

"But you saw what Martin did to him! He was useless back there."

"I agree. But even Martin isn't invincible. We both saw how he lost some of his power."

"Yeah, maybe. Where do you think he is right now?"

"Bobby?"

"Yeah."

"Hopefully, he's looking for Martin, and when he finds him, he'll be able to get rid of him."

"And you think that if he stops Martin, that'll stop the others, too?"

"That'd go along with what we talked about earlier."

"But what about my dad?"

"Your dad? I don't—"

"Would it kill him, too, or do you think we can save him before Bobby gets to Martin?"

He cupped her shoulders "Emily, I wish . . . dammit, I don't think we can save him. I wish I could say I thought that was possible—"

"What about Bobby All? What about him, Ray? He brought Martin back from the dead, from the ashes. You'd think it'd be a simple matter—"

"Then why hasn't he done it to himself, Emily? Why is he still a vampire?"

Her facial muscles tightened as she shrugged away from him. "I'm surprised you don't know, Ray. Because he doesn't want to change, that's why. But I think if you gave my father the chance, he'd take it. Bobby's just pure evil. He only agreed to help us destroy Martin so he could save his own hide. My father may be altered, but he can still be saved."

"Even if that's true, you really think Bobby's going to agree to something like that?"

"You're making fun of me, Ray, and I don't like it."

"No, I'm not making fun of you. I would never do that! I just think you've been blinded by love, that's all."

"God that's so freakin' clichéd. Maybe so, Ray, maybe I am, but that doesn't mean I'm gonna accept what's happened to my father and leave it at that. That I won't explore every possibility to get him back. And if that means begging Bobby All to help me, I'll do that, too. I'll get down on my hands and knees and beg!"

He wanted to convince her that she didn't have a prayer of saving her father, but any argument he could come up with seemed pretty weak. Better to change the topic and get back to it at a better time.

"You know the cops had to have picked up on this by now," he said. "There have got to be all kinds of people missing and murdered. And I'm sure official phones are ringing off the hooks with complaints about screams like we heard in the park, and wives complaining about how their husbands have changed, and husbands doing likewise about their wives."

"Maybe we should add our names to that list," she said.

"Maybe we should."

Emily glanced at the ceiling. "What about here? How many people in this building do you think have been affected?"

Beta rubbed against Ray's legs. "Who knows? None, I hope. You know, this'd be simple if we were dealing with a flu, or something. Go on down to Bellevue and just get a vaccination."

"Yeah, well, it's not the flu, and they're not gonna stop it with a needle in the arm. Look, Ray, I'm awfully tired."

"Me, too. Dead on my feet. Sorry. Do we dare go to sleep, though?"

"Why not? The rules, remember? They gotta have permission."

Ray nodded at the cats still asleep on the couch. "What about them? You want me to just kick 'em off?"

Emily looked at the cats, then back at Ray. "They're okay. We can share . . . it's a big bed."

She thought she saw him smirk.

"And don't get any ideas," she said. "That's the last thing on my mind, and it should be the last on yours, too."

Ray shrugged. "Wish it was that easy, but unfortunately—"

The buzzer rang then, leaving the moment in tatters.

"Jesus," Ray said, "who the hell can that be?"

She crossed to the intercom. "Who is it?" she asked.

"It's me, Bobby. Let me in, please."

She glanced at Ray.

"What do you want?"

"If you let me in, I'll tell you."

The blood pounded in her ears. She thought about the screams she had heard in the park.

"I don't know, Ray," she said. "I really don't think he wants to hurt us. I say we let him in."

"I don't think we've got a choice. If he wants to be an ally . . . that's kind of like leaving a Doberman to guard the meat, isn't it? Go ahead, let him in."

Emily pressed the button. A half minute later, there was a knock on her door.

She opened it.

Bobby's grin, measured and joyless, made her wonder if she'd done the right thing, but as he stepped inside and said, "Your father's one of *them,* Emily," she understood that they had just joined forces.

"You know that for sure?"

"Why else would he disappear the way he did? You lost Martin, I take it? I heard the sirens, so I just assumed—"

"Actually, he got stolen," Ray said.

"Stolen?"

"They took him."

"I guess I can take the blame for that. I should have done it myself. I won't make that mistake again."

"My father," Emily said, "you said he was gone?"

Bobby looked at her. "We watched the car drive away

and just moments after that, your father said, 'I do love her, you know, I really do.' Then he just walked away. The sirens though, I don't understand—"

"I set him on fire," Ray said, a hint of pride in his voice.

Bobby seemed amused. "You set him on fire? Ray, I fear you've made a mortal enemy of Martin now. But how did they rescue him? I don't understand."

"Larry rescued him, Bobby," Emily said. "My father's driver risked his life to save him. He ran over a hydrant and the water put the fire out."

Bobby smiled. "Martin must be a sight now! Well, our first priority is to find out where they've taken him. We'll worry about getting rid of him once we find him."

Bobby looked out at the park.

"You have some ideas about that, don't you?" Emily said.

Bobby turned. "A hunch, maybe. You see, if Lenora knew how to restore Martin, then she also knows how to destroy him."

"Really? Then I guess you'll go—"

"No, I think I should stay here, close to Martin. If I left, I'd probably find it very difficult to return. I'd be safe away from here, at least for a while, until the rest of the world . . . we're not a totally unsympathetic race, you know? We've got our heroes and our antiheroes. We've even got histories, just like humans. I can't allow all that to be destroyed."

"The way I see it," Ray said, "you're telling us that you've got a weak constitution."

Bobby smiled lightly. "Quite the contrary. If my will were weak, I'd give in to my weakness. I'd leave this city and let Martin destroy it."

Ray let out a large, resigned breath. He didn't have much of a choice. "I'll go, then," he said. "Just tell me where I can find her."

Bobby paused. "You realize, of course, that finding her is no guarantee of success. She's a very strange and malicious woman. I often wonder if the partial reanimation of

Martin wasn't just a practical joke on her part. You have to understand that."

"Look, if you're trying to talk me out of going, you're doing a pretty fair job of it."

"I'm just being truthful with you. If you want to be successful, you've got to have all the facts. I'll write a kind of letter of referral for you. Maybe it'll get her attention, at least."

"Are you sure about this, Ray?" Emily said.

"Hell, no! But someone's got to do something. I suppose you could go, but there's probably as much danger there as here. And you'll be safe here with Bobby. She will be safe with you, won't she?"

Bobby looked confused. "You two really don't understand my kind, do you? No, she *won't* be safe with me. I won't risk *my* welfare for *hers*. She's nothing to me. In some other time and place she'd be a meal and that's about all. Now, if you're asking me if I would harm her—no, I wouldn't. Does that answer your question?"

"You're truthful, at least."

"One of my many fine qualities. Now, if you have a pen and paper, Emily."

"Hang on."

"I assume you'll be leaving today, Ray?" Bobby said.

"I'll check the airline schedules, but yes, today sometime."

Emily found a pen and a piece of paper in a kitchen drawer. She gave them to Bobby.

"This should help," Bobby said, and began writing.

When he was done, he handed the paper to Ray. 'Please speak with this man,' it said. It was signed, "Bobby." Below that was Lenora's address in Tampa.

"It's a start," Ray said.

"I wish there were more I could do, but as I explained . . . now if you'll excuse me, there's someone I'd like to see. Good luck, Ray."

* * *

Ray called for flight times while Emily stared out the window. More than anything, Bobby's explanation of why he would not be the caretaker of her safety gave her a better understanding of his kind than anything that had happened so far. Simple enough—Bobby, and those like him, were totally immersed in self-preservation.

"United's my best bet," Ray yelled from the kitchen. "There's a flight leaving for Tampa at twelve-forty."

Emily turned and looked at him. Would that be the last time they'd see each other? She watched as he wrote down the flight information. *Godspeed,* she thought.

Twenty-eight

During and after the fire, Martin coped with his pain by thinking about the past. He thought about the time before he'd become a vampire, when he and Bobby were children and members in good standing in The Sad Café. But pain being what it is, something as mind-altering as a drug, Martin's mental excursion was not without a few surprises.

Mingled with memories of his youth were the strangest and most compelling visions imaginable. One second he and Bobby were talking about how The Sad Café was going to handle a situation—usually school related—and the next he was leading a crowd of vampires down the streets of Hunt, a blood-red, two-fanged crown upon his head. And there were Judd Lucas and Steven on the curb, and there was the dwarf doing little back-flips and cackling like a lunatic. But even then, the images hardly remained constant. While he marched through town, the buildings of Hunt began to stretch and fatten and the streets became crowded with taxicabs and bicycles and pedestrians.

But even as the village of Hunt stretched and expanded and finally became New York City, Martin's role didn't change, his blood-red crown still sat upon his head and on each side of the street he could see people in authority: the police and the mayor, and firemen in their shiny red hats.

And there were other people there, too—journalists getting all the who, what, where, and whens. Seeing these peo-

ple, he'd point at them and someone from his brood would
step out of the crowd and either kill that person or alter
them, depending on how much use they would be to him
in his quest to become the King of New York.

Funny, he thought now, how when that was going on, he
was able to decide who could be useful and who couldn't,
he was lucid enough to make those decisions. He'd had
these strange visions while they'd carried him away from
the burning car, and although he caught occasional glimpses
of reality, by the time lucidity returned—at least to some
degree—he had no idea where they had taken him.

He could guess, though. He loved to guess. He worked
his senses. His eyesight, although limited, owing to the im-
mobility of his eyes, took first crack. There wasn't any light
from any source, so he saw virtually nothing, a fact that
left him a little downhearted. But he did sense that this was
a very small room, extremely small. He felt a little angry
at that—was that any way to treat a king? His sense of
smell took over for a moment: the air was musty and stagnant, punctuated only vaguely by the odor of . . . grease?
And something else . . . pancake makeup. *Yes, pancake
makeup and lipstick.* There were people in this building.
His kind. He couldn't see them, though. They were in another room. He could hear them talking about him, plan-
ning. He could hear them with his ears and telepathically.
The telepathic noise was distinguishable from the spoken
word because it always seemed to come with a moderately
powerful echo, almost as if the person's thoughts were
bouncing off the walls of his brain.

Adding all these things up, however, didn't help Martin
guess where he was. Not because Martin wasn't bright
enough, he was; it just seemed that his ability to concentrate
had been somewhat affected. *Probably by the fire,* he decided.

As he tried to weigh all this information, the past came
back to him again. And there he stayed for a very long

time, the past and the present bobbing and weaving, both doing their best to get the upper hand. But unfortunately for Martin, neither could get the upper hand, and as it happened, Martin was still involved with these warring images when his brood filed into the room.

The last person Martin saw was David, placing a solid and vaguely human shaped cover over him. As it happened, his images at that moment were of The Sad Café. It was Halloween. Bobby was going to be a ghost, and he had decided to be a mummy.

There was a certain amount of comfort in that memory, so he lived it and breathed it, and for a while, as he and Bobby scared the bejesus out of his mother's landlady, he even forgot about how much he hated Bobby.

In the room, meanwhile, the assembled were comparing notes.

"He's confused, that's obvious," a man said, a lawyer dressed in a gray suit. "But I think it's obvious what he wants us to do. He wants us to move right now."

"I don't know," a woman about forty with salt-and-pepper hair said. "The images I get are awfully convoluted. I saw kids and a jack-o'-lantern and a fireman. Can you imagine?"

A boy about ten said, "I saw an old lady's eyes bug out." The image had obviously intrigued him.

"Well," the lawyer continued, "I think it's obvious what we have to do to make sure that Martin eventually ascends to his throne. We have to take action now. *Right* now."

"I don't think that's wise," David said. "This is a big step. If we act now, a lot of us will die."

"I don't agree," the lawyer said.

"Of course you don't, but you'll do what I say. We can't have anarchy. And avoiding anarchy isn't going to be easy. It's in our nature, subservient one second, murderously spontaneous the next. It's the bloodlust, of course, the virus.

We all know we can't just kill anyone at any time, that we'd only draw attention to ourselves if we did. But some of us do it anyway, those who can't control themselves. It's getting out of hand.

"And we've made the news, folks. They're saying it's the summertime heat, that the murder rate always shoots up in the summertime. Well, it won't be long before they hit on the real reason. And now this has happened to Martin, making him incoherent and babbling. Hopefully, he'll be better tomorrow evening."

"And in the meantime?" the lawyer said.

"Getting anxious?"

"I know I am," another man said.

David looked at him, recognized him. There was a woman standing beside him. "Louis," he said. "Good to see you."

Louis nodded.

"Everyone, listen up," David said. "Louis was my first, so I guess he should be third-in-command, behind Martin and me. Any objections?"

A little mumbling, but no objections.

"Good. Then tomorrow night we'll meet back here and check in on Martin again."

"What if he hasn't changed?" the lawyer said.

"We'll talk about that tomorrow, if we have to."

Everyone filed out then and went home, leaving Martin alone to think and to wonder about what it was in here with him that was so awfully old.

Bobby couldn't help but notice the eastern sky and the blush of early morning. The sun would be up in an hour or so. Oh he could probably find sanctuary easily enough, but he didn't want to hide just anywhere. He wanted to be comfortable. And if memory served, an old high school friend had taken up residence in this city. He probably should have looked her up before now.

It took him only a little while to get to the Plaza Hotel on Fifth Avenue. Once there, he went inside and asked for her room number.

"The name, sir?" the desk clerk said. He seemed put out.

"Cynthia Lucas." *Funny,* Bobby thought, *that she kept her married name.* He thought about Judd Lucas and the boy.

"Room five-oh-five, sir." The clerk smiled like a mannequin.

Bobby saw his carotid throbbing, reminding him that he hadn't eaten in a while. "Thanks," he looked at the clerk's name tag, "Maurice."

The wooden smile turned to plastic.

Bobby walked to the elevators. "Maurice, huh? Yeah, right. And my name's Bram Stoker."

Cynthia had returned from Bayonne, New Jersey, just minutes earlier and she was getting ready for bed.

She always dined out of state, mainly because she had actually learned to like New Yorkers, at least most of them. She rarely changed a victim now. It was becoming quite a chore to find new hiding places for the bodies.

A knock at her door shot her with curiosity.

"Yes?" she said.

"Cynthia? It's me, Bobby."

"Bobby?"

"How are you?"

She rushed to the door and opened it. He grinned at her and she grinned back. "Come in, Bobby. My goodness. What brings you to New York?"

He looked closely at her. "Martin."

"Martin? I don't understand. I thought—"

"He was. Well, as destroyed as we can be. Lenora—I never told you about her—she restored him."

She saw him give her the once-over. She knew what she looked like—her once luxurious blond hair had the look of straw, and her eyes were hollow and dark.

"Cynthia, is something wrong? You don't look well."

"You always were observant. I'm not sleeping well, Bobby. I think it's the dreams."

"What kind of dreams?"

"You'll just laugh."

"I promise, I won't laugh."

"In my dreams I'm no longer, well, as vital as I should be. That is, I don't have fangs, and—this is really weird—I can't move. And you know how I've always been so vain—"

Bobby smiled. "It's what I admire most about you."

"Well, in my dreams I've got this awful indentation in my head, right here by my temple. It's terribly pronounced and very unattractive."

"You've picked up on Martin's thoughts, Cynthia. Being in somewhat close proximity, you picked up his telepathic messages. Obviously, Martin thinks about things a lot. He couldn't look in a mirror and see the concavity in his skull. That, you probably picked up from someone he saw. One of his 'children.' But from the look on your face, you obviously don't know what's happening."

"What *is* happening? I don't understand."

"After Lenora restored Martin, we made him part of the carnival—you remember the carnival?"

"How could I forget?"

"We made him part of the carnival because Lenora's restoration hadn't been total. That is, Martin was paralyzed. Even his fangs were blunted. So we dressed him up in a costume we thought the kids would like—the blood of children always tastes better, don't you think? Anyway, what we didn't realize was that although he was physically paralyzed, his mind was certainly active. He had—has—the ability to manipulate his kind with his thoughts."

"Like a blind person can hear better, that kind of trade-off?"

"Exactly. Anyway, he had a dream as a kid, he wanted to be King of New York, and while he was under our supervision, he did what he could to manipulate our thoughts, to make us do what we had to do to see that his dreams came true."

"Bobby, if he did that—"

"Then it would be the end of our kind, I know. Then there'd be a war between humans and vampires. That's why I dumped him in a peat bog before we got to New York. Unfortunately, someone found him and brought him here anyway."

"Wait, I don't understand. If he's paralyzed, how—"

"A blood tear, Cynthia. The man who found him drank a blood tear. Well, that man created another and he created another. A normal progression, except for the fact that Martin's creatures are like him. They have a concavity in the sides of their heads, and their fangs are stunted. As near as I can tell, they savage their victims to draw the blood. Very nasty.

"Anyway, Martin escaped while he was being taken away by two mortals, or rather, he was rescued by a crowd of his creations. Where he is now, I don't know. But we've got to find him. We have to destroy him, Cynthia. If we don't, we might cease to exist as a race. His dreams of conquest will be our undoing."

Cynthia looked out the window. "Our search will have to wait. It'll be morning soon. You'll stay, won't you?"

"I was hoping you'd ask."

A large Siamese cat sashayed into the room and jumped on the sofa.

"That's Prinzi," Cynthia said. "I picked him up on the waterfront."

Bobby didn't like cats. "I'll sleep on the sofa," he said.

"On the sofa? I wouldn't hear of it. You'll sleep with me. I am tired, though, Bobby, so . . ."

"Of course. Cynthia, wake me up if you have another dream. It may help us find Martin."

"You're right, it might."

Engrossed as they were in seeing each other again, they didn't notice the sun sector onto the horizon. A beam of light came dangerously close to Cynthia's leg. She jumped out of the way, but Prinzi, who found precious few sunbeams anymore, fell onto his side directly in its path and filled the room with his loud and contented purr.

Twenty-nine

"Goddammit, Chris, get in here!"

Chris Gedney, the mayor's administrative assistant, dropped what she was doing and hurried into her boss's office. She had to wait because His Honor was reading the newspaper. The tight set of his jaw seemed to indicate that he hadn't been reading the funnies, either.

He looked up at her and she couldn't tell whether it was the afternoon sun or the fire in his eyes that caused his American flag lapel pin to glitter.

"What is it?" she said.

Ed Lawrence turned the paper toward her and back-handed it the way he might a mosquito. "D'you see this, Chris?"

"What, sir?"

"This story, that's what!" He looked beyond her, at his open office door. People were listening, pretending to work.

"Close the door, Chris," he said evenly, gritting his teeth.

Jesus, Chris thought, as she closed the door. This job could make her career, and she was blowing it. She was supposed to run damage control for Ed Lawrence, a job she usually did pretty well, but she'd obviously fucked up this time.

"Can I see that, sir?"

Ed smiled a supercilious smile. She hated that smile.

"You know this guy, don't you?" he said, a rigid finger pointed at the byline. "This Sam Sturgess character."

She sure did know him. In a biblical way. At least, until last New Year's Eve, when they'd broken up because he wouldn't practice safe sex. She understood immediately why His Honor had asked about their relationship. She was the leak—at least that's what he thought. But she hadn't been the leak, although she'd been tempted. Personally, she thought Ed had fucked up royally by keeping the lid on this thing. A crowd of weird-looking people all gathered around the Empire State Building in the wee hours for no apparent reason was definitely something people should know about.

She had learned about the gathering from the mayor himself. He felt she should know just in case word got out. She'd fought the urge to tell Sam about it, though, because she knew she'd probably get blamed if he published. Now it looked like she'd held back for nothing.

"Yes, sir, I, uh . . . we dated. It's over, but yes—"

"Chris, your personal life is your concern. The welfare of this city is mine! How'd this hack get hold of this information?"

She hated Ed right now. If she knew how Sam got hold of the information and didn't stop him, she'd be just as guilty as if she'd leaked it herself. "Sir, I don't know, I just don't know," she said. Mayor Lawrence read people well.

Ed glared at her for almost a minute, then he said, "Read it, Chris. Go ahead, take a look at what your ex wants New Yorkers to read. Jesus, I feel like having him fucking arrested!"

Chris took the paper from him and started reading the editorial.

A series of bizarre events culminated at about one-thirty this morning when a score of people had an impromptu get-together in the shadow of the Empire State Building.

The event would have been newsworthy even if His

Honor, Ed Lawrence hadn't been there. But it was newsworthy for the following reasons.

First was the disparate nature of the crowd. Included in their number were noted professionals, an athlete of some renown—whose name will go unmentioned—blue-collar workers, and even children. A diverse assemblage if there ever was one. The question, of course, is why? What drove these people to congregate around the Empire State Building at that hour of the morning?

Second, it seemed that some of those people had deformities of the skull. If only one person had had this deformity—an indentation in the skull—it wouldn't have been newsworthy. But there was more than one. A lot more.

Third, there was the presence of Mayor Lawrence. Why would he be called out at that time of night just to observe a nonviolent demonstration?

Fourth, there was a lingering odor, sour and pungent, that dissipated only after everyone left. It smelled like copper, like blood.

As we all know, there's been an increase in the crime rate of late. Murders in the last week have multiplied tenfold. Sources indicate that the number of missing persons has quadrupled. Is there a link between this bizzare event and the rising crime rate? We call upon our mayor to keep his constituents informed. We call upon him to tell us why he was there.

Mr. Mayor, the ball is in your court now. What you do with it is up to you.

"Christ, he never could write," Chris mumbled, when she got done.

"Now, I know it sounds like he was there," Ed said, "but I doubt it very much. He's just protecting his source, that's all. And this phone's going to start ringing off the hook real soon. What do you propose we do about it?"

Chris smiled and realized how foolish it looked. "Well, sir, as we all know, this particular paper tends to overdramatize. I say we defuse the situation by simply making, shall we say, an indirect reference to that reputation."

Ed's face softened. "You're right, of course. I was so pissed off . . . Sure, just make some offhanded remark about the credibility of this rag and let New Yorkers have a good laugh on them. Some anti-administration zealots out there might not be convinced, but who cares?

"Chris, I think we should get the jump on this. Prepare a press release right away. Say, I don't know—say that I've seen this article, and although I hold both the paper and the journalist who wrote the article in high regard, I refute categorically the implications. Say that I was there because . . . because there was a bomb threat, or something. You know what to do. Then, at the end, make a reference to a story they ran a couple of weeks ago. You know the one?"

"You mean the story about the face on Mars?"

"Yeah, that."

"But that's true, sir."

"I know that, Chris! But the average New Yorker hears something like that and they get a bad case of the giggles."

"Sir, maybe it'd be best if we waited, just to see if we *do* get a public response."

"No, no, I've been mayor this long because I've always been one step ahead. If I jump in now, I can *stay* one step ahead. Now, get on it."

"Yes, sir."

She turned to leave and Ed said, "Can you believe that guy, Chris? Trying to link the crime rate with that demonstration. Who the *hell's* he think he's kidding?"

Ever the politician, even with his staff.

Chris returned his smile, added a shrug, then left.

As she sat down to write the press release, a shiver ran

up her spine. Even here people were out. Sure, they'd called in sick, but these were people who *never* called in sick, the kind who prided themselves on going in even if they were at death's door.

How long would it be before a real newspaper started asking questions? And how long would it be before the person sitting next to her would call in sick?

You're an honest and devoted public servant, Bill Kranepool told himself. At least, he'd always fancied himself one. *But what does that mean, exactly? Who am I devoted to? The public at large, or Ed Lawrence in particular?*

Staring at his reflection, a beard of shaving cream on his face, he knew he had to be straight with himself. If he wasn't, he'd see it.

He slid the razor along his cheek, stretching the skin by contorting his lips. When he did that, the horror of the night before came rushing back to him.

First of all, you're loyal to yourself, he thought. *You've got a family and a kid in college. Dartmouth ain't cheap. Loyalty definitely starts at home.*

That was a lie, though, or a stretch, at least. He had gone into public service all those years ago because he gave more than two shits about people in general. Most people got a raw deal from their government—God, didn't he know that? So he told himself he was going to do what he had to do to change that. Of course, being a cop, even the top cop, wasn't like being an elected official, but he was privy to the wheelings and dealings. He knew who was greedy and who wasn't—and wasn't that a damn few?

Ed Lawrence, now he's one greedy son of a bitch. And the public, damn, the public should know! Maybe not about Ed himself, but about last night. And that piece in the paper isn't going to do it, either.

Bill stood up and came to a decision. He was going to

give Ed a day, that was it, a day, then he wanted him to tell it like it was. And he was going to tell him so in a few short hours, at the charity function they were both attending at the Met. Jesus, he really hated opera, all the fat broads and Viking costumes.

Bill ran the blade over his other cheek, pleased with himself for having made what he thought was the right decision.

He pulled back from the mirror a little and reached for his styptic pencil.

"Fucking self-sacrifice," he muttered. "Jesus, if I never see another drop of blood again. . . ."

Sam Sturgess slammed the phone down. "Son of a bitch!" he said.

"Crawling out of the woodwork, huh?" another reporter said.

Sam glanced at him, then looked back at the phone. It was ringing again. *Jesus,* he thought, *it hasn't stopped ringing since the story hit the goddamn streets.* "You want to take this?" he said to the other reporter.

"No way, pal. This is your baby, you change it."

Sam snapped up the receiver. "Yeah?" he said.

"So is this the last of the great vampire hunters?"

"Harry, did you get that information?"

"Sure did. That limo I saw is registered to something called the Anglo-American Arts Foundation. It's got offices in the Empire State Building. As for the woman, her name's Emily Kane. Looked her up in the book. A doctor of psychiatry. As far as what they stuffed into that limo, well, it could have been an artifact, but from where I was standing, it sure looked like a body dressed up to look like a vampire."

Silence, at least within a few feet of Sam's desk.

"You're sure?"

"Hell no, I'm not sure. I was a long ways away and there

wasn't a lot of light, but you got my closest guess. Here's the kicker, though, Sam. The coup de grâce, as they say. There were a couple other guys there, too. One of them I recognized right off, being the avid reader that I am."

"Who, Harry? C'mon—"

"Ray Timmerson, Sam. And the other guy—this is gonna knock your drawers down to your knees, so if there are any women—"

"Get to it, dammit!"

"The other guy was Bobby All, Sam. Your old pal Bobby All."

Sam remembered when he investigated the events in Hunt, New York—Bobby All and Martin, and he had asked Judd Lucas a long list of questions. He hadn't gotten anywhere, but he'd left town with a very sour taste in his mouth and a very firm belief in vampires. Now Harry was telling him that Bobby All was in town. The focus of his earlier investigation was right here, hobnobbing with the upper crust. Well, fate had puckered up and smacked him a good one. And Harry, good old Harry, who had helped him with his earlier investigation, was due a bonus for this.

But what the hell was Bobby All doing here, in New York City? And why was he hanging around a psychiatrist and a writer, and why were they transporting a body in a limo? This had Pulitzer written all over it.

"I got a Franklin with your name on it, pal," he said. "Good work, Harry, damn good work. Uh, you didn't follow the limo—"

"You're not going to believe this, I tried to follow them, but my new BMW wouldn't crank."

"That's okay, Harry, I've still got that Franklin. Keep in touch, okay?"

Sam hung up, the name Kane on his lips. He pulled the phone book out of a drawer and found both names. David Kane and his Anglo-American Arts Foundation, and Emily

Kane. He tried David first, got a recording, then hung up and looked up Emily's number again.

KANE, EMILY, PhD

· DEPRESSION—ANXIETY

· DEPENDENCY—LONELINESS

· ADULT PSYCHOTHERAPY
Clinical Psychiatrist. NYS License.

He dialed the number. A woman answered.

"Dr. Kane, my name is Sam Sturgess. I write for the *Herald.*"

"What do you want?"

He had a smile in his voice. "I want you to explain what you were doing with Bobby All."

"Bobby All? What are you talking about?"

"It's true, isn't it, Doctor? It's true. I can hear it in your voice. You were seen, Doctor, you and Ray Timmerson and your father. The limo was registered to him. Now, you want to tell me everything, or do I just write the story as I see it?"

"Look, I don't know what the hell you're talking about. No responsible paper—"

"Hey, Doc, this is the *Herald.* Responsible journalism and the *Herald?* C'mon! But I'll tell you what, I'm gonna give you a chance to tell your side. I've waited this long to tell the world about Bobby All, I guess I can wait to get all the facts."

She had to stop him from writing the story, even if it was only the *Herald.* They had to get rid of Martin quietly and let this thing defuse just as quietly. "Okay, I'm not saying there's any truth to what you say, but I will meet with you, just to set the record straight. I don't want you coming here, and I don't want to go there. Why don't I meet you somewhere?"

"Okay. The Met's putting on something called *Cavalleria Rusticana*. Starts about eight. How will I know you?"

Emily thought a moment, then said, "I'll have one of Ray's books with me."

"A good writer. I've read all his books. Eight sharp. Be there or I just go ahead with what I've got, and believe me, I've got a lot. I'll be waiting outside."

Thirty

Ray pulled over and compared the address Bobby had given him with the address on the mailbox. A match.

"Here I am," he said. "Wish to hell I weren't."

He looked down the long driveway, at the cavernous ruts that peppered the road to the house, and decided to walk the rest of the way.

A canopy of cypress trees protected him from the late-afternoon sun during the two-hundred-yard walk, and he was glad for that. He was sweating enough as it was.

When he got close enough, he stopped and took everything in. The building itself was about eighteenth century. And it looked like it hadn't had any maintenance since then, either.

Shadowy grays dominated the two-story house, seen only through tall circling cypress, and there were full-length porches on both floors. A wide, slow-moving stream to Ray's right snaked toward the house without making a lot of babbling-brook noises.

When he got close enough, he was able to make out weird designs over each of the four windows on the front of the house, a series of odd, doll-shaped cutouts. Of course, whenever he heard the word "voodoo" the first thing he thought about were dolls and a few strategically placed pins.

He shook his head and smiled. *Maybe Bobby had sent him on a wild-goose chase. And why the hell not? What did he care? Christ, Ray, to put your trust in someone like that! You should have your goddamned head examined!*

He heard chickens and saw a garage when he got closer. The door to the garage was open, a black car inside covered by a thick layer of dust.

He stepped onto the porch and rapped on the screen. The chickens scattered to the treeline as soon as knuckles hit wood.

Eight o'clock arrived warm and dry. People lingered on the steps of the Met in small bands, satin and silk lightly reflecting the glittering chandeliers.

Sam Sturgess stood on the third step up, a slightly pained expression on his thin, bearded face. If he was lucky, maybe he could interview both Emily Kane and the mayor. Lawrence's limo would be pulling up soon anyway, and he most definitely wanted to hear what he had to say about the article.

He looked around. Apparently, a few people knew what he was up to. So what? They'd read the article and they knew his face. They could whisper and point all they wanted because when he finally did confront Lawrence, he couldn't just brush him off. He'd have to at least say something.

The mayor's limo pulled up at about the same time Sturgess saw Emily. He glanced at Lawrence, standing on the curb and primping, straightening a godawful flowered tie and smoothing down what little hair he had left. His wife stood next to him. She had on a blue gown.

A simple choice, Sturgess thought. *The big news is standing over there dressed in a tan shift and black pumps, one of Timmerson's books in her hand and a real worried look on her face. Hizzoner can wait.*

Sturgess gestured to Emily as they started up the steps.

Emily smiled wanly.

"Let's not talk here," he said. "Over there, by the band-shell."

Out of the corner of his eye he watched Lawrence and Kranepool bound up the steps to the Met. *Not together,* he thought. *Well, isn't that interesting?*

"Mr. Sturgess," Emily said, "I don't know what you saw, or what you think you saw, but I do know that I don't want my professional name dragged through the mud by your newspaper. If you do that, you'll get a lawsuit slapped on you that'll make you think corporal punishment is just a kiss on the cheek. I'll ruin you, Mr. Sturgess. You and your newspaper. Do we understand each other?"

Sturgess knew a bluff when he heard one, and Emily Kane was definitely bluffing. "Dr. Kane, we've been sued before and we'll get sued again. You see, when there's news, we print it. It's that simple. Now, I'm not going to tell you we'll go easy on this, because as far as I'm concerned, it's big, really big. But I will let you tell your side. That's the least I can do."

The stage manager, a dapper and tall man pushing fifty, had the look of a cornered fox. "Where is my Lola?" he said. "Has anyone seen my Lola?"

The assembled, all in costume and waiting for the over-ture to start, didn't have a clue. They had a large cast to-night, most of them villagers. The opera itself was set in the mid-1800s and the villagers wore the bright Italian peas-ant dress of the period.

The opera's guest star, Cecile Seine-Boothman, hadn't ar-rived yet and the opera was supposed to begin in fifteen minutes. "Has anyone seen Miss Seine-Boothman? Please!" the stage manager pleaded.

Not only did no one know where she was; they didn't care, either. She wasn't exactly beloved. "Pain in the butt" was a phrase that really got a workout at the Met, and no one would feel too badly if she'd twisted an ankle or maybe gotten run over by a taxi. It'd give the understudy a chance, they'd say.

But just when it appeared they'd get their wish, in walked the star, moving slowly, precisely, blamelessly, as if she still had an hour to get ready.

"Ah, there you are," the stage manager said with a smile. "We were beginning to worry."

"Worry keeps you on your toes," Cecile said.

Myron's smile wilted.

"This is neither the time nor the place," Ed Lawrence said. "I came here to enjoy myself, do you understand?"

They were in the men's room. Bill had half-dragged Ed in there a couple of minutes earlier. There was an attendant on duty, an old man who only looked half asleep. He made a few dollars selling gossip to the local scandal sheets. He knew when to listen.

Bill Kranepool swallowed hard. On the way here he had made a commitment to himself. Ed was not going to bully him. He was the chief-of-police, the public standard bearer, not Ed Lawrence, and if he thought the public should know about what had really happened, then he would see to it that they found out.

"And I hope you enjoy yourself," Bill said. "But I feel it is my duty to tell you that if you don't go public with what happened, I will." *Good, Bill, keep it formal, on the up and up. Let him know—*

"You what, Billy?" Ed said evenly, the tiniest of smiles on his mouth.

"I said, Your Honor, that if you don't tell them, I will personally see to it that the public knows about what happened. Don't forget, I am chief-of-police, and according to the law—"

"You're right, Billy. The public *should* know about what

happened. Tomorrow, first thing in the morning. We'll see what we can do about getting to the bottom of this then. How's that?"

Relief washed over Bill Kranepool. He'd been willing to risk his job, and now, by God, he didn't have to.

He reached a hand out to Ed and the two men shook on it. Then they went back to their wives.

The bathroom attendant waited a minute or so, then put an OUT OF ORDER sign on the door, went to a phone, and called the person he thought should know about the conversation.

A waiting room? Ray thought. *Incredible!*

A very short, very black woman dressed in colors bright enough to guide the blind had let him in a little earlier. "Who are you and what do you want?" she'd said.

Not knowing what else to do, Ray showed her Bobby's letter of referral. The woman read it like she was reading the phone book—very unconcerned—then opened the door and let him in. "Follow me, please," she said. "Lenora is busy now, but we have some magazines. Do you like *American Farmer?*"

She took him down a long dark hall to a large, paneled room. Not a window anywhere and a smell that combined sweat, animal droppings, and moldy wood, a real holiday for the nose. There was a crucifix on the wall and magazines were piled onto a coffee table, *American Farmer* included; there were also a few ancient *Sports Illustrated*s.

Six people, each of them as black as the woman who'd answered the door, sat on plain wooden chairs around the room. One man had something inside a wicker basket making noises like a mouse caught in a vacuum cleaner. Ray smiled at him and the man smiled back.

Ray watched the woman leave, then sat down next to a young and pretty woman breast-feeding her baby. He looked into faces, and everyone he looked at looked back at him.

That had been four hours ago, and over that time everyone had been taken care of except him. He looked through all the magazines, he even searched for someone who could move him up in the pecking order. All he found were two very large men who'd politely asked him what he was doing. "Waiting, that's all, just waiting," he told them.

For what, though? he asked himself now. He hadn't seen anyone for at least an hour. What the hell were they waiting for? Foul-smelling place! Jesus, how'd he let himself get roped into this? Voodoo, vampires. Ten minutes, he decided, he'd give them another ten minutes, and then he was outta here.

"Isn't she supposed to be inside the village church?" the mayor's wife said.

Ed knew this opera—they usually combined it with *I Pagliacci*. Not tonight, though. The guest singer, he'd heard, had stipulated in her contract that it not be combined.

"Tell you what, Sharon, I'll certainly be glad when this is over. She's not in very good voice tonight."

"Yes, I noticed that. Pity. Such a wonderful opera."

The fact that Miss Seine-Boothman had not joined the others for the church scene did not go unnoticed by the more astute patrons. There were quite a few whispered comments. Choreography plainly dictated that she be surrounded by peasants and inside the church for this particular aria. The storyline didn't make a lot of sense otherwise.

Sharon Lawrence leaned toward her husband. "Someone said something to her," she said.

"Stage manager, probably."

"Good, there she goes."

Cecile Seine-Boothman moved hesitantly toward the church set.

"Yeah, she's going, but not very willingly," Ed said.

"Would you be quiet, please!" a man behind them hissed.

Ed turned and smiled and the man, recognizing who he was, apologized.

A young woman who had a five-year goal to be an understudy, but who now was just part of the village peasant cast, noticed it first. Miss Seine-Boothman, tall and beautiful and very self-assured, suddenly looked frightened. And her voice had started to crack.

"Oh, God," the young woman muttered. "What's happening to her?"

By now, everyone knew that something was terribly wrong with their guest star. Her gaze darted from one villager to the next and her singing had gone completely south.

It didn't take long for the crowd noise to drown out her singing altogether.

"What the hell?" the mayor said. He shot to his feet. Two rows down, Bill Kranepool did the same. They looked at each other briefly, just seconds before Miss Seine-Boothman filled the hall with a discordant and agonized scream that seemed to paralyze everyone.

The would-be understudy, as afraid as anyone, screamed right along with the star, and within seconds, members of the audience joined the chorus, their screams continuing until Miss Seine-Boothman herself stopped screaming and stumbled off the stage, lurching past stagehands and the stage manager and then disappearing altogether, leaving only confusion in her wake.

Thirty-one

For the last twenty minutes, Sturgess had been talking to Emily about his investigation in Hunt, New York. His story had come full circle, to Harry and what he'd seen around the Empire State Building. He wanted her to fill in the details. He wanted her to tell him about what they had spirited away in the middle of the night, shortly after the crowd around the Empire State Building had dispersed. Suddenly, she shifted her gaze. Sturgess saw the surprise on her face and turned. "What the hell?" he said. He glanced at his watch. "It's still got an hour, at least an hour. What the hell . . . ?"

He saw the mayor and the chief-of-police. The mayor's wife was with him. "Don't leave," he said to Emily. Then he ran off toward the crowd.

The mayor's limo pulled up just as Sturgess got to him. "Mr. Mayor, why are you leaving? What's going on?" he yelled, as he glanced around—lots of people crowding around, getting in the way. Noise and speculation, none of it coherent. An insane moment on the steps of the Met.

The mayor and everyone with him got into the limo and left, and Sturgess didn't have a word on his notepad.

Sturgess watched the car pull away. "Shit!" he mumbled. A man nudged him. "Hey, what the hell's going on?" he said to the man. "Where's everyone going?"

The man turned and looked at him and pushed his glasses back onto his nose. "There was an incident," he said.

"What kind of incident?"

"Miss Seine-Boothman became ill. You didn't see?"

Sturgess shook his head.

"Well, as I said, she became ill—"

"Yeah, yeah. She throw up? What? Fall down?"

"Sir, who are you?"

"Press."

"I see. Well, I was in back, so . . . she screamed. She lost her voice—"

"I think we should ask for our money back," the woman with him said.

"Yes, dear. Anyway, she screamed, that's all. In my professional opinion, I'd have to say she suffered a nervous breakdown."

"It was during the church scene," the woman said. "Miss Boothman hesitated outside the church. She wasn't supposed to do that, you see, and when she went inside, she . . . well, as my husband indicated, she became ill."

"Now, if you'll excuse us," the man said.

"Wait, where'd she go? Where is she now?"

"I'm sure I don't know. Now, if you please."

"Damn! Sorry."

Sturgess saw Emily out of the corner of his eye. "Did you hear that?" he said.

"Yeah. So?"

"Doctor Kane, I've done research, you wouldn't believe . . . Vampires and churches don't mix, Doctor, that's what I learned. Vampires usually go insane inside a church. It's the good-and-evil thing."

"You know, when I was a kid, I usually got sick inside a church, too," Emily said. "I think it was a combination of fasting and poor lighting. You don't suppose she missed a meal, do you? And, you know, come to think of it, singers usually *do* fast before they perform. Did you know that?"

"Doctor, people usually just faint when they go without

eating. They don't often scream and run off. That takes energy."

Emily could only look at him. "S'cuse me," she said, and lost herself in the crowd.

The woman who'd shown Ray to the waiting room reappeared. She had a sandwich on a plate, ham-and-cheese. She pushed the plate toward him. "Lenora sends her apologies, Mr. Timmerson. She thought you might be hungry."

Ray looked at the sandwich. Sure, he was hungry, but the smell in here didn't exactly stimulate his appetite. The sandwich looked pretty good, though. He took a bite. "Guess this means she won't be seeing me anytime soon, huh?" he said.

The woman smiled. "Your patience is admirable," she said.

"And growing short."

The woman left and Ray was alone. He looked at his watch. It was a little before ten.

"What a night," Ed said.

"That poor woman," his wife said. "What do you think happened to her?"

"Wish I knew."

Ed and Sharon were in their bedroom, getting ready for bed. It was almost midnight. The phone hadn't stopped ringing since they'd returned home, so he took it off the hook.

"Look, I'm gonna have a nightcap. Care to join me?" he asked.

"Ed, you know you don't sleep well when you drink before bedtime. And tomorrow's going to be a very busy day for you. I think, well, for tonight at least, you should forgo a drink."

"Yeah, you're probably right," Ed said. "Damn, I just remembered."

"What?"

"Morgan's still in his ball."

Morgan was their grandson's hamster. They were taking care of him while Ed's son and his family were on vacation. Morgan's ball was a hollowed-out soccer ball-sized chunk of plastic with a screw-on cap. Once inside, Morgan was a prisoner. But he also had the run of the house, at least wherever he could roll his ball to. Their grandson got a real kick out of watching Morgan smack into things, as did Ed.

"Oh, leave him," Sharon said. "He falls asleep in that thing all the time, anyway."

Ed considered doing that, but poor Morgan had been in there for the last eight hours with no water and nothing to eat. "It won't take a minute," Ed said.

Sharon crawled under the covers, just a sheet tonight. "Suit yourself," she said.

Ed stepped into his slippers and padded down the stairs and into his study, a dark-paneled dungeon of a room toward the back of the rambling Gracie Mansion.

Morgan had rolled his ball into a corner.

"My deepest apologies," Ed said, as he picked up the ball. He winced at the smell.

Morgan looked back at him, his tiny head bobbing up and down from weakness, his pinpoint eyes reflecting the light like lasers.

"Chad would never forgive me if something happened to you," Ed said to the hamster.

He opened the cage, then put the ball inside and took the lid off. Morgan wandered out, his nose working furiously. It took him only a few seconds to find his food, placed inside half an egg carton.

Ed heard the doorbell ring. *Probably just the press,* he thought. They couldn't get him on the phone, so they actually had the nerve to come to the house.

He left his study, went to the front door, and looked through the peephole.

No one there.

"Who is it?" he snapped. "It's late, dammit!"

"Mr. Mayor, it's me, Chris."

"Chris? What the—"

She moved. Ed could see her through the peephole. "Look, I know it's late," she said, "but . . . can I come in?"

Funny, Ray thought, *how people who practice voodoo are also so devout.* Where had he read that? Trouble, of course, was that Roman Catholicism was important to each rite of voodoo, even the sacrifices. *Here, God, here's a fat young woman, now help me with my mortgage payment.*

Ray looked at the crucifix again, into the eyes of Christ. He looked away, feeling somewhat like an interloper.

He fidgeted, crossing and uncrossing his legs and trying to shake the feeling that someone was watching him. *Where the hell is she,* he wondered, *and why the hell are they making me wait like this?* Another glance at his watch. Three minutes to twelve. Three more minutes, that's all he'd give her.

The door opened and a tall black woman dressed in cut-off jeans and a red halter top came into the room. She didn't look at Ray, she just sat down next to him.

Ray looked at her. *Extraordinary,* he thought. Her skin was the color of chocolate and flawless, and her features were perfect. She looked like a life-sized ceramic doll. She had on a pair of hoop earrings the size of silver dollars, and her hair was cut short.

"Lenora?" he said, after the silence stretched longer than he felt comfortable with.

She touched her fingers to his lips and smiled. "Shhh," she said, just loudly enough to be heard. "Be still a moment, Ray Timmerson. Be still and let me take you in."

Ray shrugged. He'd waited this long, he could wait a little longer.

It was precisely midnight when Lenora finally spoke to him again.

"Tell me why Bobby has sent you."

During the last six hours, Ray had worked hard on what he was going to say to her when they finally met. What he *did* say didn't even come close to what he'd *wanted* to say. "Martin, that's why. He's gotta be stopped. Bobby thought you could help."

"Stop Martin? Stop him from doing what, Ray?"

She seemed amused.

"Look, I gotta ask you right out. Did you . . . oh, Jesus, is it really possible—"

"To restore ashes to life?"

A mind-reader.

"Yeah! Is it?"

She looked at the crucifix on the wall, a smile of great satisfaction on her mouth. "There was a time when I would have said no to that question, Ray, but that was before I became a mambo. That time has long passed."

Ray hadn't really wanted to hear that. "How's that possible, though? It just doesn't make sense."

She looked at him, her expression unchanged. "Such knowledge can not be gained simply by asking. There is a price. There is always a price."

Ray smiled and fumbled out his wallet. "Thought so," he said. "How much?"

Lenora chuckled lightly and put her hand on his wallet. "A white man, like yourself, it is rare, very rare. You will become an initiate."

"Initiate? Uh-uh, sorry, lady. Just give me whatever it is I need, that's all you gotta do. Then I'm outta here."

"I'm afraid that's impossible, Ray. As I said, the information you desire comes with a price. Your initiation is that price."

For Ray, the word "initiation" conjured up images of streaking campus cuties and taking a bath in pig shit. This

initiation wouldn't be anything like that, but an initiation
was still only an initiation. As long as they didn't hurt him,
and as long as it didn't take very long, he could probably
handle it.

He sucked in a breath and let it out. "When? Now?"

"I suppose we could start now."

"Great. How long? A couple hours, maybe? And what
do I gotta do?"

"No, Ray. It takes a week."

"A week! You gotta be kidding! Sorry, that's impossible,
not to mention I'm not gonna do it. A week? Jesus . . ."
He looked at her and sighed. "Can't you give me an abbreviated version, or something?"

Ray had expected a compromise, three days at the outside, maybe four. What she said confused him.

"Till morning, then. Then I will provide you the information you need. Agreed?"

Ray's answer didn't come quickly. *She had been in a big
hurry to appease him. Why?*

"What do I have to do?" he said.

"Lie on a cot, that's all."

Ray smiled. "C'mon, lady, I'm not stupid."

"There's more, but that would spoil the surprise."

"And when it's over, I'll be able to just get up and walk
away, right? I won't be harmed in any way?"

"No."

A night, Ray thought. Till the sun came up, then he'd be
on that plane back to civilization with whatever he needed.
"Okay," he agreed.

Lenora took his hand into her own and stood up. "Come
with me, then," she said.

Ray went with her reluctantly, but also with a writer's
sense of wonder.

Once outside, they walked through the backyard to a
small motorboat pulled onto the shore of a large marshy
area. The night was black and still, alive with the sounds

of mosquitoes and frogs. Ray thought about the Louisiana bayou: Cypress trees rising from the swamp, leafy dark branches drooping like huge capes. An oily sweat rose on his forehead.

"Where are we going?" he said, as he climbed into the boat and sat down. He wished to hell he could see better. Then again he wondered if he really wanted to see what was in here with him.

"You'll see," Lenora said. "There is one thing, though. From now until morning, you will speak only when spoken to. That is part of the initiation. Do you understand? Nod if you do."

Ray nodded and Lenora pulled the cord and started the motor.

Thirty-two

Emily went over the precautions she had taken: strings of garlic around her door, holy water on the nightstand, a crucifix around her neck. She didn't know if these traditional measures would really protect her from her father and the others, but they were all she had.

She sat up in bed, waking up Beta in the process. He looked at her, his eyes catching what little light came through her open window.

"How you doin', pal?" she said.

Beta squeezed his eyes shut and purred.

"Not too many troubles, huh? Wish I could say the same."

The phone rang then; she let the machine answer it. "Hi, this is Dr. Emily Kane. I can't get to the phone right now, but if you'll leave a message after the beep, I'll get back to you as soon as I can. Thanks."

"Emily, this is Bobby. I was wondering if you'd heard from Ray. I ask because I think I have a line on Martin. Give me a call at 555-2245."

Emily hustled out of bed and picked up the phone before Bobby could hang up.

"Bobby? Are you—"

"Oh—you're there—"

"What was it you were saying about Martin?"

"I'd rather tell you in person."

"When will you be here?"

"Within the hour."

"I'll be waiting."

Emily hung up and went to the window. While she looked out at Central Park, she heard another scream, very similar to the ones she'd heard earlier, and she instantly started thinking about—of all things—the Nazi occupation of Poland. How much longer did they have, she wondered. Days? Maybe hours?

At about twelve-thirty, Ray saw a building loom from the darkness. At about the same time, Lenora turned the boat toward land and toward the building.

It sat on a small knoll, and from here at the water's edge, Ray saw what he thought was a steeple, the dark point spearing the night sky.

"A church?" he asked.

"Quiet!" Lenora ordered.

After they got out of the boat, they walked up a slight incline toward the small white church. Lenora led the way, using a well-worn path that snaked through the underbrush.

"Damn mosquitoes," Ray mumbled. If only he had a nickel for each bite . . .

Lenora stopped when they got to the church. "Go in and make your confession," she said.

"My confession? But I'm not even Catholic."

"That doesn't matter, you still have a black soul. The confessional is on the right."

A black soul? Ray thought. *What is it with religious types?* He opened the door anyway and went inside.

A wave of candles near the altar cast a buttery, inconstant glow throughout the interior, onto the stations of the cross that ran down each side and onto a statue of Christ that rose above the altar.

Ray saw someone go into the confessional. *The priest,*

he thought. *A voodoo priest.* He swore he could hear the pitter-patter of little feet. *Rats, probably.*

Wishing to hell that this was all behind him, Ray stepped into the confessional and sat down. As soon as he did, the small door between him and the priest slid open. He could barely discern an outline through the wicker screen.

"What are your sins, my son?" A gentle but firm voice.

My sins, Ray thought. Well, that would take some thought. It probably didn't matter what he said, though. "Well, Father, I swore, let me see, five times last week, and I had prurient thoughts at least twelve times—"

"Do not make light of our ways, Mr. Timmerson." A little less gentle now.

Jesus, what the hell do these people want? "Sorry. Let me try again . . ."

"I'm listening, my son."

Ray said what he thought the priest wanted to hear and when he was done, he was told to say ten "Our Fathers" and a like number of "Hail Marys" for his penance. "But remember," the priest added, "you must pray in silence."

"No problem."

Ray left the confessional, sat in the closest pew, and leaned forward onto the kneeler. He didn't recite his penance, he just sat there long enough to make it look as if he had.

After a suitable time, he made the sign of the cross just in case someone was looking, and went outside. Lenora was waiting.

"I am told you made a good confession," she said. "Now it is time for your bath."

Before he could say anything, Lenora took him by the hand and led him back to the boat. Ten minutes later, they pulled onto shore again.

After a short walk through the underbrush, they stopped at a mudhole no bigger than a wading pool. There were a few huts close by. The embers of a dying fire glowed like feral eyes near the entrance to one hut. Ray thought he heard talking—chanting, maybe—inside. *God, I'm sweating like Secretariat.*

"Take your clothes off," Lenora said. She was all white teeth and eyes in the dark.

Ray balked. People were born naked and too many of them died that way, too.

Lenora sighed. "You may leave your underwear on, if you wish," she said, "but you'll only get them dirty."

They looked at each other for a moment, then Ray stripped entirely and waited, covering himself with his hands.

"Sit down," Lenora said, nodding toward the mudhole.

With his mind's eye, Ray saw his body covered by leeches or whatever else called a Florida mudhole home. Again he balked.

"Go on," Lenora said, "it's safe."

Ray looked closely at her, wishing he could see the expression on her face better. He had to trust someone, though, and he didn't have too many choices.

Reluctantly, he stepped into the mudhole, sloshed into the waist-deep middle, then sat down. Before his butt even touched ground, he let go with a sigh of pleasure. He'd heard about mud baths and how good they could feel, but he never thought it would be orgasmic. *The heat,* he thought. *Sitting down in this mud is like jumping into a cold shower on a hot July day in the city.*

Two women appeared from the bushes then, but Ray hardly noticed. Let them get their own mudhole.

They started chanting—Ray did notice that. *Hymns,* he thought. *Nice voices, too.* Something fell on his chest. He picked it up. A leaf, sweetly scented and tiny. A shower of leaves fell on him and Ray thought about dream images and the afterglow of sex. He could handle this kind of initiation any day of the week. And the lying down part, God, he was really going to like that. He was beginning to feel a little tired anyway. Waiting around always made him tired.

He lay back against the side of the mudhole, a whisper of a smile on his mouth, and closed his eyes.

Seconds later he saw something on the dark lids of his eyes: a small boy with an eye gouged out. Nothing there but black space rimmed by scar tissue.

Sam Sturgess looked up at what he thought had to be Emily's apartment, the only one lit. It was just a dull glow, almost like a night light.

He checked her box number and rang the bell. His plan was simple enough—just keep bugging her until she cracked.

The door buzzer sounded and Sturgess felt a little anxious. She'd opened the door without so much as a "Who's there?"

He went up the stairs to her apartment and knocked on the door. It opened seconds later.

"You?" Emily said. "I thought . . . *get out!*"

"Wait a second, just hear me out."

Emily looked past him and down the hall.

"Waiting for someone?" Sturgess asked.

"No, of course not—"

"Then why'd you just let me in without asking who I was?"

She had to get rid of him before Bobby arrived, but if she made him leave, they just might run into each other. She had no choice. "Get in here."

Sturgess stepped into the apartment. "That for him?" he said.

Emily lifted the cross off her neck and looked at it. "It's just a cross—"

"You weren't wearing it earlier. You're waiting for Bobby All, aren't you, Dr. Kane?" He looked past her, at the door. "Garlic, huh? New decorating tip?" She saw him look at the vial of holy water. "Armed to the teeth. Pretty convincing."

Emily didn't say anything, but just took the string of garlic down, lumped it together with her cross and the holy water, and then put everything in a kitchen drawer while Sturgess watched. As soon as she closed the drawer, the doorbell rang again.

"Dammit!" she whispered. "Into the closet, quick, get into the closet!"

Sturgess didn't move and the bell rang again.

"Didn't you hear me? Get in the closet!"

This time Sturgess did as he was told, leaving the door open a couple of inches.

Emily switched on the intercom. "Hello?" she said.

"It's me."

"Come on up."

"There's someone with me."

"Someone with you?"

"Cynthia. I told you about her, remember?"

"Is she a vampire, too?" Emily almost blurted.

"Does your invitation extend to her as well?" Bobby said.

Invitation? Emily thought. *Jesus, she is a vampire!* "Of course, sure, I'm looking forward . . . let me get the door. Hang on." *Christ, I hope I don't sound as nervous as I really am.*

About thirty seconds later, she heard a knock at her door. She glanced at the closet, saw it was open slightly. She rushed over and pushed it closed. "Keep it shut!" she whispered.

No answer.

"You hear me? Don't open this door!"

She went back to the front door and pulled it open. When she saw Cynthia, the first thing she thought about was someone stepping out of a week-old grave. Her skin was the color of milk, and there were huge dark circles under her eyes. And the eyes—the eyes—like emeralds lying in two feet of muddy water. Despite all that, Emily still managed a smile. Cynthia just looked at her.

"Come on in," she said, as she pulled the door open wide.

Cynthia looked at Bobby and he at her, but neither one moved.

"Is something wrong?" Emily asked.

"Garlic," Bobby said. He crossed his hands in front of him.

He probably wouldn't believe her if she told him it wasn't for him, just the others. Or would he?

A bead of sweat rose on her forehead and her mind raced. For some insane reason she remembered being in a school play in the third grade. She'd done a good job of acting back then. Could she do it again? "Pasta night," she said with a grin. "Linguine with garlic and tomatoes."

"Really?" Bobby said, studying her. "You didn't know our kind despises the smell of garlic?"

"No, I really didn't. I apologize. If I'd known—"

Bobby shrugged. "I suppose we can tolerate it for the time being. What do you think, Cynthia?"

Cynthia nodded lightly.

Bobby closed the door behind him and looked around the apartment. Then he said, "Cynthia lives in New York. She's been dreaming about Martin, or rather, she's been dreaming Martin's dreams."

Emily's gaze shifted from Bobby to Cynthia, then back to Bobby. "And that's how you got a line on Martin?"

"In her most recent dream, Cynthia detected the odor of what she thought was grease and makeup, which leads us to believe that they've hidden him—"

"In the theater district. Broadway. Am I right?"

"Exactly. But the theater district is very large, as you know. It won't be easy to find him."

Beta came into the room then and stretched. Being social.

"Then what are you going to do next?" Emily asked.

"Well, hopefully, Ray will be successful. And hopefully,

he'll be back soon. First we find Martin; then, when Ray comes back with Lenora's potion, we destroy him."

"That simple? Christ, it sounds too simple. They'll be guarding him, you know." She spoke very softly, hoping Sturgess couldn't hear them.

"Yes, I know. That'll make him easier to find."

By now Beta had moved around the furniture to a point between Emily and the closet. Emily could see the beginnings of a smile play at the corners of Cynthia's mouth as cat and vampire stared at each other.

"Is there anything I can do in the meantime?" Emily asked.

"Just let us know if you hear from Ray. You have the number?"

"Yeah. You'll let me know if you find him, right?"

"Of course."

Beta had shifted his attention to the closet. Emily watched as Cynthia, smiling now, moved toward him slowly, mumbling something about what a nice cat he was.

Christ, they're only about fifteen feet away, Sturgess thought. He had the door open a crack, just enough to see everyone. He saw something else, too. There was a mirror to his right, on a diagonal wall. Cynthia and Bobby should have reflected in that mirror. They didn't. Proof enough for anyone. He'd had nightmares, but he'd never been as scared as he got when the mirror didn't reflect. And now a vampire was moving toward him saying, "Here, kitty, kitty, kitty." *The cat! Jesus, the goddamned cat definitely knew he was in here. It was going to give him away!*

"What's his name?" Cynthia said. The cat was back on his haunches, his tail swishing.

Christ, Sturgess thought, *I could just reach out the door and pet him if I wanted to. If I could actually move!*

"Beta," Emily said.

Cynthia was within five feet of the closet now, and Beta even closer. Sturgess watched Cynthia squat down to pet him.

"Beta. What a lovely name," she said.

Sturgess swore he could hear his heart ramming against his ribs, and the sweat ran down his cheeks in rivers.

Then he realized something—the cat was purring. *Jesus,* he thought, *the goddamn cat's purring! A fucking vampire's gonna pick him up and he's fucking purring!*

Beta moved closer to the closet and rubbed his face against the door, pushing it within an inch of being closed.

"You keep his food in there?" Bobby said.

"Catnip ball," Emily said.

"I think he likes me, Bobby," Cynthia said.

"Cynthia's a cat lover," Bobby said to Emily. "Why don't you get that catnip ball and let him play with it? She likes that kind of thing."

Emily grinned stupidly.

Cynthia got up. Beta was only a few feet from the closet now. *Can she smell me?* Sturgess wondered. *Oh, God, she can! She can smell me!*

"I'd rather have him like me for me," Cynthia said, "not because I've got some drug."

Maybe if I caught her by surprise, Sam thought, his eyes working furiously as he tried to figure things out. He swiped at the sweat on his nose as he remembered the garlic and holy water. *And don't forget the cross, Sam. The cross is the thing you really need!* If he could just get to it, shove the door open and make a beeline. That's all he had to do.

He raised both hands, although not easily. Cynthia was only a few feet away now. He could smell the blood. If he could just knock her over, and then, in the confusion . . .

Cynthia picked up the cat. They looked at each other. Sturgess saw the back of Cynthia's head and he heard her say, "He likes me. Look, Bobby, he really does! I told you I didn't need that catnip."

His body filmed by sweat, Sam watched Cynthia move back to where she had been, next to Bobby, the cat in her arms snuggled there and happy.

"May I keep him?" Cynthia said, as she rubbed Beta behind the ears.

"Well, he's . . . sure. Why not? I've got more cats than I know what to do with anyway. He, uh, he likes Nine Lives."

Cynthia smiled coyly. "Don't we all?" she said, as she rubbed the cat against her face.

On the way out, Bobby said, "I'll be in touch. And remember, if you hear from Ray—"

"Yeah, I know, I'll call."

After they left, Sam Sturgess slid to the floor like molasses down a jar.

Thirty-three

Ray snapped his eyes open, hoping the boy with the missing eye would just go away, and not at all believing that he would. He was almost right. What he saw now wasn't quite as vibrant, more an afterimage than anything. The boy's outline seemed to pulse, as if it were backlit, and in place of his missing eye there was only a cavernous hole. He had his arms outstretched, beckoning, pleading.

But then the images faded and disappeared, leaving only the inky blackness of night and the fiery embers.

Sure, Ray thought, relieved, *an afterimage.* He'd just gotten a little carried away. And being as tired as he was . . .

The sweet smell of the leaves came back to him like someone barging into a room and his eyelids felt suddenly heavy, far too heavy to keep open.

"Wake up, Ray Timmerson, wake up!"

"Lenora?" Her voice had traveled an awfully long way to get to him.

"Wake up!"

Getting his eyes to open was like chipping away at a wall of granite with a feather. But he did finally manage to, and when he did, he saw one of the women standing next to him, with a white tunic spread wide; Cleopatra's slave girl with a towel. Or was that Marc Antony's?

"Get out," Lenora demanded. "You can imagine later."

Thankfully, his body wasn't nearly so heavy as his eyelids. He even felt a bounce in his step as he pushed himself to his feet and got out of the mudbath.

The woman with the tunic reached out and wrapped it around him. There was a drawstring in front. Ray tied a bow, then they took him into one of the huts. *Candles,* he thought. *So many damn candles.*

Lenora pointed at a simple white cot. "Sit down," she ordered.

Ray sat and watched by flickering candlelight while Lenora combined a variety of ingredients: mashed grains, wine-soaked bread, the blood of sacrificed fowl and animals. He had no idea what they were, but even from across the room he could smell the thing. He squinched his nose and Lenora smiled.

After she was done mixing, she wrapped the ingredients in sacred leaves, then dumped the concoction into a red kerchief.

He felt his eyes close again and seconds later the kerchief and everything inside was wrapped around his head. The smell had been bad enough from across the room; it was almost unbearable now. He made a grunting, disgusted noise and reached for the kerchief.

Lenora grabbed his wrist.

"Do not touch it!" she said. "If you take it off before the initiation is complete, the initiation will be over and you will be asked to leave. Is that clear? Nod if it is."

Ray sucked in a deep breath, realized how dumb that was, and nodded.

"Good," Lenora said, a smile in her voice. "Lie down on your left side."

Sleep right now, Ray thought, *would be a gift from God.* He lay down on his left side and waited, wondering what the hell was going to happen next.

He didn't wait long.

"Because this is—how did you put it?—an abbreviated initiation," Lenora said, "there are parts we will not do."

He heard a chicken squawk. He thought about death row. "And there are parts we will do."

He was positive he heard her chuckle.

He couldn't see her, but he knew she was only a few feet away. He turned his head a little, out of reflex, and as he did, he felt the chicken peck at his nose and lips.

He'd never moved as fast as he did then. He tore the wrapping off his head, threw it onto the dirt floor with a sickening splat, and jumped to his feet. "Okay, dammit, that's it!" he said. "I've put up with enough indignities to last a lifetime. Now you've got a goddamn chicken pecking at my goddamn face! No way, lady! No . . . fucking . . . way!"

Suddenly he felt light-headed. Standing was almost impossible. He plopped back down onto the cot. He could see Lenora in the candlelight glow; she had the chicken. He couldn't be sure, not swaying like he was, dizzy as he was, but he thought he saw her wring the chicken's neck and then pull its head off.

He couldn't even imagine what happened next; he could make out a few telltale sounds, though.

Lenora pulled a handful of feathers from the chicken's body, doused them in the chicken's *own* blood, crossed the room, and plastered the feathers against Ray's forehead with all the force of a healing evangelist. Chicken blood dripped into his eyes and Ray was as helpless as a wooden Indian.

She started reciting prayers: Paternoster, Ave Maria, the Credo, prayers for the mightiest God, the Catholic God. When she was done, she went on to psalms, and then, finally, to strict voodoo chants.

His senses reeled—with chicken blood in his eyes, voodoo chants he couldn't even begin to understand, the sour and coppery odor of blood. And everything he touched felt like rubber; his skin, the cot. *Drugs,* he thought remotely. *The leaves. Dear God, would he see the morning sun or was he going to die . . . ? This wasn't any initiation. They were going to sacrifice him to some goddamn voodoo god!* He saw himself lying on an altar, surrounded by voodoo priests. *Oh, God, why me, why me?* his mind screamed. What the hell had he done to deserve this?

Silence. Then, "Drink this, Ray. Drink it all. This will complete the job the leaves only started."

Ray saw a container being lifted to his mouth. He gestured feebly and tried to push it away. "Poison," he muttered.

"No, Ray. It's not poison."

The liquid, in a silver chalice, sloshed like molten metal.

"This is his body, Ray, and this is his blood. Take, drink, and see what you must see."

She spoke in hushed, almost reverent tones.

"No," Ray mumbled. "Poison."

"Take, drink." She moved the chalice close to his lips. "This is his blood that you have come for. Drink, Ray. Drink."

The chalice was cold on his mouth, the taste of blood sour. He felt a gag coming on and someone tipped his head back. The blood flowed freely now. It felt warm against his throat. There wasn't a lot, thankfully.

Ray expected that he'd have to stay on this cot for the rest of the night, that he'd have to endure a few visions the likes of which—in truth—he had conjured up with a few illicit drugs when he was working on one of his horror novels. But when he felt himself being lifted and then carried out of the hut and to the boat, he suspected that visions would be only part of what he would experience tonight.

He moaned when they put him in the boat, as they laid his head back against what he thought was a pillow, but was, in reality, only his shirt, rolled over. He could see the black, starlit night through breaks in the cypress as the boat puttered along.

Lenora looked down on him from the front of the boat.

In his stupefied condition her face looked like a reflection in a funhouse mirror; when she moved, she moved in stuttering bursts.

"What do you see, Ray?" she asked. "Tell Lenora what you see." Her voice was low, then high. It warbled, then it was constant.

Ray didn't see anything, just black sky and a few stars . . . wait. What was that? There was someone up there, in the top of the tree. He was sitting down and he was inside some kind of hut. Or a fort, maybe. A kid's fort. Sure, had to be. There was a poster of Rowdy Roddy Piper, and there was Hulk Hogan. Funny, Ray thought, how he could see the boy and everything around him like they were really there.

Out of the corner of his eye, he saw Lenora look at the same tree. "See something, do you, Ray?" she said. "You want to tell Lenora what you see, Ray? Sure you do."

He hadn't heard much; he was too interested in the boy. He looked anxious, like he was waiting for someone. *Probably one of the members of the MTD,* Ray thought, *whatever the hell that is.* He tried to shift positions when he thought about the MTD, when he didn't know why he'd thought about it.

The boy got up then, took a long swig of beer from what looked like a quart container, wiped his mouth with his sleeve, mumbled something Ray didn't understand, then crossed to the door and opened it.

And there was Martin. Whole and animated and grinning and wearing that same stupid vampire suit with the black skull buttons. "Food, need food!" he said gruffly. Apparently the boy heard the same thing, because he backed away quickly—too quickly. He fell down, reaching out with his skinny arms to catch himself, his eyes as big as an owl's. Martin came inside then, still muttering something about needing food. But then, just as Martin bent to the boy, the image faded, then disappeared, and the boy's screams retreated into nothingness.

Ray didn't know if he was happy or sad that he didn't

see what Martin did to the boy, but he didn't have a lot of time to work through that because by the time they got to where they were going, Ray had seen a host of visions, some vile, some not. A few were actually pleasant.

"You wanted to know how Martin was restored from ashes, now you will find out," Lenora said.

She helped him to his feet and together they moved through the woods for what Ray thought was a very long time, Lenora walking, Ray stumbling and shambling and just doing what he could to put one foot in front of the other. He had no real sense of the present, no sense of being anywhere. And when Lenora spoke, her words still had that inconstant, broken record quality.

But he knew very well where they were once they reached their destination. They were in a backwoods graveyard, and although his ability to comprehend was minimal, he saw that it was a very small, very old graveyard and that the caskets were all above ground.

Morning, New York City

Mayor Ed Lawrence turned and looked at his wife. She looked back at him and smiled. Then he reached out and stroked her cheek, as he had done every morning for many years. This time she responded a little differently. She didn't wrap his wrist and moan lightly, pleased at his gentle touch. This time her head hinged back because her neck was broken.

"Necessary, I'm afraid," Ed told her. "We gave you a choice and you chose death. Pity."

Across the room, Chris Gedney parted the drapes slightly, then pulled them closed again. "Not a cloud in sight," she said.

"What?" Ed asked.

"It's going to be sunny today. I'd suggest you take an umbrella to work with you."

"Won't that look strange?"

"Ed, your skin was always very sensitive to bright sunlight. I'm sure no one would notice. We don't want to take chances. We'll be going ahead with the plans soon, and you're the man who can keep the authorities off our backs. We don't want anything happening to you, now, do we?"

"I suppose not."

Ed got out of bed.

"You want me to take care of Sharon?" Chris asked.

"No," Ed said. "It's the least I can do. We were married a very long time, you know."

"Yes."

"Oh, you said that Bill—"

"Yes, last night. Into the fold, so to speak."

Ed grinned. "Great. Think I'll take a shower. Oh, this scab." He rubbed his neck. "It'll go away, won't it?"

"In time."

"What do I do in the meantime?"

Chris shrugged. "Keep your shirt buttoned."

Tampa, Florida

Ray was awakened by the same hissing sound he'd heard the day before. This time, the same man he had seen the day before, the man with the wicker basket, sat to his right. The other chairs in the room were taken, too. It was over. He was alive and it was over. He was back in the waiting room.

Then he remembered his dream . . . or hallucination—whatever. He'd been a cannibal. He had eaten and enjoyed human flesh. There had been a basement room and he had been lying on a cot. There were people in the room with him—children, mostly, except for a dead woman with rats around her, nibbling . . . and he remembered what Lenora said about how Martin had been restored . . .

"Good morning."

Lenora was in the doorway, a cup of steaming coffee in her hand. Ray could only look at her.

"You will be leaving today?" she asked.

Leaving?

"Ray? Will you be leaving today?"

"What? Yes. Today. But what—"

"Martin's blood, of course. You drank Martin's blood. We saved some and you drank it. It will help you find him. He is in your veins now, you and he are . . . blood brothers. Sorry, my sense of humor—"

"Oh, God, I'm not—"

"A vampire? No. As a matter of fact, Martin's blood should act like a vaccine."

"But what about when we find him? What then?"

Lenora nodded at the chair to Ray's left. There was a container of Morton's salt on it. He picked it up.

"Salt? I don't understand."

"Touch it to Martin's lips when you find him. He is, essentially, a zombie. Salt on the lips of a zombie will kill him. Have a nice trip back, Ray."

Ray shot to his feet. "You put me through all that and all I needed was a pinch of salt?"

Lenora smiled, pleased with herself. "Yes, that's all. Now, go. I'm sure there are people waiting for you. And already we have heard news reports, even down here. People are dying in New York City, Ray. Lots of people. You'd better run off and save them."

She went back through the door, laughing like a mad-woman. The others in the room seemed oblivious, as if this kind of thing went on all the time.

Ray picked up his container of salt, ascribing some re-mote secret power to it—surely it wasn't *just* salt—and left.

Thirty-four

VAMPYRUS! the headline screamed. The word took up half the page.

"Incredible," Ray whispered. "How in the world . . . ?"

"Buck and a half, pal," a man behind the news counter said.

Ray dug into his pocket and took out a wad of bills, folded out a five, put it on the counter, and sat on the nearest bench, not bothering to pick up his change. His plane had arrived at JFK just fifteen minutes earlier.

The byline belonged to Sam Sturgess. "Vampyrus," Ray muttered, shaking his head. "Where the hell'd you come up with that term?" The print in the story was so large, Ray didn't have to put on his reading glasses to read the story.

Take a careful look at the person next to you, Mr. and Mrs. New Yorker. That person could be infected. He could be a vampire!

As we all know, there has lately been a marked increase in the crime rate, murder especially. Cases of missing persons have risen dramatically as well. Just last night, at the Met, famed lyric soprano Cecile Seine-Boothman ran from the stage screaming, having suffered what one doctor said was probably a nervous breakdown. She hasn't been heard from since. Did she really suffer a nervous breakdown, or has she, too, been infected?

Mayor Lawrence, who was in attendance last night, was asked to apprise New Yorkers of the situation and to allow them to make personal choices concerning their own well-being. A mysterious virus is passing through the city, and New Yorkers are turning into vampires . . .

Ray looked up; he'd heard a woman screaming. He looked up just in time to see people running toward him, yelling and obviously very afraid. He got up quickly, avoiding people as they raced for the exits.

When the crowd finally thinned out, he saw a blond man about thirty, dressed in a gray suit, bent over a young woman dressed in a pleated blue skirt and a white blouse. Her black purse hung off her arm. Ray could see the woman's face—they were only twenty yards apart—her dark hair corkscrewed over it, her eyes open and vacant. The man was at her neck, ripping at it with his teeth like a dog with a meaty bone.

"Freeze!" Ray heard then.

He saw two cops, their weapons drawn. They stood about ten feet apart and about that distance from the couple. The man either didn't hear them, Ray thought, or didn't care. Ray thought, he too, didn't care—not about anything except what he was doing. The cops moved a little closer and again Ray heard them order, "Freeze!" Still no reaction.

The cops didn't wait. They fired, the shots echoing in the corridor. The man reeled and pushed himself up. They shot him again and Ray dived for cover, slamming his elbow into the bench he'd been sitting on. He peeked over the top, absently rubbing his bruised elbow, and the cops fired a few more shots. The man hadn't gone down, not even close. They shot again and cursed, and he just stood there and took it, fabric flying everywhere, little clouds of smoke puffing out of their guns.

The two cops looked at each other, as surprised as if they'd just won the lottery. Ray wasn't the least bit surprised. He knew damn well what was going on, what they were trying to kill. Blanks would have been just as effective.

The cops each got onto one knee, taking better aim, and after they sighted in as precisely as they could, fired again.

The man's suit flew apart and the cops just looked at each other and fired again. Three more shots tore into the man and still he didn't go down. By now the cops looked like little kids in a playground full of bullies. They got to their feet and started backing away, yelling at the man that he'd been shot and that he should get down, that they were cops.

The man took a moment to look down at the girl, blood oozing from her neck and onto the floor. Then he turned and ran. He ran right past Ray, who slid behind the bench, the two cops in hot pursuit, one reloading, the other barking orders into a walkie-talkie, the air squawking with static.

"Holy shit!" the man behind the news counter said.

After the cops were out of sight, Ray joined a crowd of people around the girl. "Christ," he said. "She can't be more'n nineteen years old!"

An old, leather-faced woman about a head shorter than Ray looked up at him.

"It's vampires, you know. The city's overrun with vampires," she said. She waved airily, then looked back at the dead girl, and Ray saw a tear roll down her cheek. "Goddamn vampires!" she said.

"Emily, if you're there, answer the phone. Pick up, dammit!"

Ray didn't know that Emily had just stepped out of the shower.

"Okay, I'm going to hang up now, Emily—you hear me?"

"Ray? Where are you, Ray? Thank God!"

"I'm at the airport. Christ, you wouldn't believe . . . are you okay?"

"Yeah, fine."

"Do they know where Martin is yet?"

"I don't know, I . . . maybe. Bobby and a woman, Cynthia, they're out looking for him. She had a dream or something, I don't know. Ray, did you see the paper?"

"Yeah."

"He knows about Bobby All, Ray. He even investigated what happened in Hunt. He was here last night when Bobby and Cynthia came over to tell me about Martin. He hid in the closet and listened . . . you know the mirror in my living room?"

"Mirror? I don't—"

"He could see the mirror from the closet—"

"No reflection, right?"

"That's right. He didn't see their reflection. Neither did I, Ray. Funny, isn't it?"

"Funny?"

"You know, how you hold out hope that something isn't true, that vampires really aren't living in our fair city, but when you see visual proof, when tradition bangs down your door and says 'Gotcha,' well, it makes you pretty damn paranoid, Ray."

"Emily, just take it easy. Where are they now?"

"Maybe they're together, at her place, wherever that is. I don't know. The mayor's called a press conference for six o'clock. Sam Sturgess called and told me."

"I'll be there before then. See you soon."

Thirty-five

The phone rang again a few minutes later. Emily picked up. "Ray?" she said.

No answer.

"Ray, is that—"

"Emily?"

Her father.

"Dad? God, Dad, where are you?"

"Emily, I . . ."

"What, Dad?"

"Last night . . . I managed to put it off for a couple of days, maybe a couple of days."

"Put what off, Dad?"

"The coronation, Emily. Martin's coronation."

"Dad, I don't un—"

He hung up.

"—derstand."

David glared at the phone. He had wanted to tell her that he loved her, he had wanted to say that he would be home very soon and that everything was going to be all right. He hadn't said anything, though, and he knew why: he wasn't going to be home soon and he didn't know if he really loved her anymore. He certainly didn't believe that everything was going to be all right. People were going to try to kill him soon, the others, too. A real slaughter. Even the mayor's press conference, when he'd told everyone that things were under control, wouldn't put that off much longer. And how much longer would it be before the feds started poking around? Then they'd have a real problem. Of course, telling that to Martin's brood would be like talking to stones. He'd have to try, though.

He saw Louis and Lesley. He could start with them. Just explain to them that they'd have to be patient. They'd understand. They were still rational beings.

He started toward them, wishing he felt a little more energetic. He was going to need all the energy he could get.

Thirty-six

"Dammit, Ray, where the hell are you?"

Emily had settled her gaze on the relative calm outside her window. Ray was supposed to have been here at least a half hour ago, and as the hour came and went, her fevered brain conjured up a lot of possibilities, none of them good. He'd been attacked by a taxi driver, or maybe he'd taken a bus and one of the riders . . . or maybe he hadn't even made it out of the airport.

A cab pulled up. A man got out. "Please, please . . ." It wasn't Ray. She sat down on the couch.

But sitting in the middle of her living room, petting her cats, only made her feel claustrophobic, so she got up and started for the window again. She made it about halfway there before she heard the buzzer, and as coincidence would have it, the phone rang at the same time. The buzzer was probably Ray, but the phone? Her father, maybe? She decided to answer the doorbell and let the machine get the phone.

"Ray?" she said.

"Yeah, let me in, Emily."

He sounded a little frantic, like someone wanting in from the cold. She heard her telephone message playing in the background. She pressed the button and let Ray in.

As she started for the front door, she heard Bobby's voice on the phone. "Emily? Have you heard from Ray yet? Give me a call as soon as you can. I'm at the same number."

A knock at the door. She opened it and Ray looked back at her, a container of salt in his hand.

She looked at it and said, "What's with the salt?"

Ray pushed past her and turned around. "I heard a man's voice," he said.

Emily glanced at the phone, then looked back at Ray. "That was Bobby. He wanted to know if you were back yet."

"Did you talk with him?"

"No, I let the machine get it. It was that or leave you outside. Is everything okay, Ray? You sounded scared."

"Yeah, I'm okay. I never did like walking around this city, and I like it even less now. Imagination really gets in the way, you know? Not to change the subject, but Lenora came through."

"She did? Where is it?"

Ray held up the salt again. "Right here," he said.

Emily looked confused. "I don't understand. How can salt—"

"Well, essentially, Martin's a zombie. And according to voodoo law, salt can kill a zombie. All we've got to do is put some in his mouth, on his lips."

"A zombie? Ray, he's a vampire, not a zombie."

"I know. I mentioned that, too, but don't you see, Emily? Vampires, to begin with, are undead. Living dead. And so are zombies."

"I don't know. What did you have to go through to get this from her? Or did she just prescribe a dose of salt when you walked in?"

Ray couldn't help but grin. "Emily, you don't want to know what I went through. What I went through is one of the reasons I take this seriously." He looked at her for a moment, leaving his next thought unspoken.

"What, Ray?" she said. "Something else happened, didn't it?"

"Lenora had . . . well, she had some of Martin's blood.

She forced it down my throat, said it would help me find him. She called us blood brothers." He smiled, obviously to help relieve the tension. "I had visions, some really weird stuff."

"Oh, my God, you're not—"

Ray shook his head. "No, don't worry, I'm not—if I can believe Lenora, at least."

"If you can believe Lenora? Ray, she's a goddamn voodoo queen. Not someone I'd call overly credible."

"Look, maybe we'd better give Bobby a call and tell him I'm here."

"Ray, I don't think you understand the seriousness . . . you drank Martin's blood! A vampire's blood. That's how it works, isn't it?"

"I don't know, I just . . . maybe I don't want to know. All I know is that I had visions, sure, but I haven't experienced any symptoms. Look, I still reflect." He pointed at his reflection in the mirror. "And that's garlic I smell, isn't it? Doesn't faze me in the least. I like the smell of garlic. What else, what else? The kicker, yeah, I didn't ask you to let me in, did I?"

She looked at him. He was right . . . for now, at least.

He smiled at her and cupped her shoulders. "You have nothing to fear from me, Emily. Nothing," he said.

He hugged her then and she hugged him back. Still, she couldn't help remembering that Bobby had said pretty much the same thing to her—she had nothing to fear from him, either.

Thirty-seven

Emily couldn't shake the idea that she was strolling through a dream. Here she was, in the lobby of the Plaza Hotel, because she and Ray were going to have a meeting with a couple of vampires, a meeting where they would discuss another vampire who was totally paralyzed and could be killed only with a little Morton's salt given to them by a voodoo queen. A dream? No. One step lower than that. A nightmare, a big, boldly intrusive nightmare, one she might never wake up from.

"Five forty-four, right?" Ray said.

"Yeah," she said, distracted. "I wrote it down."

The elevator doors opened and an older couple got off. The woman wore a scarf around her neck and the man had a tall collar.

"C'mon," Ray said, "let's go."

They had walked from her apartment. She was getting used to long walks. It took them about forty minutes. On the way she noticed that traffic wasn't as heavy as it should have been and that some restaurants and stores had closed early. She heard sirens almost constantly, ambulances and police cars. If the city hadn't already reached a state of chaos, it was getting there in one big hurry.

Emily kept remembering what her father had said about Martin's coronation and about putting if off for a couple of days. With luck, a couple of days, that's what he'd said.

Maybe they were approaching something other than simple chaos. Maybe this was more like Armageddon. The ultimate conflict, good against evil.

The elevator stopped. She got off and walked with Ray down the hall to Room 544. Ray knocked on the door. It opened almost immediately.

Bobby looked at them. "The potion," he said. "Where is it?"

Ray took a small container of salt out of his pocket and gave it to Bobby.

"Sugar?" he said sarcastically, as he held it up to the light.

"Salt," Ray said.

Bobby looked at him. "And?"

"And what?"

"Salt and what? It's gotta be fortified by something, some catalyst. It's not just simple salt, is it?"

"Yeah. Just salt."

Bobby dropped the container to the floor as a look of anger flashed onto his face. He balled his hands into fists. "She toyed with you, Ray. I told you she'd do that. I told you to be prepared for that. She toyed with you, and now there's nothing we can do."

For one brief dull moment Ray thought maybe Bobby was right. Maybe she *had* toyed with him, made a fool out of him. But he'd always had the ability to know when someone was lying, and as far as he could tell, Lenora hadn't been lying. "Bobby," he said, "the way I understand it, vampires are like—"

"Zombies? Is that what she said, Ray?" He was smiling. "She told you that vampires are like zombies, and as everybody knows, salt kills zombies. Is that right?"

Ray's faith in his ability to read people had slipped a little. "Yeah, something like that," he said, trying to sound more self-assured than he felt.

"Then if I eat some of this salt, I'll die, right?"

"I don't really know. I guess if it were that easy, there wouldn't be too many vampires around, would there? What if you ate out and you didn't pay attention to what you were ordering?"

Bobby grinned; on him it looked threatening. "I admire your chutzpah, Ray, but only to a point. Don't push it!"

But Ray did push it. He was tired of being scared. "Then why don't you swallow some and we'll see?" he said, leaning into Bobby.

"Maybe I have an explanation," Emily said.

Cynthia came into the room then, Beta in her arms, his eyes half closed with pleasure.

"Really?" Bobby said. "Do tell."

"Martin's been affected by a voodoo rite. He's what he is now because of Lenora, right? That's true, isn't it?"

"You're on a roll," Bobby said.

"Well, what if he's only part vampire and the other part zombie? That makes sense, doesn't it? Some kind of hybrid."

No comment.

"And as far as you trying to prove that you're mightier than Ray by eating salt, Bobby, well, that'd be rather childish, wouldn't it?"

Ray saw a look of amusement on Cynthia's face. Obviously, Ray thought, Bobby didn't know what to say. She was right and he was wrong, and that didn't sit well with him. Killing himself trying to prove him wrong would be ridiculously foolhardy, though. No way he'd admit that he was wrong.

"You two stay here. Cynthia and I—" Bobby began.

"I don't think so!" Emily said.

"You don't think so?"

"You know the last time you and Martin got it on, you lost, Bobby. He overpowered you as easily as you could overpower me. And he'd probably do the same to Cynthia, too." Cynthia just smiled at her while she rubbed Beta against her cheek. "What if he senses you coming and mentally dismisses you? No, we all go look for him, all four of us."

Bobby nodded. Cynthia asked if she could take Beta, and Emily suggested that maybe that wouldn't be good. Cynthia pouted a little and put the cat down next to his food bowl.

They left a little while later.

David Kane thought back to when Emily had been small, when they'd lived in Connecticut. She had been somewhat precocious, but she had also been a normal, happy child. He might be able to see Connecticut from here, if it weren't so dark. But he could still see the green-and-tan split-level they sold so quickly. He thought about his son Hal, and that if it hadn't been for him . . . no, this wasn't Hal's fault. Pinpointing blame was useless, anyway. It wouldn't undo anything.

He'd never been so frightened. What was going to happen to him now? Was he going to stay like this forever, trapped in this body? Or would they find a cure? Would Emily find a cure? She might—if she lived through what was going to happen. He smiled. Leukemia was a cinch compared to this. But even leukemia, apparently, hadn't been able to stand up to what had surged into his system when he'd drunk that blood tear.

Looking out at the lights of the city, David drifted and drifted and finally settled into the past, to a time when this was all in the future . . . when he didn't have to think about it or live it.

And the past, it did sparkle so.

Martin liked where they'd taken him. At least there was something to see here. And they were obviously preparing him for his coronation. Why else would they have left him here, stage center, looking out at all those empty seats that would soon be filled with cheering subjects, applauding his ascension? He could see people in the balcony and some seated in the orchestra pit. Guards.

There were people looking for him, he knew that—Emily Kane and Ray Timmerson among them. They'd certainly caused him a lot of pain. *Something special for them,* he thought. *Something worthy. Death would be like a sip of good wine once he got through with them.*

He was small and bald and obviously frightened, his face drawn and pale. His audience, about two hundred people gathered at DeWitt Clinton Park, were just as frightened. "I say we've got no choice," he said. "We've got to arm ourselves. If the city's finest won't protect us, we've got to protect ourselves."

A woman toward the front tried to get the crowd's attention. She was about thirty and darkly pretty. There was a teenaged girl with her. The woman waggled a finger at the crowd. "Know what I heard?" she said. "I heard the mayor said there's nothin' wrong. He says it's the heat. He said it was an aberration, that it's the heat and the full moon, and that once we don't have a full moon, everything's gonna be okay."

Someone mumbled something like, "What is an aberration?" but he didn't get an answer.

"Now, some of you folks know me," the woman continued. "I'm a peace-loving person. Hell, I never even owned a gun, won't even have one in the house. But I bought a gun today, and I'll tell you what—I didn't mind forkin' over a couple hundred dollars for it, either. A couple hundred dollars for my life is pretty damn cheap!"

She nodded, obviously satisfied with herself, and another woman got the crowd's attention just a few seconds before a man tried to do the same thing.

She waved her hands to ask for calm. Silence took about ten seconds. It fell like a coffin lid onto the crowd.

"I heard what may or may not be a rumor—that whatever has happened is confined to Brooklyn, Queens, and Manhattan. Now, I've got a sister who lives on Staten Island and she said nothin's happening over there, not a damn thing. I have a police scanner, and from what I can tell, it's all confined to a large but specific area: the theater district and Central Park, and maybe a dozen or so blocks around there. Why that is, I don't know. Maybe these things are getting together, you know, like an offensive. I don't know. But you know what I think we should do . . . ?"

A crowd twice as large had gathered in Brooklyn, right in front of Lesley Charleton's office. People were using the back of a pickup truck as a podium.

The current speaker was a young black woman with an intensely resolute look on her face. "My brother, Arnold, he's a vampire!" She nodded slowly, hardening her point. "I know it like I know my own name. Sure, he goes out in the sunlight, but only for a little while, then he scurries back into his room like a whupped dog. And I swear this on my mama's grave—Arnold used to be a vegetarian, but you know what? He's not anymore! The thing is, he doesn't even eat it—he just sucks the blood out and then throws the meat into the garbage!" She crossed herself and raised her right hand. "I swear that's the truth! The God's honest truth!"

Four others had climbed onto the back of the pickup, and each one had a wife or son or daughter who had come up missing or dead or maybe turned into a vampire.

The next speaker, an older black man with a paunch, offered a solution. "For reasons I don't understand," he began, "the police ain't doin' nothin'. So I say it's up to us. I say we *find* these things and *kill* 'em before they kill *us!* Are you with me?"

The crowd roared and fists were thrust skyward. Some people raised their weapons.

When the crowd quieted down, a young Italian man said, "Where are they, though, Andre? We don't know where the hell they are!"

No one in a lynch mob wanted to hear the voice of reason.

"Hell if I know," Andre said, "but it don't matter! We'll find the fuckers! They're *somewhere* in this goddamn city, and we'll by God find 'em! Isn't that right?"

The crowd roared again as a boy about twelve jumped onto the back of the truck, a police scanner in his hand. He almost fell back, but Andre grabbed him by the arm. His name was Kyle, and just like a lot of other people, he had some things to say about where the violence had begun to center.

This scene replayed itself a dozen times in Manhattan and Queens and Brooklyn. Some people even went home and sharpened up wooden stakes before they went back to rejoin their respective vigilante groups, having heard that a wooden stake was the only thing—other than a silver bullet—that would kill a vampire.

When they were all together, they went out to look for the vampires. Some went in the right direction—although they wouldn't find anything tonight—and some went in the wrong direction. They went blindly, all of them, like starving rats, death on their minds and righteousness in their hearts, as healthy a mob as ever had formed.

One of these crowds found Bobby and Cynthia near the Broadhurst Theater on Forty-fourth Street, near Times Square. And when a man put a mirror up to Bobby's face— just as he'd done to a hundred others during the last two hours—he actually took Bobby by surprise.

The very small crowd at the Broadhurst, there to see the play *Sight Unseen*, were leaving the theater when they heard, "A vampire! Jesus, I found one! He didn't reflect, he didn't reflect!"

The man, his eyes owlish and scared, pointed a rigid finger at Bobby. At first the vigilante crowd seemed stunned that they had actually found a vampire, but their bloodlust most definitely needed satisfying. They turned on Bobby, yelling, "Vampire, kill him! Kill the vampire!" almost in unison.

Bobby, being what he was, was much faster than a crowd of novice vampire hunters. He ran into an alley, and when the crowd flooded in there to get him, he jumped onto a rooftop.

"My God," the man said, as he looked around at nothing in particular, "a vampire! I found a *real, live vampire!*"

He showed the mirror to the gathering crowd while they told him what a great job he'd done and clapped him on the back and generally made him feel like a hero. "I saw, too!" a woman said. "I saw him hold the mirror up. He didn't reflect, either. He was real. *Real!*"

"Wait," another man said. "He wasn't alone. There were two women and a man with him. I'm sure of it!"

"Back to the theater!" someone yelled. "We'll get the sonsabitches, we'll get 'em!"

The crowd pushed back to the street to search for more vampires.

By then, Emily and Ray and Cynthia had made a hasty and well-advised retreat.

Thirty-eight

At Emily's apartment, Ray said, "We still have a few more to go." He was talking about the theaters they'd missed, having gotten sidetracked by a crowd of what Cynthia had alluded to as "Fucking vampire hunters." He ran down the list. "Near as I can remember, we checked out the Golden, the Imperial, the Royale, the Booth—"

"And if we check out the rest, we're going to come up empty, too," Cynthia said. She went to the window. "Where's Bobby? Where the hell is Bobby?" she mumbled.

"Why do you say that?" Emily said. "Why do you think we'll come up empty?"

Cynthia turned. "My dreams. Sometimes I remember them, sometimes I don't. Sometimes it takes me a while before they come back. The latest came back entirely just a few seconds ago, and you know what I discovered? A musty, stagnant odor. Places like the Booth and the Royale wouldn't allow that. No, they've hidden Martin in a deserted building, an old theater. That's where we have to look."

"But it's not safe—at least, not for you."

Another crowd paraded past the window. "I can take care of myself," Cynthia said. "Don't ever doubt that. I know how I look sometimes, how foolish . . . I can take care of myself."

"I don't doubt that, but I don't know of any old theaters

in the area, and the only place we can find that information is at the historical society, and they're not open until—"

"The sun comes up," Cynthia cut in, her tone hollow and vacant. She turned back to the window. "I used to enjoy the sunlight," she said. "Now it's my mortal enemy. Did you know that even seeing it on television is painful? Strange, huh?" She turned back. "Go ahead and get the information you need and tomorrow, when Bobby's back, we'll find Martin and destroy him."

Cynthia said nothing and neither did Ray, but they both knew that tomorrow night might be too late. They'd have to get the information they needed and then continue the search without Cynthia or Bobby. They would have to destroy Martin alone.

"Good enough," Emily said.

"Then if you'll excuse me," Cynthia said, and started for the door.

"Where are you going?" Emily asked.

Cynthia turned and smiled. "Regardless of circumstances, I still have to eat."

That said, she turned and left.

Emily and Ray just looked at each other a moment, then sat down together on the couch. Seconds later, Ray put his arm around her, and within a few seconds they fell fast asleep. They didn't wake up until the morning sun edged beyond the windowsill and touched their eyelids.

The White House

"Troops are moving into position, Mr. President."

The president looked at his chief-of-staff. "Tell me, Keith," he said. "Hypothetically speaking, do you believe in evil? Do you believe that poor girl we saw had been touched by evil?"

"Are you asking me from a theological—"

"No, I don't think so. Do you believe that evil takes specific forms? C'mon, Keith, you've heard the rumors!"

Keith didn't know what to say. The president was asking him if he believed in vampires, and although he had known the president since childhood—and they'd certainly had some good times watching horror movies together—this scenario was a far cry from two kids munching popcorn and watching Godzilla trample Tokyo.

"Vampires, Mr. President?"

"Yes, vampires. Do you think it's possible that they could actually exist?"

"I hope not, sir. I sincerely hope not. No, no, of course not. That's ridiculous to even . . . no, sir. I don't."

That answer seemed to placate the president. "I don't think so, either, Keith. You say troops are moving into position?"

"Yes, sir. From Fort Dix and Camp Drum."

"All major arteries must be severed, all tunnels blocked off."

"Yes, sir, the commanders understand that."

"Good. Now all we can do is wait and do what we can to keep the rest of the country from learning too much. You've prepared a press release?"

"Yes, sir."

"I'll want to see it."

"Of course."

"And the health authorities have been notified?"

"Yes, sir. Everything's in place."

"Good. Very good. Let me know when the troops are in place and wait for my orders."

"Yes, sir."

Keith left the Oval Office, and although his mind was full, one image stood out: Christine Fuller as they'd seen her on tape, deformed and paralyzed. Then he thought about what the president had asked, whether or not he believed in vampires. There was a time he wouldn't have hesitated when asked a question like that.

* * *

While troops were being hurried into position, Ray picked up yesterday's *New York Times*. He wished he could sleep, but he had only slept as long as he had because his body had almost shut down. Thankfully, he hadn't dreamt, either—at least, that he could remember.

Emily had put on a pot of coffee. She was in the kitchen hunting up some sugar. She'd run out, she'd told him, but she had a few restaurant packets lying around somewhere.

Ray flipped to the theater section, having scanned the news—all bad for New York; there just wasn't enough space to fit all the violence. The Yankees, who were on a road trip to Kansas City, had won again, though, and that was something, at least. Normal stuff.

He read the listings, only vaguely hearing Emily slap the cupboards closed. *Temper, temper,* he thought. She was losing it quick, but she was allowed. He stopped scanning, his attention drawn to a strangely worded ad: *See it free at the Manhattan Punch Line Theater, a new production of* The Man who Would Be King, *with an all-star cast. First performance tonight at midnight.*

"Emily?" he said.

"Yeah?"

"The Manhattan Punch Line Theater, isn't that closed down?"

She came into the living room. "It's off Broadway. Not real big, a coupla hundred seats. I went there once years ago. I thought it was still open, but it could be closed down. Why?"

Ray turned the paper toward her. "It's open now and there's a new play being staged. *The Man Who Would Be King.*"

He saw her eyes open wide. *"The Man Who Would Be King?"* she mumbled. She looked at him. "That's Martin, Ray, I'll bet anything. Martin is there, waiting for his coronation."

Thirty-nine

"I don't believe we're taking a taxi," Ray whispered. He nodded toward the driver. "What if he's one of them?"

"I'm sick of walking!" Emily said. "And you know I'd like to have some energy left when we get there. Anyway, if he *was* one of them, we'd have known by now."

"You've got the salt, right?"

"Ray, you've asked me that at least a hundred times. *Yes.*"

"You know, even if we *do* find him and it *does* work, there's no guarantee that the killing'll stop."

"I know that, but can you think of anything better?"

"Sweet Jesus," the driver said.

"What?"

He turned slightly. "The city's under quarantine. It just came over the radio. Jesus, a goddamn quarantine! I gotta get home!"

He slammed on the brakes and another taxi bumped them from behind. *"Out,"* the driver said, turning. "Don't worry about the fare, just get out."

They were at Thirtieth and Lexington, still a long way from Greenwich Village, home of the Manhattan Punch Line Theater.

Ray grabbed at his neck. "We're in the middle of the goddamn street!" he said.

"I don't give a rat's ass if you're at the goddamn Smithsonian Institution! Get outta my cab!"

Ray looked around; traffic was moving pretty slowly now. He wondered how many people knew they weren't getting out of the city anytime soon. "C'mon, Emily," he said, taking her by the arm. "Thanks loads, pal!" he said to the driver as they got out, his eyes moving frantically as he tried to pick out a route that wouldn't get them killed.

Ray had a vision of it all ending right here. Everyone was looking for a faster way to go the next fifty feet, then slamming on their brakes and looking for another route. Bumper cars on Broadway.

By the grace of a higher power, they made it to the sidewalk quicker and easier than Ray thought they would.

He caught his breath and looked around. Word about the quarantine had spread like the plague. Horns blared and curses fouled the air, and when a man came running out of a wholesale clothing outlet, they heard even more news. "The mayor's killed the governor!" he shouted. "Ed Lawrence killed the governor!"

Not a lot of people heard that, just those within ten yards or so, because the racket on the street had risen to ear-splitting levels. It was a madhouse without walls.

"Maybe this *is* Armageddon," Ray mumbled, feeling suddenly humbled by the enormity of what was going on around him.

"You up to a mild trot?" he asked. He squeezed her hand.

She looked at him. "I haven't been doing exercises every morning for nothing," she said. "I'm up to it. Can't get any worse than this."

They trotted off, the sidewalks now an obstacle course of scared and confused New Yorkers, some of whom, Ray thought, would be alive tomorrow and some of whom would not.

Ed Lawrence had been summoned to the governor's mansion to explain his action—or inaction—concerning the escalating violence in the city and also to be informed that the city had been put under quarantine. In a fit of panic and with a powerful sense of purpose, he had attacked the governor and then fled to the basement. Once there, and in a very secluded and dark corner, he began to feel a lethargy crawl over him. He wondered if someone had slipped him a mickey.

"No way this place is open," Emily said.

They were standing outside the Manhattan Punch Line Theater. Litter had collected around the chained and padlocked doors. Old posters were taped up inside the ticket window. *If they are having a show here,* Emily thought, *they'd have to hire a whole army of Merry Maids.*

"He's in there," Ray said. "I can feel it!" He looked at her. "I guess it worked, huh?"

"What worked?"

"You know, the blood Lenora made me drink."

Out of the corner of her eye, Emily saw two men standing in the shadows inside a hardware store across the street, their heads hidden in the arch of a painted window sign that read, GREENWICH VILLAGE HARDWARE.

"I think we're being watched," she said.

The two men had moved a few steps back, as if they knew they'd been noticed. "I think you're right," he said. "Well, that proves it, doesn't it? He's here. Martin's here. Why else . . . ?"

Emily smiled at Ray and took his hand. "We're tourists, okay? Just tourists. By the way, you got any suggestions? Other than buying plaid shorts and black socks?"

Ray smiled at that. "We could storm the place."

"Wouldn't be much of a storm with two people."

"There's gotta be a way in. They got in, why can't we?"

Emily looked past Ray at a tenement two buildings down. There was a young girl on the stoop playing with a rag doll, feeding it invisible food from an invisible spoon. "Talk about coincidence," she said. "Ray, my Aunt Doris lives just two buildings down. God, I haven't seen her in, I don't know, at least three years. She's gotta be in her seventies by now."

"I don't understand. What's that—"

"Look, I know how this is gonna sound, considering the circumstances."

"Jeez. Sorry for being so slow. You want to see if she's okay, right?"

"Just take a few minutes. Give us a chance to catch our breath, too."

Ray glanced at the little girl and the building behind her. "Sure, okay," he said. "Maybe we can get something cold to drink, too. I'm parched."

Emily's face brightened "Great. Thanks." She put her hand on Ray's arm. "He's in there, right?" She hadn't lost her smile. "Martin's really in there."

"I'd stake my life on it," he said.

"Well, then, let's go get a cold one."

Aunt Doris lived on the third floor of the five-story tenement. Emily remembered that much, even though she hadn't seen her for a while.

They stepped past the pigtailed little girl, who glanced at them briefly, then stepped into the outer foyer. Mailboxes were on one side, buzzers and apartment numbers on the other.

As soon as they started looking for numbers, the little girl got Emily's attention. She moved to the door for a better look.

The little girl had her doll turned over on her knees. She was giving it a spanking. *A fairly brutal spanking,* Emily thought.

"Don't you do that anymore!" she scolded. "Do you understand? You can't do that anymore!" She shook the doll viciously, then held it close to her face and scolded it some more.

Emily noticed something then that made her shudder—
the fangs on either side of the doll's mouth, drawn in with
red crayon.

"Ray, look at that," she said.

Ray looked at the doll and frowned, then let out a breath.
"Try the door, Emily."

Emily gripped the knob—the door was locked. She
looked up her aunt's name, found it, pressed the buzzer.
Nothing. A low apprehension began to build in her belly.

"Try them all," Ray said.

She did. Still nothing.

"Guess no one's in the mood for visitors," Ray said.
"Can't say I blame them."

They started to leave. The two men left the hardware
store. Ray and Emily went back inside.

The two men moved toward them quickly from sunlight
to shadow.

Emily nodded toward the little girl. "I'll bet she's got a
key," Emily said.

"She might, if she lives here."

Emily opened the door about a foot. "Hi," she said.
"What's your name, sweetie?"

The little girl turned and looked at her with big, probing
blue eyes. "Shannon," she said, as if she liked her name.

"Well, Shannon—I wonder, can you help us?"

"Who are you?"

The two men were closer now; they'd stopped in the shade
of a hot dog vendor's umbrella.

"My name is Emily, and this is Ray. Shannon, do you have
a key, dear? We wanted to visit my aunt, but she doesn't
answer. She's an old lady, and, well, we're a little worried
about her. You understand, don't you, dear?"

Shannon frowned. "Are you vampires?" she asked. "My
daddy's a vampire. He went away. I'm waiting for him to
come home and not be a vampire anymore."

Words failed Emily for a moment. Finally, she said, "No, we're not vampires."

The two men had moved away from the hot dog stand.

"Can you open the door, sweetie? Please?"

The little girl shrugged. "Sure," she said and got up, leaving her vampire doll on the step. She looked back and pointed a disciplinary finger at it. "And you be good while I'm gone; do you understand?"

By now the two men had started across the street. When they were about halfway there, the girl slipped the key out of her jeans pocket, stepped past Emily and Ray, and unlocked the door. "Is your daddy a vampire, too?" she asked, as she pushed the door open.

Emily and Ray hurried inside. Just as the door closed behind them, the two men rushed up the steps and pulled the outer door open.

Shannon frowned. "Who are they?" she said, to no one in particular. She shook her head slowly, ponderously, as the larger man grabbed the doorknob. "Oh, they're bad! They're vampires, too! I can tell. See their heads? They're just like my daddy. See their heads?"

Emily and Ray didn't stick around long enough to look at their heads. They ran for the stairs. Glass shattered as they pulled the stairway door open.

Taking two steps at a time, they made it to the third floor in record time, the two men close behind. They had planned to go straight to the roof, but that didn't seem too wise right now. *Our only hope is Aunt Doris,* Emily thought. *Maybe she's been in the shower, or maybe she isn't answering the door anymore.*

She pulled the hallway door open, then shut it as quietly as possible. Her aunt's apartment was about midway down the hall.

"It's open," Emily whispered, nodding at her door.

Noise on the stairs. "Inside," Ray whispered.

Emily looked back at the stairway door. They were here.

"Hurry!" Ray said.

They made it into the apartment at about the same time the two men stepped into the hallway. Emily eased the door shut, holding onto the knob so they wouldn't hear the click as it closed.

"They gotta be in one of these apartments," she heard.

Footsteps, heavy and plodding.

Ray tapped her hand. She looked at him and he shook his head. At the same time, he mouthed the words, "Don't let go, let me have it."

Carefully, precisely, Ray replaced her hand with his own. "They're getting closer," he whispered.

"Anything?" one of the men said.

"Not yet."

"Shit!"

This guy was on their side of the hallway, Emily thought, the other guy was across the hall. As soon as she thought that, she saw a shadow at the bottom of the door, just enough time for Ray to grip the knob. Emily held her breath as his knuckles whitened. If the guy on the other side wanted to, he could just rip the knob off with his hand.

Just when she thought Ray's strength would give out, she heard the guy on the other side say, "No one here, either. Guess they gave us the slip. C'mon, let's retrace our steps."

As soon as they were out of earshot, Ray let go of the knob and turned. He leaned against the door, eyes closed, his breath coming in short, quick volleys.

When he opened his eyes, Emily was about halfway across the room, moving toward a half open door. "Aunt Doris," she said almost at a whisper. "Are you in there, Aunt Doris?"

She pushed the door open and Ray watched as she raised her hands to her mouth and let go with a small, shrill cry.

Ray rushed to her side. Her gaze had settled on a woman sitting in a rocking chair near a window. *Aunt Doris,* he thought. Her head was lolled to the side and her eyes were open. Her gray hair had streaks of blood running through it. A small-caliber handgun lay on the floor in front of her like a fallen knickknack.

Emily went into the room and knelt beside her. Half of Doris's face was bathed in sunlight, the other half in shadow. "Suicide," Emily said. She looked at him. "She killed herself, Ray. Look at her throat. One of them got to her."

The closer Ray got, the more he realized that Aunt Doris really had killed herself. Her throat had been torn away—in the fashion of the pseudo-vampires. He saw a note on her lap.

He watched as Emily looked into her aunt's vacant eyes and picked up the note. She read it quickly, then put it back down on her lap again. "She killed herself rather than become one of them," she said. "She said . . . she said there are better places." She looked at Ray with tears in her eyes.

"I'm sorry, Emily," Ray said. "God, I'm sorry."

The tears, he knew, were for her aunt and her father. He even wondered if maybe David hadn't done this to her.

"C'mon," he said, taking her by the arm. "We've got work to do."

Emily wiped away a tear. "Wait a second," she said. She went to the window and looked up toward the roof. "About ten feet. I don't know about you, Ray, but I think I can handle a ten-foot jump."

Ray knew what she wanted to do: she wanted to use rooftops to get to the Manhattan Punch Line Theater.

No noise, Ray thought, as he opened the door to the hallway and stuck his head out. He looked north and south. No one there. He signaled to Emily.

They climbed the two flights of stairs to the roof quickly but quietly. The warm sunshine that greeted them was as welcome as a spring thaw.

"They can't stay out in the sun too long," Ray said, "so we're relatively safe out here."

They walked to the edge of the building and looked across to the other side.

"Yeah, about ten feet," Ray said. "I'll go first."

"Okay."

Ray went back to get a running start, all kinds of things running through his head. What if he tripped? What if he got a cramp on pushoff? What if he just couldn't jump that far? What if they stayed here?

About thirty feet, he calculated. *That should be enough of a running start.*

He shook his arms in front of him, then sucked in a breath and let it out. "Ready. Set."

"Ray?" Emily said. "Be—"

"Go!"

"Careful!"

On the way across, he looked down at the alleyway, about a thousand feet below, and he actually felt like he was flying. He thought about how sky-divers must feel.

His knees buckled slightly when he hit, but he didn't fall down. He turned toward Emily after he got his balance back. "A snap," he said. "Come on! Just like falling off a log."

"You *would* say falling."

"You know what I mean. C'mon. Nothin' to it!"

Emily moved back about the same distance Ray had, broke into a dead run, and leaped the ten-foot span with a couple of feet to spare, actually more room to spare than Ray had had. She rolled when she hit and then bounced to her feet like Mary Lou Retton.

"You okay?" Ray said.

"Yeah, fine. Piece of cake."

A few seconds later, they found out that the Manhattan

Punch Line Theater was only four stories tall, not five, like the building they were on. They would have to jump over ten feet and down the same distance.

"You up to it?" Ray asked.

"I sure as hell hope so," Emily said.

"Good, 'cause look over there." He pointed at a door on the roof of the theater. "With luck it'll be open."

"What the hell are we waiting for, then?"

"Wait a sec."

"For what?"

Ray tilted his head back. "Who knows," he said, "this might be the last tan I'll ever get. The last time I'll be able to feel the sun on my face."

"C'mon, Ray, you gotta be kidding."

He looked at her more seriously than she liked. "Not this time, Emily. Not this time."

For the second time in the last hour, Emily felt a tremble shudder through her. He was right. So right in fact, she joined him.

And for the next few minutes, they stood very still, their heads tilted back, their eyes closed, basking in the warmth of the midday sun.

Forty

The door wasn't locked. Not only was it not locked, the knob was missing.

Ray yawned the door open and a flat, pungent smell leaped out at him. He reeled, holding the back of his hand to his nose. "Good God!" he said.

He waited a few moments to catch his breath.

"Have we got the right address?" Emily said.

"Yeah."

A little fresh air diluted the odor enough to be manageable, but when they looked down the stairway and saw yet another door, Emily said, "I wonder if we only made it through the first wave."

"Maybe."

She started down, but he stopped her. "Okay, Emily," he said, wiping back tears, "I've let you come this far, but from here on in, I go it alone. You'll be safe if you stay out here in the sunlight—"

"You've gotta be kidding! I haven't come this far and gone through what I've gone through just to be a spectator! C'mon, Ray!"

Ray took her by the hand. "Emily, the danger beyond that door . . . you can't even begin to imagine—"

"Ray, two pairs of eyes are much better than one. And you don't honestly believe I'd let you go in there alone, do you?"

Ray looked at her. He was out of words, and she was probably right, anyway. "Okay, c'mon, but stay close, understand?"

"You don't have to worry about that."

They started down, but when they got to the bottom of the stairs, frustration settled in. The door was locked.

"Shit!" Ray mumbled.

"I'll second that."

Ray felt the door—old and thin. "If only I were a few pounds heavier . . . oh, hell, we got no choice."

"Ray, what are you going to do?"

He rammed a shoulder into the door. It flew open, spraying bits of wood everywhere, and slammed back against the wall with a concussive *whump*.

He reeled again. As they had guessed, the odor here was twice as bad. Ray felt his stomach churn and the bile rose in his throat. Emily retched her last meal onto the wall.

It took him a while, but when he finally started thinking clearly again, Ray said, "They heard us, Emily. How could they not? We sounded like a goddamn SWAT team!"

"Maybe, but we've come this far."

Light streaming into the open door exposed what appeared to be a bedroom.

"It was probably a private residence at one time," Emily said.

The blast of sunlight also exposed something else, the cause of the odor. A young woman dressed in only her underwear lay on her stomach on a neatly made bed. She had flowing blond hair, and her left arm was turned under her body.

"No signs of struggle," Ray said.

"There wasn't any struggle," Emily said. She picked up a prescription bottle, the cap off. "Just like Aunt Doris, Ray."

Emily went around to the other side of the bed, blinking back tears. The woman's eyes were open. She closed them, looked at Ray a second, then turned the woman's head slightly. The concavity had started, although it wasn't nearly as pronounced as the ones they had seen on others.

"She killed herself while she still could, Ray."

Emily pulled the bedspread over her—instantly cutting the smell—and made the sign of the cross.

"How many others?" she whispered.

"I'd hate to even guess," Ray said. "C'mon, let's go."

The open bedroom door led to a short hallway. Ray tried a light switch—no juice. "Damn," he said.

"Wait," Emily said. "Did you hear that?"

"What?"

"Listen!"

The dull roar of small talk drifted up to them.

"Sold out," Emily said. "Sounds like there's hundreds of them down there."

Ray looked at Emily, Emily at Ray. His shoulders sagged, as did hers. "How can we get past all those people, Ray?"

Ray's eyes brightened.

"I've got an idea," he said. He reached into his back pocket and took out his comb.

"What are you doing?" Emily asked.

"Just shut up a minute."

He ran the comb through her hair and pushed it to the right side of her head. "It's the only way," he said. "If we want to get to Martin we have to become vampires, we have to socialize with those things."

"Ow!" Emily cried. "Gimme that!"

She took the comb from him. When she was done, she gave it back. "How do I look?" she asked.

"Like you're trying to hide something."

"That's the look we want, isn't it?"

Ray combed his hair the same way and when they were done they moved down the hallway to the living room.

They could see the building next door through a window. The kitchen was on the left. They moved through the living room and tried another door. It opened onto a hall and another set of stairs to the left, about twenty feet away. Another window at the end of the hall, painted black, left the hallway in deep shadow.

"Still got the salt, right?" Ray whispered.

Emily rolled her eyes.

"Hang on a sec," Ray said. He took out his trusty matchbook and lit one, pleased that it took only one try. The hallway lit up and now they could actually see a picture on the wall, a painting; standard stuff, a mountain-and-stream scene. It didn't do much to brighten things up.

"How many matches left?" Emily asked, as they started down the hallway.

"Enough," Ray said.

They stopped at the top of the U-shaped stairway. "Stay here a second," Ray said. "Let me take a look."

"Don't get any wild ideas!"

"Don't worry."

Ray started down the stairway and Emily watched as the light faded, leaving her in almost total darkness.

She tried to control it, but her imagination ran wild; they were in front of her, behind her, above and beneath her. She could still hear the roar of small talk, louder now, as she imagined Ray drawing closer to the source. "Oh, God, hurry, Ray," she mumbled.

Seconds later, as if Ray had heard her, she saw the quivering matchlight.

"How you doin'?" he whispered. "You all set?"

Emily let out a breath and nodded less than confidently.

"Good. C'mon."

She moved down the stairs to join him, staying only a step behind as they moved toward another door.

"We're going to have to be real careful," he whispered. "There's a helluva crowd out there, but it's only lit by candlelight so we've got a chance. Looks like the balcony hall-way."

"Maybe there's another way, Ray."

"I don't think so, Emily. I think we found the only way."

They stopped at a door. Ray gripped the knob and pushed the door open a few inches. What they saw then could have been a scene from a New York night on the town. Under quavering candlelight they saw groups of people and people in pairs, and some alone. Some had drinks in their hands, some didn't.

Ray took Emily's hand and squeezed it hard.

"We've got to wait for just the right . . ."

Two men walked within a few feet then, their backs to them, and stopped. They could hear the two men talking.

"Everyone should be here by midnight," the man on the left said. He took a sip of his drink.

"It's going pretty well," the other man said.

"It'll be touch-and-go, what with the quarantine, but it'll happen. Look, there's Oscar."

The two men moved away then and after Ray surveyed the scene, he whispered, "It's now or never," and pulled the door open.

They stepped into the crowd as nonchalantly as they could, Emily fully suspecting that they'd been seen. But when one minute passed and then another, she realized no one had seen them.

They moved through the crowd slowly, avoiding eyes and avoiding conversation, all of which seemed to be centered on Martin and his upcoming coronation. No one seemed worried that it wouldn't happen because of the quarantine or the resulting military intervention.

The hallway was about fifteen by fifty. The entryway to the balcony was about in the middle. They had almost made it there—where they hoped to see much more than they could from where they were—when a man dressed like a waiter stopped in front of them and smiled. He had a tray of drinks. "No thanks," Ray said, smiling back. "Just had one."

The waiter's smile faded.

"I haven't had any yet, though," Emily said. She picked up a glass and took a sip. Her first reaction was to spit it out, but somehow she fought that reaction and even smiled. Then she swallowed.

The waiter moved away.

"It's blood," she said.

"I thought so. Don't put it down. They'll suspect."

They realized something then—they were the only two people here who had bothered to cover the sides of their heads.

"Shit," Emily muttered. "Their heads, Ray."

"Yeah, I see. Any suggestions?"

"I say we get outta here and rethink this thing."

"I'm with you."

They started back to the stairway door, but at the same time, Emily saw the waiter nodding at them while he talked with two men.

"Ray, aren't those the same two guys—"

"Uh-huh. Damn! We've been made. Don't run, but don't dawdle, either."

They picked up their pace, brushing against people; a man spilled his drink. "Hey, watch it!" he said, as he brushed himself off.

"Sorry," Ray said, smiling, showing a lot of teeth.

A couple of seconds later they heard, "Stop them!" The order came from one of the men who had chased them.

"Move it!" Ray yelled to Emily.

Emily was in front, the door just ten feet away. She felt a hand on her arm; she kicked out and sent a woman sprawling, grabbed the doorknob, pulled open the door, and started up the stairs, Ray right behind.

A *thud*—she looked back—Ray was on his stomach looking up at her, being dragged backward.

"Run, Emily," he yelled. "Get out, get out!"

"Ray!" She started back to him.

"Run, Emily, run!"

So she ran, and with Ray's pleas echoing in her ears, she made it to the stairs and to the hallway. But in her haste, she ran past the apartment and to another door, a door she thought led into the apartment. She yanked it open, hurried inside, and promptly banged her forehead against a shelf.

She lost consciousness in seconds.

When she finally came to, her thoughts ran wild. She was dead—no, not dead. They found her and threw her into a basement or something and they were waiting till later to kill her, maybe even sacrifice . . . or maybe she'd been unconscious for a second and they were out in the hallway right now, looking for her.

None of that was true, though, and when she waited a while, listening and hearing nothing, she realized that. She was still alive and this wasn't a basement—it was a broom closet; she'd bumped her knee into a mop bucket.

What now, though? she thought, as she rubbed the goose egg on her forehead. Maybe she should make a run for it. But she couldn't do that, either. Somehow, she had to finish what she and Ray had started. And who the hell knew what was going on outside? She might be worse off out there.

Well, one thing for sure—she couldn't spend the rest of her life in a broom closet. She got up slowly, feeling for the shelf, and pulled the door open.

The hallway was totally dark. The sun had gone down. *How long have I been out?* she wondered. *Hours, at least.*

She stepped out of the closet and took a few halting steps, feeling in front of her like a blind person. She imagined someone grabbing her hands and pulling her close. "Got you now!" they'd say.

"Not yet, you don't," she said.

Her foot collided with something hard; she almost fell down. She steadied herself and let her toes do the walking.

A body? Was it . . . oh, God, not Ray! Please don't let it be Ray!

She knelt and ran her hands over the body. Hard as stone beneath what felt like a silk suit. *Thank God—it's not Ray.*

She thought about checking for a pulse, but that seemed a little silly, so she stepped over the body and moved slowly down the hallway.

She wished she had the matches. She felt a door. The apartment? She tried it. It was the apartment, but where could she hide in there? And why should she be hiding in the first place? She was here to kill Martin, and she couldn't very well do that cowering in some dark corner.

You're hiding, she told herself, *because they're probably looking for you. And that makes sense.*

But they sure weren't looking very hard. Were they looking at all? She couldn't even hear the small talk anymore. Still, she'd probably be better off if she stayed here for a while, just to make sure. *Under the bed, maybe. Sure, under the bed, like a kid at a Halloween party.*

She went into the apartment and then back to the bedroom. The light was better here because the moon was out. She saw the bedspread, the body underneath it. "No, no, not in here," she said. She looked back toward the living room and thought about Ray, that maybe he was only being held prisoner, although more macabre visions tried to push that one aside. "Ray," she said, "God, Ray, please be all right. Please, please don't be . . ."

Her head began to throb and she lost her balance for a moment. Having no choice, she sat down next to the dead woman, and wondered if she had a concussion. It'd be a miracle if she didn't, as hard as she'd conked her head.

She wanted to lie down, but she knew that wouldn't be wise, even a little foolhardy, so she just sat on the bed next to the dead woman and thought about her father and Ray and going to plays when you didn't have to worry about your life being in danger. *Not to mention your soul.* So many things to think about . . .

Emily was lost in a bittersweet world of memories, and the time passed quickly—first an hour, then two. It was her bladder that finally brought her back to reality: she had to pee. She looked at her watch, illuminating the dial, realizing then how long she'd been sitting on the bed and also realizing that lost in thought, she probably wouldn't have heard anyone come into the apartment anyway.

She got up and looked for the bathroom, counting her blessings as she did. She peed, but she didn't flush, remembering a little ditty her dad had told her years ago. "If it's yellow, keep it mellow. If it's brown, flush it down." They'd had a water shortage at the cabin, so they only flushed when the toilet had a full load.

She left the bathroom and almost out of instinct checked her pocket for the Tupperware container of salt. She held it out in front of her and listened for sounds. All she heard was the wind.

"Okay," she mumbled, as she put the salt back into her pocket, "it's obvious that for some unknown reason they're not looking for you, so you should probably be looking for Martin. Deal?"

Her other self had a few misgivings about that, but that part had already pleaded its case and lost. It was time.

With a deep, nerve-settling breath, she went through the living room and to the front door. She listened for movement. When she didn't hear anything, she opened the door, looked both ways, then stepped into the hallway. About a minute later, she started for the stairs, remembering Ray being dragged backward and then out of sight . . .

She felt a certain pride about how little noise she made—she had no idea she could move so quietly.

When she got there, she put her ear against the door. *So quiet,* she thought. *Too quiet. Too damn quiet . . .*

She pulled the door open just slightly. No one there—and

that, she thought, was plenty strange. Not long ago you could hardly move in there. The candles were out, too, although she saw light flickering from a doorway to the balcony.

She stepped into the hallway and stood very still, her eyes panning. She felt pretty good about the fact that she hadn't seen anyone yet. *But there's probably a reason for that.* They could've moved Martin while she wandered through her very long daydream, or maybe the theater was deserted now. Or maybe there was a war going on outside. *Plenty of reasons.*

She stared at the flickering light, if only because there really wasn't anything else to look at. That's where the answers were, though, more than likely. *Now, Emily, all you've got to do is find the courage to actually step into that doorway.*

She hitched in a breath and let it out. "Move it, Emily," she whispered. "Get your ass in gear, woman."

It didn't happen right away, but eventually one foot did follow the other, and when she got to the entryway, she stuck her head around the side.

The scene that opened before her made her wonder if she hadn't fallen asleep, if she wasn't just dreaming. As far as she could tell, every seat here and below was taken. And now she saw the reason for the dull, flickering glow—a wave of candles on the stage, easily a hundred feet away. Martin was on that stage, a crown on his head.

Emily stepped back into the hallway and braced against a wall. Her heart felt like it was going to explode. *They're here, every damn one of them, just waiting for Martin's coronation!* Oh, God, what could she do against two hundred vampires?

But even as she wondered about that, she reconsidered what she had seen, and when she got the full picture, she got a little puzzled. She cocked her head to the side, her face lined with curiosity. *If Martin was about to become*

*King of New York, why wasn't anyone shouting his name
or applauding his ascension? Why hadn't she heard "Long
live the king," or some bullshit like that?*

It took a while, but eventually she screwed up enough
courage to have another look, and when she did, she realized something very odd—no one was moving. For some
reason, none of the people in this theater were moving. As
if they were all somehow . . . paralyzed.

Her face felt suddenly hot. *Like Martin,* she thought.
*They're all like Martin! Martin can't move, and they can't
move, either!* She remembered the body upstairs, how cold
and hard . . .

She stepped all the way into the doorway and waited for
someone to notice her. There were two young women on
her right, their hands joined together on their laps, as close
to her as anyone. She tapped the closest woman on the
shoulder.

Nothing.

She gave her a push and all she did was lean to the right
and bounce right back. She felt suddenly chilled. It was
true: none of these vampires could move!

She smiled and chased the chills away. Had she ever been
this happy? This relieved? *Hell, no! Never!* "Long live the
king!" she yelled. "Long live Martin!"

Her words echoed through the balcony and died a lonely
death.

And what about the others? Was the city littered with
paralyzed vampires?

"Hold on, Emily," she said, putting her hands out in front
of her. "Don't count your chickens . . . if it's true, how
long are they going to stay like this? No guarantees, Ray
said, remember?"

She went to the edge of the balcony, past young and old
people, rich and poor people, all paralyzed, some looking
down at Martin, some looking to the right or left or at each
other. She looked closely at Martin. From the back of the

balcony, he had appeared to be standing. From here, she could see that he'd been propped up on a wooden platform.

She wrapped her hand around the container of salt. "Hungry, Martin?" she yelled to him.

She went back into the hallway beyond the balcony, looking for a way down.

Martin saw Emily appear at the back of the theater and move toward him. Did she actually think he was afraid of her? How could he ever be afraid of a mere mortal?

It had happened almost at once, as he'd ordered it. It would have happened eventually anyway, so he had mentally ordered their paralysis as soon as they were all seated. Now his subjects were all like him, those who had made it here, at least. But he really wished he didn't have to hear them, wished he couldn't still read their thoughts. They were all so afraid. Their faces didn't show it—some were actually grinning—but their minds screamed at him: "Help me, Martin, please help me! What's happened to me, Martin? I can't move, Martin, I can't move! Help us, Martin! Please help us . . ."

But she could still move—Emily Kane could still move. Her boyfriend had gotten what he deserved, but Emily Kane was still human.

He watched as she moved to the front of the theater and then turned right, toward the stairs, watched until she'd left his periphery, reappearing again seconds later in front of him, just a foot away. He could see the top of her head and her eyes, but nothing else. He had heard her say, "Long live the king," and "Are you hungry, Martin?" which hadn't made any sense at all.

Now she said it again, a touch of crazy happiness in her tone.

* * *

"Are you hungry, Martin?"

She snapped the cover off the container of salt and flipped it away. But she waited a moment, wondering if anything would actually happen if she went through with it or if Lenora had played the ultimate practical joke on everyone. Of course, there was only one way to find that out. "They say that too much salt's not good for you, Martin. Let's hope so." That said, she poured a liberal amount onto Martin's lips, took a step back, and waited.

The silence hummed; she felt a thousand pairs of eyes boring into her. She watched Martin, waiting for some sign. But what? He could be dead right now, for all she knew. Her head started to throb again. He could have died without a lot of fanfare, that was definitely one possibility.

After another fifteen minutes passed, she decided that one of two things had probably happened. He *had* died, or Lenora, as Bobby had suggested, had made fools out of them.

She reached out and touched Martin, wondering what she'd feel. She felt exactly nothing, just another stone cold being like the one upstairs—like the ones behind her—watching while she tried to kill their king, watching like dummies in a store window.

"I hope you're dead, Martin," she said. "You have no idea . . ." Again her words echoed and again they died a lonely death.

She left the stage wondering and hoping and started up the center aisle, trying her best not to look at the people on either side. What if she looked and one of them moved? What if one of them turned his head and smiled . . . ?

It was about halfway back, near three small children, when she heard something behind her, a kind of shuffling. She didn't bother to turn, but she did stop, and when she stopped, she smiled. "Go away," she said. "Whatever part of my imagination is back there, just go away."

She waited a moment, listening. She heard another shuffle, like a thousand hungry insects moving along the floor toward a pile of spilled garbage.

"Didn't you hear me? I said—"

"Food, need food!"

Her eyes bulged and her skin erupted in gooseflesh. She wheeled, her breath caught in her throat

Martin, grinning, his fangs the size of walrus teeth, his eyes feverishly intent, stood only a few feet away. He reached out to her and Emily screamed loudly.

"Food, need food!" Martin said.

Her legs were almost useless, but she did manage to fall onto her rear end and crabwalk slowly up the aisle, Martin moving ever so close, arms outstretched, fangs glistening, hungry for a proper meal.

And now Emily was certain she could see the others turn and grin at her, certain this had all been a big practical joke on her and that at any moment Martin would sink his teeth into her neck, that he would rip her throat out and suck the juices out of it while they all applauded.

But something happened then that gave her hope. From the balcony she saw a flutter of movement, something floating down.

Bobby All?

He landed between her and Martin as softly as snow and she heard him say, "Salt, I would never have believed it possible."

Her legs finally decided to work. She pushed herself to her feet and ran to the back of the theater, very much expecting that Martin and Bobby would begin a fight to the death with her as the prize, at least for Martin.

And although they began to pose as if there was going to be a fight, the fight never got started.

Martin started forward, spouting something about how he was going to tear Bobby apart, when he stopped suddenly and a very surprised and pained expression passed over his face. Even Bobby looked surprised.

"You're dying, Martin," Bobby said finally.

Martin looked at himself, then at Bobby. "Help me!" he said.

Bobby just smiled and shook his head.

The disintegration began at the tips of Martin's fingers. His hands dissolved into something that looked strangely like fairy dust and the residue floated soundlessly to the floor. Wide-eyed with fear, Martin could only watch as it continued up his arms, his face ever changing, ever more fearful as the decomposition continued, until finally all that was left of him was a pile of gray-white ash about halfway up the aisle of the Manhattan Punch Line Theater.

Bobby looked back at Emily, and she at him.

Emily's nerves had about had it, but she had enough sense to ask Bobby one question. "My father and Ray, Bobby—where are they?"

Bobby looked at her a moment and shook his head. Then he gathered up the residue that was Martin and let it cascade into his pocket.

Emily heard movement behind her. She turned quickly and stared into the scared faces of two soldiers who couldn't have been more than eighteen, the barrels of their M-16s leveled at her.

"Please don't move, lady," one of them said, his voice quavering. "I don't want to kill anyone else today."

But she did move; she turned to see if Bobby was still there. He wasn't, and in his place, she saw a wisp of smoke spiraling languidly toward the ceiling.

Forty-one

Emily was on her back on a cot and the first thing she saw was a slowly revolving fan above her head about twenty feet up. She glanced to the left and right—more fans.

Jesus, where in the world am I? she wondered. *What's happened to me?*

What had happened came back to her. She remembered winding tendrils of smoke where Bobby had been standing, fascinating all by itself, but when she heard a collective moan from the crowd of vampires, followed by actual movement from first a few and then everyone she could see, she forgot all about Bobby and his little vampire tricks. "Holy shit!" she'd heard from behind her—the soldier who'd told her not to move. What happened next was exactly why she was here. "Well, I got this one!" the soldier said. She tried to move, she knew that, to tell him she wasn't one of them, but she didn't make it. The soldier clubbed her on the head and then . . . then they brought her here. *Wherever here is . . .*

She tried to push herself up to get a better look, but her aching head objected.

She plopped back down, the pain in her head returning in all its wonderful glory. She'd have to move a lot more slowly if she wanted to move at all.

When her eyes adjusted, she saw something to her left that made her heart do a little dance—an old man lying on a cot not five feet away, looking at her, a half grin on his white-stubbled face. She looked in the other direction, at a younger man staring at the ceiling.

"Damn the pain!" she said. "I've gotta get outta here."

She sat up, propping herself onto an elbow, and looked around. As far as she could see, the place was packed with people lying on cots just like hers.

Of course, she thought, *the vampires!* She put it all together easily enough. Martin died, then these people came back from . . . well, from wherever they'd been. They had regained the ability to move. And then, somehow, they had lost it again. And when they couldn't move, the army had brought them here, to this . . . warehouse.

Not all the cots were taken, though, so . . . she heard movement from the far end of the building. *Thank God!* "Over here! Over here!" she yelled. "I'm okay! Thank God, thank God!" She tried to get up again, but her pain wouldn't let her.

"One of them's alive!" she heard. "Holy shit! One of them's alive? Get the general!"

Emily froze.

"Fuck the general! I'm gettin' my goddamn gun!"

Jesus, Emily thought, *I'm okay, but these guys, Christ, these guys sound real trigger-happy.* If she got up and started walking toward them, she might get her head blown off. No, she'd have to go about this slowly, a step at a time, or she'd have to try to sneak out of here. For now, though, she'd have to pretend to be one of these things, one of the vampires. And if they turned on the lights, that would probably be a very hard thing to do.

She lay down and waited. A light went on overhead; a weak glow leaving everything in shadow, with the consistency of a dream.

She saw a flashlight beam seconds later, probing through the warehouse like the light from a drunk's motorcycle. She heard footsteps and two very frightened soldiers. "Make this quick, dammit! You sure you heard—?"

"Yeah, I'm sure!"

"Coulda been Joe, you know. He likes to play jokes—"

"No, man, it was a woman. It wasn't Joe. Jesus!"

"Okay, okay, we check out the women. Wha'd you say she said?"

"Said she was okay, something like that, I don't know. Shit, man, I don't like this! Not one little bit!"

"Said she was okay, huh? I heard about some guy in Queens who got torn apart by one of these things. He said *he* was okay."

The flashlight beam got closer, the banter stopped, and Emily ordered each muscle not to move. But when one of the soldiers got so close she could actually reach out and touch him, she thought she'd scream.

He pointed the flashlight into her face and she had to fight the urge to squint. She wondered if her pupils would dilate.

"This one's a looker," he said.

The other soldier came over.

"Yeah, sure is. You imagine gettin' it on with one of these things?"

"They got a word for that, you know. Necro-something-or-other."

"Necrophilia."

"Huh?"

"It's called necrophilia. Fucking a dead person."

"Yeah, whatever. C'mon, let's get this over with. We're not supposed to be in here too long anyway. Might catch something."

Finally, the soldiers left, and for a very long time all Emily could see were flashes of light in front of her eyes.

She tried to move again after the place had been quiet for about half an hour. This time the pain was more accom-

modating. They were obviously through for the night. She'd
seen them bring in three more people.

She turned onto her stomach and looked around. "Well,
isn't that convenient," she mumbled. "An exit sign. The way
out." When, though? *Now, probably,* she decided. *No better
time than the present.*

She slid off the cot onto the floor and started crawling
toward the exit, hoping this was going to be as easy as it
looked. She had reason to think so. Obviously they hadn't
used a building specifically built to house these things—
they were using a plain old warehouse. Where was this
place, though? Manhattan? Brooklyn, maybe? *Well,* she decided, *wherever it is, I can't stay here.*

She had twenty feet or so of open space between the last
cot and the exit sign. She'd be in the open and visible for
as long as it took her to get there. She waited beside a cot
with a child lying on it, making sure no one was close
by—from here she could see two soldiers in camouflage
fatigues inside a glass-walled room looking at what she
thought was a map of this place where they'd put everyone.
They probably had her name on that list. The room was
easily a hundred feet away, though, so if she was fast
enough . . .

She crawled the twenty feet to the door, staying below the
light. From all fours, she reached for the knob, gripped it.
Locked.

"Shit!" she mumbled. Trapped. She was trapped! She
gripped the knob harder. Nothing.

She suddenly felt a little stupid, but also relieved. She
could unlock the door from the inside by just turning the
locking button.

She unlocked the door, but before she opened it, she
looked back at the glass-walled room. "Shit, where's the
other guy?" she said. Her face felt hot. *They don't like coming in here, but they might have to for routine inspections.*

She got up slowly, pushed the door open, then stepped

through as quickly as she could, shutting the door behind her as quietly as possible.

There was moisture in the air and maybe . . . the sounds of waves breaking onto the shore? Her spirits took a nose-dive. She was on an island. Beyond a tall security fence was water for as far as she could see, the full moon casting ribbons of bright yellow light onto it like a banner flapping in a light breeze. *An island!*

A sense of purpose flooded through her. She wasn't going back in there. She'd gotten to this island; she could damn sure get off. First of all, though, she'd have to get beyond that security fence, and she wasn't about to go over the top—even from here she could see the barbed wire.

She moved to the far end of the building, about a hundred yards, then stuck her head around the side. She saw four Army trucks parked in a row. *Deuce and a halves,* she remembered. *Hal drove one in the Army.* While she watched, another truck pulled up, stopped, then backed up to the build-ing. She watched while the cargo was offloaded, a cargo she guessed even before they started unloading—vampires.

Not this way, she thought. She went back to where she had been, then further, to the other end of the building. The fence hadn't been finished yet. She had a way out. She ran for the opening, expecting someone would see her, some joker out for a smoke or something, but no one saw her and she reached the woodline feeling very relieved. She didn't stop running until thickening underbrush forced her to.

She trudged through the underbrush for as long as she could, another three hours. Exhausted, she lay down and fell into the deepest sleep she had ever enjoyed.

She woke up to the sounds of birds and the sun breaking through the dense forest canopy. And although she had dozens of bug bites, the sound of a motorboat made her spirits soar. She had made it to the other side of the island.

She got up and stumbled through the underbrush, finally emerging onto a beautiful white sand beach. She stopped. She wasn't sure, but in the distance she thought she saw the skyline of New York. *Quite a swim,* she thought. *What now?*

She could still hear the motorboat, but she couldn't see it, not yet. It was getting closer, though. She went back into the bushes as the engine noise got louder.

Seconds later, the motorboat burst from the small peninsula at very high speed. And it wasn't a government boat, she saw, it was a couple of kids, a boy and a girl.

Emily ran from the bushes, waving and yelling like Robinson Crusoe. Almost immediately, the boat slowed down.

"Hello!" she yelled. *Think quickly, Emily, very quickly.* "Can you help me, please? I'm stranded. My boyfriend . . ."

The driver paused a moment, then accelerated slightly and waved, his smile as bright and as welcome as a midsummer sun.

Forty-two

It was easy to lie. Lying was such a minor thing nowadays.

She told her rescuers that she and her date, a blind date, had come to the island the night before because he had just picked up his boat and wanted to show it off, when in fact, all he had really wanted was to get her alone. When she wouldn't oblige him, he'd left her there and told her to thumb a ride back. And that, she told them, was pretty much what he had done. She knew it hadn't been very smart to go with him in the first place, she said, but everyone made mistakes.

When the subject of where she lived came up, she lied again. "What a coincidence, I'm from Jersey City, too," she said. In passing, the kids had briefly mentioned that they were from Jersey City, so when they asked her what part, she had a quick answer. She couldn't tell them she was from New York—everyone knew about the quarantine, although only a select few, she thought, knew the reason.

"Heard it's all hush-hush, some weird disease," the boy said. "Some tabloid said it was vampires." He grinned. "Vampires. They'll do anything to sell papers."

That, Emily knew, was more or less true.

But if they knew she lived in New York they might just throw her overboard or even take her back to the island.

The boat, the boy said, was new, and they were taking it on a shakedown cruise. She admired the boat properly when he told her that, and after a while, conversation leveled off and then died altogether.

They took her back to Jersey City, and after they parted company, she got a motel room to wait out the quarantine. She thought about sneaking back into the city, but for now, she saw no reason to do that. She could wait it out. She had enough plastic to last a while.

She waited eight days. Word came over television and radio within minutes after the quarantine was officially lifted. She caught a bus back to the city, wondering all the while what changes she'd see.

She smiled when she got there. The government had done a remarkably efficient job. It was as if nothing had happened. The city seemed to have the same pulse; traffic was still ridiculously heavy and the sidewalks looked like crowded dance floors.

There were rumors as to why the quarantine had been instituted in the first place, but every rumor she heard had to do with a dangerous strain of virus brought into the country by illegal aliens: Haitians or Cubans, or the Chinese.

By the end of the quarantine it appeared that any inclination toward the vampire theory had been effectively quashed.

But how many people had been killed or altered? Emily wondered. And would the populace ever know the exact figure? Would the government ever concede that hundreds of people had been taken out of the city to places like that island, within view of New York? She could tell people what she knew, of course, but who would listen? She felt like a witness to the JFK assassination, or more appropriately, the Roswell incident.

But as she got off the bus, she realized something else: if the government knew that she had been on the island, they might try to find her. They might try somehow to convince her that what she'd seen *wasn't* exactly what she'd seen. They were good at that. They could call on her patriotism and sense of duty to God and country, not necessarily in that order.

She hailed a taxi and gave that some thought before she told the driver her destination. Should she go back to her apartment? she wondered. Or should she simply leave the city and never come back? She smiled. Compared to what she'd faced, the U.S. government was just a kid trying to play ball at Yankee Stadium. They were a cocky bunch, anyway; if she decided to speak up, they had their ways of making sure no one would listen to her.

In a clear, strong voice she gave the driver her address and didn't hesitate when she got there.

Despite an outward appearance of calm, inwardly, she was a mess. What about Ray? What about her dad? The government was still in her thoughts, too, although they'd now been relegated to third place.

She pushed open the door to her apartment, expecting to find three very sick, maybe even dead, cats. They hadn't had water or food for days, after all.

"Alpha? Beta?" she yelled. *No, Emily, Cynthia's got him, remember?*

"Kitty, kitty," she said.

To her surprise, Alpha, Delta, and Gamma came prancing in regal cat fashion. She knelt to them, smiling and stroking each one and telling them how much she'd missed them. But even while she breathed a sigh of relief, she wondered how they'd survived, a puzzle that made her suddenly apprehensive.

She stood while the cats circled her legs.

She heard footsteps.

"Emily? Is that you?"

Over the last eight days she had worried mightily about Ray, and although she held out hope that he was still alive, that hope had become razor-thin. Now she was looking into his smiling and very normal-looking face.

"Ray—thank God, Ray," she said. She hugged him, enjoying the normal and very human thump of his heart.

"She was right," Ray whispered in her ear. "Lenora was right. I developed an immunity. Martin's blood made me immune."

"*Shh*," she said, touching her fingers to his lips. "We'll talk about that later. Just let me hold you for now, okay? Just let me hold you."

Ray didn't bother to respond, other than to stroke her hair.

Later that evening, after they had eaten a wonderful meal and drunk an equally wonderful wine, the topic of her father came up. Emily was certain he was gone. He could, she said, even be a prisoner on the same island she had fled eight days earlier.

"Maybe," Ray said. "Maybe not."

He was acting strange, as if he knew something . . .

"You've seen him, haven't you?" She put her glass down.

Ray just looked at her and held her hand. "Come with me," he said.

"Where? Where are we going?"

"Just come with me."

"He's dead, isn't he? You found him and he's dead."

"Emily, please. Be patient and trust me."

"I've got no choice, have I?"

Ray didn't say anything.

They took a taxi to the Empire State Building, and when they got out, Emily felt her hope soar to the rooftops. "Ray, he's here, isn't he? He's alive!"

Ray only smiled and led her into the building. But he didn't ring the bell when they got to her father's offices. Instead he took a key from his pocket and unlocked the door.

"I can't take this, Ray," she said, unable to move another step. "Is he all right or not? Just tell me, is he okay?"

Ray cupped her shoulders. "That's for you to decide, Emily."

They went through the outer office and into the artifacts holding area, the lights of the city blazing beyond as if nothing had happened.

"Well, where is he?" Emily asked. "Where's my father?"

Ray nodded toward Martin's casket and Emily felt suddenly dizzy. Her legs threatened to give out. He took her by the arm, but halfway to the casket she broke free. Ray took a step back and waited.

She moved around the casket slowly, remembering how she had reacted to Martin. The blood pounded at her temples.

And when she went around the casket and looked inside, her legs almost did give out.

Her father was there, inside Martin's casket, staring out at the city. The side of his head had the telltale concavity.

"Oh, Dad, how?" Emily said. She looked at Ray.

"I wish I could tell you how," Ray said. "I came here looking for you and found him. All I can conclude is that he knew what was happening to him and came back here. I didn't want to touch him, though. I wanted you to see him. I wanted you to decide what to do with him. I, uh, I got the key to his office in the mail, so I guess . . ."

Emily glanced frantically between Ray and her father. "How can I decide that, Ray?" she said. "How? He's my father. What can I do?"

Their gazes locked for a very long time. Finally, Ray said, "What about the salt, Emily?"

David could hear every word, and although they couldn't see his response, he said it anyway. He didn't know anything about what salt could do, he just knew what he wanted them to do.

Help me, Emily, he thought. *I can't go on like this, I can't! Help me die. Please help me die!*

Emily stepped up to the casket and stroked her father's face. "Is he happy, Ray?" she said. "Do you think he's happy?"

Ray measured his answer but when he did give it, he meant every word.

After he had given it, Emily dabbed at a tear on her cheek and said, "Thanks, Ray, thanks for helping."

If David could have smiled, he probably would have.

And the past. It did glitter so.

HORROR FROM HAUTALA

SHADES OF NIGHT (0-8217-5097-6, $4.99)
Stalked by a madman, Lara DeSalvo is unaware that she is most in danger in the one place she thinks she is safe—home.

TWILIGHT TIME (0-8217-4713-4, $4.99)
Jeff Wagner comes home for his sister's funeral and uncovers long-buried memories of childhood sexual abuse and murder.

DARK SILENCE (0-8217-3923-9, $5.99)
Dianne Fraser fights for her family—and her sanity—against the evil forces that haunt an abandoned mill.

COLD WHISPER (0-8217-3464-4, $5.95)
Tully can make Sarah's wishes come true, but Sarah lives in terror because Tully doesn't understand that some wishes aren't meant to come true.

LITTLE BROTHERS (0-8217-4020-2, $4.50)
Kip saw the "little brothers" kill his mother five years ago. Now they have returned, and this time there will be no escape.

MOONBOG (0-8217-3356-7, $4.95)
Someone—or some*thing*—is killing the children in the little town of Holland, Maine.

DON'T MISS THESE OTHER GREAT WHO-DUNITS!

BURIED LIES   (1-57566-033-4, $18.95)
It looks like lawyer-turned-golf pro Kieran Lenahan finally has a shot at the PGA tour, but a week before he is supposed to play at Winged Foot in Westchester County, his pro shop goes up in flames. The fire marshal is calling it arson. When Kieran's caddie falls in front of an oncoming train and his former girlfriend insists he was pushed, can Kieran find a connection between his caddie's death and the fire?

DEAD IN THE DIRT:
AN AMANDA HAZARD MYSTERY(1-57566-046-6, $4.99)
by Connie Feddersen
Amanda arrives too late to talk taxes with her near-destitute client, Wilbur Bloom, who turns up dead in a bullpen surrounded by livestock. A search of Bloom's dilapidated farm soon uncovers a wealth of luxuries and a small fortune in antiques. It seems the odd duck was living high on the hog. Convinced that Bloom's death was no accident, Amanda—with the help of sexy cop Nick Thorn—has to rustle up a suspect, a motive . . . and the dirty little secret Bloom took with him to his grave.

Available wherever paperbacks are sold, or order direct from the Publisher. Send cover price plus 50¢ per copy for mailing and handling to Penguin USA, P.O. Box 999, c/o Dept. 17109, Bergenfield, NJ 07621. Residents of New York and Tennessee must include sales tax. DO NOT SEND CASH.